(For more stunning acclaim, please turn page . .)

"AN ADMIRABLE NOVEL . . . A PLEA-SURE . . . RIGHT ON THE MARK . . . a rural gothic horror story wonderfully humanized . . . convincing characters . . . a sense of place."
                    —*Wichita Eagle-Beacon*

"A LOVE STORY AND A MYSTERY . . . sure pacing and evocative writing cast a spell . . . readers will remember."
                    —*Orlando Sentinel*

"ELEGANT, EVOCATIVE, COMPELLING, DEFT . . . A SPELLBINDING, PAGE-TURNING DENOUEMENT."
                    —*Country Inns* magazine

"A MASTERPIECE . . . BRILLIANT . . . PERFECTLY CRAFTED!"
                    —*Senior Lifestyle* magazine

EDEN CLOSE

A NOVEL

ANITA SHREVE

A SIGNET BOOK

SIGNET
Published by the Penguin Group
Penguin Books USA Inc., 375 Hudson Street,
New York, New York 10014, U.S.A.
Penguin Books Ltd, 27 Wrights Lane,
London W8 5TZ, England
Penguin Books Australia Ltd, Ringwood,
Victoria, Australia
Penguin Books Canada Ltd, 2801 John Street,
Markham, Ontario, Canada L3R 1B4
Penguin Books (N.Z.) Ltd, 182–190 Wairau Road,
Auckland 10, New Zealand

Penguin Books Ltd, Registered Offices:
Harmondsworth, Middlesex, England

This is an authorized reprint of a hardcover edition published by
Harcourt Brace Jovanovich, Publisher.

First Signet Printing, November, 1990
10 9 8 7 6 5 4 3 2 1

REGISTERED TRADEMARK—MARCA REGISTRADA

Printed in the United States of America

PUBLISHER'S NOTE
This is a work of fiction. Names, characters, places, and incidents either are the product
of the author's imagination or are used fictitiously, and any resemblance to actual
persons, living or dead, events, or locales is entirely coincidental.

For John

ONE

THE AIR LAY AS HEAVY AS WATER IN THE SQUARE DARK rooms of the farmhouse. The house was still, sounds indistinct and muffled, as if heard through cloth. Upstairs, in the boy's room, the clock over the desk ticked away the minutes just past midnight. In the next room, where the boy's parents slept, there was the soft rattle of an old fan, moving the thick air from outside the house to inside and over his parents' bodies. As they had done nearly every hot night that summer, they had offered the fan to the boy, but the boy, aware that summer for the first time of his parents' age, had refused to take it from them.

In the house, far from town, Andy slept on his back in his bed. He slept badly, his lips lightly parted, his body smothered by the August night. A damp sheet, loose from its moorings, covered his chest. The boy's chest was bony then, without the muscles that would come later, and he had an older boy's summer growth, as if he'd sprouted too fast and had lost the grace of childhood. He was tall now, so tall that he towered over his parents, and his unfamiliar limbs, splayed under and out from the sheet, gave his body a lanky awkwardness, even in his sleep. His skin had an August tan and had all but lost the marks of adolescence. His hair, dark brown and thick and slightly too long, against his father's wishes, was wet at the sides and the back with the heat. He turned, pulling the sheet

11

with him, as if to say, despite his dreams, *OK, now, enough of this.*

The boy's father, in the next room, sleeping on his stomach in a sleeveless undershirt and boxer shorts, moved a hand near his ear to make a mosquito go away. His mother lay beside his father, on her back, like the boy. She had thrown off the sheet entirely, but her body was clothed in her pink summer pajamas. She had curlers at the sides and top of her head. The mosquito, discouraged by the father, alighted on her thigh, and too late, in her sleep, she moved her leg against the air.

Beyond the screen in the boy's room, there was only darkness. The darkness lay over the town and along the road that led from town, and it lay over the two farmhouses that were set two miles along that road like an afterthought, with only each other for company. The two houses were only seventy feet apart, the one facing the road, the other, his own, down a short dirt drive, pointing north, overlooking an abandoned cornfield. Indeed, the darkness had come that day from the north, blanketing that part of the state where the town was and where the boy had been born. In the afternoon, clouds the color of dust had moved along the sky like thick batting, diffusing the sun until it was only heat and blotting out the moon and the shooting stars of August in the evening. The blackness folded the heat back down upon itself and pushed it through the screens and into the rooms where the boy and his parents slept.

Later they would all know and be able to say that it was ten minutes past twelve when the sounds started. It was the boy who woke first, seconds before his parents. He heard a woman cry out, and he thought, as he swam up through his sodden sleep, that it might be his mother. But when he was awake, he knew that the sound was outside, in the darkness past the screen. The boy pushed the sheet from his chest as if the sheet kept him from understanding the sound outside his window. Perhaps, too, he heard then, through the wall, his father or his mother, sitting up. Like him, suddenly alert.

The second sound was a hoarse cry, nearly a shout, from a man, and with that there was immediately the frightened squeal of another female voice, that of a child still, like himself. He heard his father's feet on the floor, the rustle of trousers, a zipper—then his mother's muffled voice, anxious, questioning. The boy moved down to the foot of the bed, where the window was. On his hands and knees, he looked out at the night, waiting for the voices to explain themselves.

There were two shots, the boy and his parents would say later. Two shots fast upon each other, so that they sounded, in the silent night of midsummer, like one explosion shattering the air. The boy knelt frozen, his hands on the sill. He knelt that way for the seconds of silence that followed the explosion, until he heard the loud voice of his father telling his mother not to move. And then calling his son's name through the wall. *Andy*. He could hear his father open the door of the closet where he kept the rifle on a shelf. Then his own door opened. His father, in his sleeveless undershirt, rifle in hand, said, *Get away from the window*. The boy heard his father's footsteps running on the stairs and the soft whir as his father dialed the phone in the hallway downstairs.

Unable to move as his father had commanded, the boy stared at the darkness outside the screen. The last sound began then. It was reedy, a high-pitched wail, rising at first like a tendril of smoke into the sky—a female voice, though nearly inhuman, gathering momentum as it rose. He imagined a woman opening her mouth, her voice rising from her in a thin, quivering stream. The boy heard his father stop dialing, listen and replace the receiver. The keening rose, sliced through the night. The boy shivered with the sound and backed away from the window. The cat downstairs jumped onto the kitchen table and started to hiss. Crows and summer birds, awakened by the unearthly cries, or perhaps by the gunshots, began to chatter and caw. And through the wall, the boy heard his mother say, as if in comprehension, *Oh God, oh Jesus*.

ANDREW WAKES from the dream in the same bed in which he was a boy and is disoriented. The dream lingers, vivid and heavy, pulling him down, causing him to swim in confusion between the night of the gunshots, when he was seventeen, and this night, the night of his mother's funeral, when he is thirty-six and sleeping alone in his parents' house for the first time in his life. He makes the dream linger longer than it might, enjoying the sensation of diving deeply into the boy's body and thoughts, hearing with the boy's ears as he has not been able to do in nineteen years, enjoying even the fear—the ability to feel that kind of fear chasing along the spine.

Andy. He hears again the exact timbre of his father's voice, and of his mother's—muffled, murmuring, anxious. There are details in the dream he hasn't remembered in nineteen years, and he thinks (briefly, because he does not want thoughts to interrupt or block his way back down into the dream) that the dream has worked like hypnosis, giving back sight and hearing that have been lost to him. In his waking thoughts he hasn't been able to see, as he can now, his father as a younger man, the shoulders still muscled under the sleeveless vest, the thin open weave of the undershirt, nearly like gauze, so unlike the thick cotton T-shirts he himself wears now. The midnight stubble on his father's face, the hard stomach lying flat beneath the undershirt. In his waking thoughts he can make his father appear only as he was shortly before he died— clean shaven, the thickened waist straining at the belt, the chest sunken, as though the center, the power, of the body had slipped. Most of the images he now has of his father's youth come from photographs, so that his father is frozen in this pose or that, that expression or this, but has no life, no voice—just as his own son's early years seem locked forever in the photographs and movies Martha, his ex-wife, has taken. His son is seven now, but Andrew cannot reliably remember how he sounded or what he said at two or at four.

He rolls over in the bed, hoping to sink deeper into sleep, to keep the dream alive. He can feel a door closing slowly. The dream is slipping away, and he is losing the feeling of being a boy, but the door hasn't entirely shut: he can still make out some of the details. He had forgotten, but can see now, the way the clouds came on that afternoon, a sour color filling the sky, turning trees and skin in the early evening light a pale, sickish yellow. And he can hear again the excited sounds of the birds just after midnight, when there should have been silence. He had forgotten the way his father held a gun, pointed straight down along the side of his leg, like a brace. And that his mother wore curlers to bed. And he had forgotten (indeed, how could anyone have retained the precise sound?) the terrible pitch of the woman's cries. At any point in the intervening years, he could have said that, yes, there was the sound of a woman crying in grief or in horror, but he couldn't have described it. Occasionally he would, when he was younger and more eager to impress, tell the story to a new acquaintance or to a woman, giving his childhood its only bit of glamour: *The man next door was murdered when I was seventeen. His daughter was raped.* But he hasn't, until the dream, been able to hear the sound.

But is the dream accurate? he wonders. Have bits been added for dramatic effect or for some psychological payoff? No, he thinks (his thoughts intruding, coming faster, taking precedence over his sleep), the dream is true in the details that are there—nothing that is there is altered (except, perhaps, the part about the mosquito, which must have bitten *him* just now and worked its way into the dream)—but like edited copy, the dream has left out certain messy or seemingly irrelevant complications.

He had forgotten, but remembers now—and this was not part of the dream—the way the heat and the dirty air raised tempers that day, like an irritant chafing the skin, causing his parents, earlier in the evening, to speak in uncharacteristically querulous tones. He remembers that night at dinner—a cold, disappointing meal of ham slices and potato salad (it was too hot to cook, or even to eat)—that when his mother once again offered him the fan, there was an edge to her voice as if she knew in advance that he would decline it and was tired of the minor triumph of her son's refusal and of the larger implication of her son's generosity. And he remembers that after the meal, she rose in silence to get the ice cream from the freezer and put the half-empty carton on the table. The dessert looked to Andy as if it would taste like the cardboard it came in, and he didn't want it despite the heat, despite his usual thirst for sweets. He got up from the table and went out the screen door, letting it bang a little harder than usual, hunching his shoulders slightly against the possibility that his father would swing open the door in anger at his son's sudden sullenness.

But his father didn't come to the door, and Andy walked on down the dirt and gravel drive to the road, his hands in his pockets, thinking that soon he would go away, to Massachusetts, to school. He reached the road and the Closes' house. It, like his own, was a simple, nearly too spare farmhouse of white clapboards. Decades ago, the two houses had been set in a farmer's family compound at right angles to each other, with the back stoops the nearest point of contact, for two brothers to call to each other, or for a mother to watch over her new daughter-in-law. Now, though they shared a common drive, the families were not related, except in that way that two families, living far from town, might come to weave their lives together. Indeed, a passerby, cruising along the straight road from town, would know, at a glance, that the two families were not related: The first house, close to the road, though swathed in lush overgrown vegetation, particularly a profusion of blue hydrangeas in August, was the more derelict of the two. There was always peeling paint, a roof that needed mending, a shutter fallen in a storm. The house behind, facing north, Andy's own house, as if to disassociate itself from the careless house out front, was expertly if humbly manicured, its own hydrangea bushes trimmed neatly to size, its surrounding lawns cut and fertilized with discipline.

Mrs. Close worked nights then, as a nurse at the county hospital, and their car, a black Buick, was not in the driveway. Andy thought, if indeed he thought of it at all, that she'd taken the car and not the bus to work. (Later—hours, days later?—Andy would know that this impression was mistaken. He would be told, or would overhear, that Mr. Close, thinking to escape the heat, had driven his wife to work and then taken the car to the movies. And when his wife's shift was over, he brought her home just minutes after midnight.)

Andy might have wondered then if Eden was at home with her father or was out. He was not able to say later if he saw lights on in the house or not, or if he did, in what rooms the lights were. He tried to explain to the police that he passed that house, looked at that house, a dozen, twenty times a day, every day of his life, so that he could not say for sure if the lights he saw in the living room or the upstairs bathroom were on precisely at that moment, or earlier in the evening, when he was taking out the garbage, or on

another night entirely when he had passed by his own
screen window and had looked out.

He walked to the road and stood there, looking up
and down. He had no plans for the night. He wore a
white T-shirt and dungaree shorts and was letting his
hair grow, despite his father's sharp comments, long
enough for college. The road was flat as far as he could
see in either direction. That time of night, after dinner, there were few cars on the road: a family in a
station wagon going out for ice cream; an older boy,
like himself, about to pick up a girl; a grown man
escaping the dishes, heading for the package store.
Strangers used the road too, passing through from
towns and cities he did not know to other towns and
cities. And occasionally there might be a trucker who
had a night delivery off the highway.

Across the road, in the fading ocher light, were the
cornfields of a working farm; the farmhouse lay on
another road, parallel to his own. Sometimes Andy
saw MacKenzie and his son, Sam, on tractors, working the fields. Sam didn't play sports at school because
his father needed him in the afternoons. The drying
and brittle cornfields rose like briers for several acres
in both directions, lending the two farmhouses on Andy's side of the road even more of a sense of isolation
in August than in December. The corn was feed corn
for dairy cattle. Andy was glad his own father was not
a farmer.

That evening Andy stood there, alone on the road,
hearing only a distant barking of a dog, the faint whine
far off of a car along a highway, the clatter of dishes
in a dishpan, a faucet running in his mother's kitchen.
He looked east and south, across the cornfields, as he
had been doing for weeks since his acceptance at college had arrived in the mail, thinking of leaving, of
getting out, yet afraid, too, of the leaving and of what
might lie ahead. Already he had a sense of leaving for
good, though when he spoke to his mother, he talked

often of his vacations, of Thanksgiving, of returning
to teach at the junior college in the county. But he
knew, even then, that this wasn't true, that he would
return for Thanksgiving and for Christmas and probably for the first summer vacation, but that he would
really never come back. That what he was to be lay
not behind him in the small rooms of the farmhouse
but across the cornfields he could not, this month, see
over.

His mother called to him. He turned. He saw her
framed in the screen door, the yellow light of the
kitchen behind her. He saw the red smock she wore to
cover her heavy breasts and abdomen, the bottom of
her shorts cutting into her thighs. And, standing in the
road, he saw, too—the vision surprising him—the
younger woman she had once been, as though he knew
for certain he was leaving all of them. He saw the
young woman of the photograph albums she kept on
the coffee table—her long thick hair and the white collar of her high school picture; the ivory satin of her
wedding dress seen through a blizzard at the church
door (his father holding a fur jacket over her shoulders); the dazed expression of sensual pleasure in her
eyes as she cradled her infant, himself, in her arms.
He always thought of her, in the photographs, as beautiful, and he was startled for a moment to realize—to
realize he was *capable* of realizing—that she had no
beauty left at all. The subtle color of the once auburn
hair was already gone, replaced by short, too bright,
reddish curls.

And then, because he was seventeen, he had another
realization—one that had possibly been lurking below
the surface all along but now became, like many of
the insights he was having that summer, a conscious
thought: Even though you could love someone as much
as he had loved his mother and she him, her only child,
you could leave her if you had to. You could even look
forward to leaving her.

"Your show is on," his mother said behind the screen.

He went in then and upstairs to shower, to wash away the smell of gasoline that lingered from his summer job at the Texaco station. After the shower, he sat downstairs in the living room watching the rest of the TV show with his parents, not because he wanted to (he would have preferred to be alone in his room), but because it had been the family ritual for years to watch one TV show together before bed. He was very conscious that summer of rituals, and he didn't want to break any of them. He knew his parents would soon be lonely without him, and though he sometimes felt himself wanting to begin the separation, he didn't like to think about his mother's face or his father's tight smile after he had gone. There'd been a time, not so long ago, when the family rituals—the elaborate pancake breakfasts on Sunday morning, the deliberate choreography of the holidays, the small triangle of the supper table—had been the highlights of his days and weeks and years.

Yes, he now sees, his father had already taken off his shirt and was wearing only the sleeveless undervest and trousers. His mother fanned herself with a magazine and got up during a commercial to make them all lemonade. (Oddly, near dawn, they all sat around the kitchen table and drank the remaining lemonade together after the police and the ambulances had gone. How like his parents not to think of whiskey or brandy first in a crisis, as he would now—*does* now.) They all went up to bed after the show, shortly past ten o'clock (he remembers having said so to the police), his father winding his watch as he walked up the stairs, as he had nearly every night Andrew could remember; his mother hoisting her weight up the stairs by her grip on the banister, her tread heavy on each riser, short of breath at the top; and himself, as light as air, flying,

bounding, sprinting up the stairs, not an obstacle for
him as they were for his parents.

Later, after he left home, he liked to imagine that
he had looked out of his screen window, while he was
waiting for his mother or his father to vacate the single
bathroom at the top of the stairs, and had had a thought
of Eden that night—had posed a query or had seen a
silhouette of her moving across the window. But it
was, in retrospect, impossible to know if he'd thought
of her that night or that morning, or when he'd gotten
off the bus from the Texaco station. Eden had been too
much a part of his life—as much a piece of his geography as the hydrangea tree outside his window, whose
white puffy blossoms are turning now to salmon as
they do at the end of every summer; or as the way his
mother looked each morning at breakfast in her bathrobe, nursing her coffee as she stared out the kitchen
window, making, he always thought, some kind of
peace with the weather and with how the day seemed
about to unfold. He had known Eden all her life and
most of his, and though he was too young then to be
able to say with any confidence precisely how it was
he was connected to Eden, he knew that he was trou-
bled, as the days of August moved toward September,
about having to leave her behind.

HE SEES that he has pulled the sheet from the foot of
the bed during his dream—during the boyhood fear in
the dream?—and it now lies in a damp rough swath
across his chest. He brings it to his face and inhales a
musty scent; it must be years since anyone has slept
in this narrow single bed, he thinks. When he used to
visit with his wife and his son, the three of them always slept together in the double bed in the guest room
at the opposite end of the hallway—and it was, for
him, one of the highlights of those visits, their holding
each other in that soft, lumpy bed. As a general rule,
Martha didn't believe in letting Billy sleep with them

(the child-care books, she said, insisted it would make the boy too dependent), and so they hadn't, except on these rare and wonderful occasions.

Since he left home—and went to college, got married, fathered a child and separated from that wife and child—his room has evolved in the way the rooms of children do when the children aren't ever coming back. At first his mother kept it unviolated, the pennants and the posters on the walls, his desk neat, with his boyhood books and blotter, the few clothes he didn't take with him to school hanging in the closet. They were still there, he saw last night, as he hung up the charcoal gray suit he'd worn to the funeral; but she had used the closet herself, beginning when he didn't know, for her off-season clothes, if such a formal term could be applied to the oversized gaudy synthetics with orange diamonds, green stripes and pink flowers on the sleeves. She never lost the weight she vowed to lose and favored, right up until her death, large loose blouses that camouflaged her ever-swelling hips and thighs.

On the desk now is her sewing machine, and instead of the old pens and half-used notebooks he used to keep in the right-hand drawer, he found there last night an array of bobbins, fabric scraps and needles. There were other rooms she could have chosen to sew in— the sun room downstairs, where the light was good, or the guest bedroom. Perhaps, though, she wanted an excuse to be in this room, to savor some vestige of her son's presence. Or possibly she simply liked the east light in the early morning, or wished to see the other farmhouse, to reassure herself that she was not entirely alone. He tries to imagine what it must have been like for her to have a family and have it fall away: his own leaving and never really coming back except as a visitor; his father abandoning her five years ago with a heart attack. It has happened to him too— Martha and Billy have left him—though faster and without the dignity of these natural milestones. And he had not had time to be defined by the family he'd made, as she was, nor to become rooted to a place.

The still, heavy night mocks the dream, teasing it in and out of his consciousness. He wonders if the weather, so similar to that on the night of the shooting, has brought on the dream, or if it is the coincidence of lying alone in this bed. Or is it that he needs to feel his parents young and alive again, and his dream has willingly obliged? It is a mixed blessing, he thinks, to hold your past again for a few moments, as he sometimes feels when he dreams of Martha as she was (as they were together) when they first met. He wakes from these erotic dreams of his wife as if immersed in a warm bath, and then is chilled by those first few hints of reality—a tie flung over a mirror, a briefcase on a bureau, sheets he hasn't washed.

He swings his feet onto the floor and arches his shoulders. His back aches faintly; he isn't used to such a soft bed. And with Billy gone, he seldom exercises now—though his body remains, despite neglect, reasonably lean. He still has his hair too, for which he is grateful. His father, from whom Andrew inherited his thick dark hair—as well as his pale gray eyes—went bald at an early age. Andrew isn't certain, but he thinks his father may have lost his hair by the time he was forty-five.

Beside the bed, on a table, Andrew sees the sleeping pills. Dr. Ryder, his mother's doctor, pressed a vial into Andrew's palm after the funeral. He imagines the doctor with many similar vials, a drawerful perhaps, kept for similar occasions, the gesture like that of a priest with a rosary card, or of a car salesman handing you a calendar as you leave the showroom. But he doesn't want a sleeping pill just now. He feels restless.

FOUR DAYS earlier, he was in the screening room at the other end of the twenty-seventh floor, watching a videotape of an advertisement for a pain reliever his company manufactures, when Jayne, his secretary, got the call. The videotape had been especially poor, and despite the air-conditioning, he was sweating faintly when he returned to his office. As he walked in, Jayne came to his doorway with her hands clasped uncharacteristically in front of her. "There's bad news," she said quietly.

"Billy?" he said immediately, the adrenaline already shooting toward his fingertips.

Jayne shook her head quickly. Andrew slowly let out his breath. He thought he could bear anything except bad news about Billy, who was uncommonly prone to accidents—already a chipped tooth and a broken wrist, a scar over his right eyebrow. And since the child had left his keeping, Andrew's fears for him had increased exponentially. It was like the panic he sometimes had in airplanes.

"I'm so sorry," said Jayne. "It's your mother. She had a stroke just after breakfast and died almost immediately. A woman named Mrs. Close called to tell you, but I didn't want to break the news to you in the screening room. She says to call her. I have the number."

Andrew sat down. He remembers that his fingers could no longer hold a pen and that already a certain kind of numbness had set in, a disbelief in the truth of the event. He wouldn't need the number, he told Jayne. He had known it by heart since he was four, had been taught it in case of an emergency and later had used it to call Eden.

Although that conversation was days ago, Andrew is not sure even now that he has taken it in. The chaos of a funeral creates a blur inside which one can choose to remain. He has felt, alternately, grateful that his mother died so easily and so quickly; saddened that she might, even so, have known of her death, if only for a moment, and may have called out to him, her only son; relieved that he will no longer have to think of his mother as lonely; and horrified that the burden of being utterly alone has finally passed to him. He has no parents now or any family of his own to go home to, to create rituals with.

He walks from room to room upstairs, switching on lights as he walks, naked but for his shorts. The contradictory feelings have come in gulps, unexpectedly assaulting him and then leaving him to move about in the curious kind of peace that tending to business has always offered him. Like a good secretary to himself, he has made lists: lists of people to call and tasks to be completed to get to this day, the day of the funeral, and a long list of chores to accomplish before he can leave the farmhouse and the town. The list contains notes such as *call auctioneer, call real estate agents, do gutters, select mementos.* He imagines the sorting out, the auctioning off of the furniture, the minor repairs to the house and the arrangements to sell it will take him a week, and he called Martha to say that he will be upstate another seven days. When Martha offered to come to the funeral, Andrew said no, Billy was too young. Their presence, he thought, would distract him. Billy's trusting face and sturdy body would enthrall him as they always did; with Martha, there would be a tension that would inhibit every movement, so that thinking about his mother at all would be nearly impossible.

He has imagined that in lists there is control, but as he walks from room to room, the house seems about to slip from his grasp. His mother's room, now too bright under the overhead electric light, the room she left at dawn one morning five years ago to find her husband cold as tiles on the bathroom floor, the room she then slept in alone, is a labyrinth of snares and complications. There are only so many boxes of things Andrew can rescue from his and his parents' past to take back with him to his apartment in the city. And he sees at once that unless he hardens himself or designs a selection system, he might spend an entire day just in here.

Should he, for instance, take the quilt his mother made when he was ten—a year of her labor (he can recall it clearly) each night after supper, the basket of pieces beside her, her plump fingers nimble with a needle? What will he do with it? He has no wife to give it to, no closet big enough to store it, for it is a massive thing: It kept his parents warm even on the bleakest January nights.

And what of the oak chest of keepsakes at the foot of their bed, things his own mother saved from her mother, and doubtless things that his grandmother saved from her own mother's house? Such a process of distillation, like the corridors of endlessly repeated, though smaller, images in two mirrors; and such a burden, he thinks, these cartons filled with the leavings of lives gone before you. Will Billy one day open drawers in his father's apartment (depressing thought! Will Andrew now progress no farther in his domestic life than his expensive, cheerless condo?), taking objects that seem to contain some essence of his father, or of his own past, and bring them back to his own drawers and closets in Greenwich or Santa Fe?

Andrew picks up the watch his father wore and wound every night going up the stairs to bed. He knows he will take this, a watch his father inherited from his own father, but what of the Omega lying beside it on his father's bureau—the surface of the bureau undisturbed but for dusting? The Omega was a gift to his father when he left the dairy at his retirement. Andrew did not come to the retirement dinner—there'd been a critical business trip, a trip Andrew has always regretted making—and he doesn't know if his father ever even wore the Omega or if he would want it saved.

Andrew's father was plant foreman when he retired. But for most of the forty years he spent at the dairy, he drove a truck. (At his mother's insistence, the more accurate title ''milkman'' was seldom used in the house.) Andy was always asleep when his father left for work (at a punishing three forty-five in the morning), but when he returned from school, the truck would be there, and if he had a friend with him, they would clamber up into it with its bright green and red Miller Dairy sign, competing for the privilege of sitting on the high burnished leather seat and placing their small hands on the oversized steering wheel, the stem of which came all the way from the floor. Andrew remembers his father's gray overalls with the red embroidered script on the pocket, and the way, in winter, his father would wear so many layers underneath for warmth that he looked nearly stuffed. It wasn't until Andrew went to college and the boys around him spoke of their families that he first thought of himself as a WASP. But so humble were his father's circumstances (and, in truth, the circumstances of all his father's ancestors, most poor farmers) that Andrew wondered for a time if there might not be such a category as failed WASP. Andrew remembers vividly the afternoon his father came home with the news that he'd been promoted to foreman at the plant, releasing him from his position as a driver. He is not sure he ever saw his mother quite so jubilant—the way she kept kissing his father and throwing her arms around him and laughing, as if it were another era and she'd won the lottery.

He sits on the edge of the bed. He wonders who made the bed, for it was here that his mother was found. He assumes it must have been Mrs. Close, who came to his mother after the phone call. (''Your mother called Edith Close at about eight this morning and said she had a terrific pain in her head,'' Dr. Ryder revealed in his hoarse, authoritative voice on the phone the night Andrew arrived. ''By the time Edith got dressed and went over, your mother had already passed away. She found her upstairs. It was a massive stroke, mercifully quick. Be glad for that. But you watch yourself, Andy, both your parents dying of cardiovascular diseases in their sixties; you watch your diet.'')

As he sits on the bed, he thinks that a marriage seen when you're a parent too, an adult, is a different thing than the one seen from boyhood. He wonders if his parents were happy together, if they slept touching or apart (he doesn't really know; they were always private and silent in this room, and he has no memory, as other children do, as Eden said she did, of mysterious and unexplained parental sounds) and whether they had ceased to make love. His parents were older than most when he was born; his mother was thirty-one. She had, she said, nearly given up on a baby before he came, and there was a time when this caused him to imagine that he was adopted, like Eden, despite the fact he looks so like his father that he can't, even today, go into town without a man or woman there saying it: *the image of your father*. Still, as children can be, he was obsessed for months (or perhaps it was only weeks) by this notion of adoption; so much so that he conceived the idea that the two families had gravitated to the two farmhouses set apart from the town because there was about them this unnatural link.

He looks at the marriage bed and sees, suddenly and unbidden, the image of a woman rolling over, turning her back on the man. But it is not his mother he is seeing; it is his wife. He doesn't want to think of Martha just now. He gets up and shuts off the light.

The brandy, kept for company, is in the cabinet with the meat grinder over the fridge. He pours himself a generous amount in a jelly glass. The kitchen, he reflects, sitting on a white-painted wooden chair, is nearly unchanged since he was a boy. And as it did then, it gives the appearance of having been scrubbed raw. It is a farmhouse kitchen, ''modernized'' during the thirties, with a green-speckled linoleum floor, a

white porcelain sink and stove and kitchen table, all
with rounded edges. There are painted surfaces every-
where—the white tongue-and-groove boards of the
walls, the pale green of the old Hoosier cabinet, the
four unmatched white chairs at the table. He thinks
about the kitchen in the house in Saddle River he
bought with Martha, where Martha and Billy now live,
and about the shiny, stainless-steel refrigerator in that
kitchen and the expensive quarry tile on the floor and
how remarkably cold—literally cold—the floor is there.

When he arrived the evening of the day his mother
died—by car, having driven the 270 miles north from
the city—and walked in the back door (as did everyone
who entered the house), the kitchen appeared as it does
now; there were no leavings of a half-eaten breakfast,
as he had feared to see. Edith Close again, he imagines, silently officious, cleaning up the clutter of death.

Thinking of Edith Close, he remembers again, and
abruptly, the terrible sound in his dream of a woman
crying. He swirls the golden brandy in the jelly glass
and recalls the sequence of events, an exact sequence
he has not thought of for years. His father again picked
up the phone and dialed the police. Then he went alone
through the kitchen, out the door and up the drive, his
rifle tense along the side of his leg. Andy heard his
father's unhurried footsteps on the gravel and the heavy
patter of his mother running down the stairs. Andy
pulled on his shorts and went downstairs to be with
his mother, partially out of a desire to protect her,
primarily out of a need to be in her presence. She was
standing at the screen door, peering out at the darkness. Despite the heat, she had put on a robe (pink
seersucker with lace at the edges, he sees now), knowing that there would be the police soon. The shrill wail
had stopped; they both knew it had been the voice of
Edith Close, but neither yet had the courage to imagine precisely what had caused it. Andy moved closer

to his mother, and she shifted slightly so that he, too, could see out the screen door into nothing.

"I told him to wait for the police," his mother said, her voice tight with strain. It was a strain he is now familiar with, the strain of cautious women with good sense, a voice men often choose to ignore.

"He has a gun," Andy said, knowing instantly she would not for one minute think that a help.

"A gun!" his mother cried. Her voice rose like the other, as if it, too, might spiral up into the night. Was this freedom a special province of women? he wondered. "What good is a gun in the pitch dark? You can't see a hand in front of you out there."

"He'll be careful," Andy said. But he didn't know if this was true. Was his father, in a crisis—a life-threatening crisis—a cautious man? He had never witnessed his father in physical danger; he doubted that his father knew himself how he would react until each footstep was taken.

He could feel the tension in his mother's body, a static current running along her arm, causing even his own arm to raise goose bumps. She stood with her hands clutching her robe closed—still, intent, warding off, as if by her will alone, the sound of another gun-shot. His father would say later that he felt no danger, but Andy thought his father must already have been forgetting his fear when he said it. Had his father not imagined the consequences of being seen by a gun-man, possibly a murderer, on the dirt drive as the man ran wildly into the cornfields?

Andy and his mother saw the flashing lights just a split second before they heard the siren, coming fast along the straight flat road from town. One, two police cars, an ambulance following—the town's entire force. And then another vehicle, half a minute later: the fire chief. The vehicles swung into the drive and over the lawn, spewing themselves every which way like children's toys, leaving the drive free for the ambulance.

The police cars and the ambulance lit up the night with eerie flashing beacons, red and blue, out of sync, so that Andy could see through his own screen door the back door of the other farmhouse and the bedroom windows upstairs to the north and west, awash in the unnatural pulsing lights. Two policemen ran from one of the cars to the back stoop and into the Closes' kitchen. From the ambulance, turning around and backing down the drive to the Closes' back stoop, another man alighted, swinging open its wide rear door.

"I'm going out there," Andy said suddenly.

"You stay here," his mother insisted. "Your father said."

But Andy was already through the door and down the steps. He put his hands in the pockets of his shorts and walked toward the edge of the circle created by the ring of official cars. The humid night was thick with mosquitoes; they whined at his ear, and he slapped at one on the back of his neck. He heard, too, the slap of the screen door behind him and turned to see his mother walking carefully down the back steps on the sagging treads, her curiosity stronger than her husband's admonition. The crows and summer birds, aroused at the wrong hour, had lost their fright and were silent now. Andy could hear the low, muffled voices of men at the front and sides of the house, searching already with powerful flashlights for someone or something, though no one outside the house yet knew what it was they might be expected to find. The headlights of a car—a Chevy?—approached the house, the driver slowing to see what the commotion was, perhaps suspecting an accident. Andy watched the car pull over. A man and a woman got out and crossed the road. They stood at the edge of the drive, staring at the scene, puzzled. And then, he knew from the soft furry breath at his arm, his mother was beside him.

Impulsively, he put his arm around her and jerked

her toward him. It was the first time he had ever touched her quite this way, from his full height, as if he were now the stronger of the two. It was a scene he thought he had seen somewhere before, on television possibly, in a show. The son, grown, towering over the mother, assuming the role of protector, steadying her while a husband is taken off in handcuffs or on a stretcher. The image, lasting only seconds, was inexplicably delicious. It was not unlike a similar and baffling feeling he sometimes has even now when he hears of someone else's bad news and has an irrepressible and horrifying urge to smile.

The Closes' back door swung open hard. It was DeSalvo, the thick-necked, heavyset police chief. Andy knew him from the hockey games. His face was pocked along his jowls. He had a son who years ago had made All State as a wing, and though his son had left the town, the father still haunted the games, as if to catch some echo—a shout skimming across the ice, a hand on his shoulder with a reminiscence—of his son's triumph. DeSalvo gestured sharply to the man standing at attention by the ambulance. As swift as skaters, the attendants slid up the back stoop with the stretcher and into the house. (Paramedics? Andrew doesn't know if they were called that then. Were they not simply volunteers, roused from their beds, as he was, by calls in the night?) His mother moved her face closer to his bare chest. Unconsciously, he braced himself for what the night might deliver next. But didn't the urgency of the stretcher imply injury and not death?

Andy could see the man and the woman at the end of the drive edging along closer to the house. A policeman was patrolling the front and spotted them too; he barked at them to move back. Andy thought he could imagine the prurient curiosity of the couple, exciting them enough to trespass, and how they would tomorrow assault whoever would listen with the details, their own status momentarily and satisfyingly enhanced. Then the policeman, turning back to his task at the front of the house, saw Andy and his mother and raised his flashlight to them. Andy brought his hand up to shield his eyes.

"You there," the officer called.

Andy, his arm still raised, nodded. It was Reardon. He saw again the diffused beacon of a flashlight against the steamed-up window on the driver's side of his father's Ford, and Reardon's face, peering and smirking in the darkness as he watched Andy's date worry her hair with her fingers. *Move along now,* Reardon had said with something like amusement or satisfaction on his face. *Not safe to park here this time of night.* Andy and his date, a girl he hadn't known well, had driven home in silence.

Reardon lowered the light. "Where's your father?"

Andy pointed to the Closes' house. Instinctively, he pointed upstairs.

"Either of you hear or see anything?"

Andy looked at his mother.

"We heard some things," she said cautiously.

"You stick around, then," said Reardon. It was an unnecessary command. Where did he think they would go?

The screen door opened, and a stretcher bearer backed out quickly. Andy heard, beside him, a gasp, and before he was even certain himself, his mother said her name. *Eden.*

He felt his thighs loosen, along with the bottom of his stomach, not so badly that he feared he might fall, but enough so that his mother felt the weight and stiffened, becoming a crutch. Their roles, so new and pure just a moment before, were again reversed; he was, after all, still her boy.

TAKING A quick swallow of the brandy, he remembers now a white bath towel, darkened by a large black stain, hiding Eden's face. She lay motionless, but Andy knew from the urgent syllables of the attendants that she couldn't yet be dead. She was covered by a bed sheet, a long flower-print one, he remembers, a sheet as smooth as glass over her body, and from that he knew she was naked underneath. He remembers clearly the way her toes stuck out from the sheet, and how the nail polish on them, in the dim light, shone as black dots. He sees, too, the long sticky clump of pale blond hair falling away from the bunched towel.

A force as primitive as running into a street to save a child made him start forward, but his mother held his arm. The attendants raised Eden to shoulder height and slid her into the ambulance as if onto a shelf. One of the men climbed in after her and slammed the door. The door wouldn't fasten properly, and as the ambulance sped out the drive (taking Eden to the same hospital her mother had left only forty minutes before), Andy could see the attendant furiously opening and closing the rear door to get it to catch. As it made the turn onto the road, the driver started up the siren, sending an electrifying wail out over the silent cornfields, summoning all who would listen from their sleep, announcing that something of importance had happened at the farmhouses two miles from town.

Andy watched the receding lights of the ambulance. The driveway was suddenly quiet, too quiet. Something about the scene he had just witnessed wasn't right, wasn't the way it would have gone on TV. He looked at the empty drive, and then he knew at least what the question was: Why had a fourteen-year-old girl been sent alone to the hospital?

It was his mother who said it first.
Where's Edith?

ANDREW FINGERS the quilted sides of the jelly tumbler and gets up to open the back door. He stands at the screen, hoping for a wash of cool night air. But as it was on the night of the shooting, the air is dense and smells unclean. When he was a boy, and the air was bad, his mother would always say, sniffing as she said it, *The dairy*. In the summer, if there was a southeast wind, the sickly scent of sour milk, mixed with the smell of cows, would float over the cornfields. But today, who can say? He doesn't know the industry of the area anymore; and if he did, he thinks, he's not sure he would recognize the odor. The smell could be that of toxic waste, from a plant not unlike the one his own company has in New Jersey. He seldom has to visit the plant, and no one ever talks to him about waste and disposal, but he knows it is a touchy subject. Periodically there are quiet suits and directives.

He takes a large swallow of brandy, draining the glass. Though the air is dull and the night black as a cave, the earth around him is noisy and alive with the castanets of cicadas, relentlessly sending out their frenzied scratchings. Or at least it sounds like scratchings. He doesn't know how they make their sounds, and it has always puzzled him how such a relatively small insect can be so noisy; he thinks the riddle is one that if Billy were with him he would bother to solve.

He looks out the screen door, down the dirt drive to the road. He thinks to himself, in the manner of a pronouncement: *This is the day my mother was buried*. He expects to feel a shudder of grief. When that does not come, he forces himself to think about his mother under the ground, as if that might trigger the appropriate sorrow. He waits for the horror of the image to assail him. But, as has been happening of late, his emotions won't cooperate. The images he tries to bring into focus are like sexual fantasies that no longer do the trick. Instead, at this moment, he is inexplicably distracted by thoughts of Edith Close at the burial. And this distraction, which feels like someone lingering overlong in his bedroom or his office, denying him badly needed privacy, teases him away from his mother.

He sees Edith standing alone, off to one side. She was the only woman there who wore a veil—a hat with a black veil from another era, even in the heat. The other women—women from the Ladies Guild, wives of dairymen—wore sleeveless summer dresses and stood in clumps, stooped, their necks bowed by what seemed to be the thickening of old age between their shoulder blades. Yet she stood erect and alone, in black, the only one there to wear that color. Not family, yet nearly that, the geographical accident of being the only neighbor having given her the status, almost, of a sister.

When he had spoken to her on the phone the night of his mother's death, she was, as she had always been, reserved with him—even if, on this occasion, for a sentence or two, a trace of something softer crept into her voice—and he found he could not call her anything but Mrs. Close, as he had since he was a boy. But at the burial, after the funeral, aware of her presence for the first time that day, he looked up and saw that she was watching him. She looked away quickly, and he remembers her standing on the hill, gazing out over the gravestones, beyond the iron fence, listening but not bowing to the prayers. He thought, or felt, how distant she had always been, even before the shooting. She seemed more fragile than he had, as a boy, known her to be—but though he knows she must be in her mid-sixties, she had at the burial the bearing of a younger woman, a bearing some women never achieve.

After the burial, everyone returned to the church. It had been arranged without Andrew's knowledge. There was coffee in a large green metal urn and brownies and cookies someone had baked, *refreshments,* a woman he didn't know whispered softly, touching his arm on the hill. When his father died, his mother had provided food at home, and he had thought then how macabre it was to entertain, to eat, so soon after you had put a man into the earth. He himself had had no appetite for days after his father's burial, as he has none now and didn't at the church today.

There were old worn green velvet drapes up on a stage and a portrait of Jesus on a wall. Metal chairs were unfolded and placed near the table with the food, as if for a children's dance. He stood benumbed, not from grief but from strangeness. People came and said soft things to him and moved away and chatted with more animation, out of his hearing, to each other. It was the strangeness of being in a room that you had known overwell as a child and that hadn't changed in any detail but now seemed as unfamiliar as death.

She came up to him and explained: *The guild thought you wouldn't want the trouble.* He understood that they saw him now as a bachelor again. She was still wearing the veil, and he couldn't clearly see her eyes. He wanted, almost maliciously, to walk out, for he thought, with a slight irritation, that someone could at least have asked him if he wanted this, but the impulse passed. It was right, he remembers thinking, that she should stand with him; she was as strange in that place as he was.

He looks at the clock over the sink. It reads twelve-fifty. He thinks he might have to resort to the sleeping pill after all, but then remembers that he can't; he's had the brandy.

He looks out the door in the direction of the Close farmhouse, but he can't even perceive its outlines. There are no lights on anywhere—not even the faint glow of a night-light. Somewhere upstairs, he knows, Eden is lying on a bed or sitting in a chair, the darkness irrelevant to her.

AFTER HIS mother had asked *Where's Edith?* they stood together, waiting. Andy had his hands in the pockets of his shorts; his mother had her arms wrapped

around his elbow. Andy knew it had to be Mr. Close
who was hurt; how else could there have been that
awful crying? A policeman opened the back door and
called to two others. Andy, straining, could hear bits
of grunts and breathless sentences. ". . . is talking
now . . . medium height, a mask, yellow shirt, she's
pretty sure . . . on the stairs . . . pretty hysterical . . .
face blown . . . Christ, you should . . ."

Behind the policeman, Andy saw his father at the
Closes' screen door, wanting to get out. His father
said something, and the policeman stood to one side.
In turn, the policeman mumbled something to Andy's
father, and his father shook his head slowly several
times—not a gesture of refusal, but rather one of disbelief.

Andy watched his father walk toward him. It was a
moment Andrew would never forget, though he
wouldn't know until years later that the thing his father
had seen, the thing that had changed his father's face
and the movements of his body, had, in the space of
a few short minutes, soaked in so deep that it would
never leave him. Even in the dim, pulsing light, Andy
could see the rivulets of sweat running down from his
father's temples. His father's walk was slow, the rifle
no longer a rigid brace—more like a heavy broken tool
he was taking to the garage to fix. When his father
stood in front of them, he looked first at Andy and
then at his wife. He spoke to her.

"Go inside now. Take the boy. They're bringing Jim
out."

"Jim?" his mother said quickly.

"It's bad. You go on in. Quick, now."

But his mother would not move. "What happened?" she demanded. "Tell me."

His father raised his arms, as if he meant to shep-
herd his family back to shelter. But when he saw she
would not move, he lowered them. He stabbed the
barrel of the rifle into the gravel, like a stick. He

looked at the ground. He sighed—a deep, exhausted sound.

"Jim is dead," said his father. "Eden's been shot, but she's still alive."

His mother brought her hands to her mouth. Andrew heard a high, strangled murmur.

"But how?" she asked. "Who?"

"I don't know. It looks like, *looks like,*" his father said, faltering, repeating himself, "and I think Edith was trying to say this, a man broke in while she and Jim were out, Jim was out, and Jim found him in Eden's room. He was"—his father hesitated, looked at Andy, searched for the proper wording—*"assaulting* Eden, and the man had a gun—we heard the shots. . . . Eden somehow got in the way . . . a struggle, I think. . . . Edith saw the man on the stairs. . . . He had a mask. . . . She found them both." His father stared. "I saw her in the bedroom . . . covered, covering . . ."

Andy watched his father's mouth tighten. He was seeing something Andy could only imagine, yet could not imagine at all. The image refused to form. Later Andrew realized that his father must, at that moment, have been in deep shock himself. How could his father, a dairyman, ever have been prepared for that scene in Eden's bedroom? Why did they think, did his father think, sheltered as he was by his homely routines, that he was any better equipped to deal with it than Andy or his mother?

His mother put her hands on his father's shoulders and laid her forehead on his chest. Along the road from town, Andy could see, and hear, a parade of ambulances and police cars, moving fast toward the houses. These would be from the county and the state, he was thinking. When the first ambulance pulled in the drive, they brought out Edith Close from the house.

The black stain was on her white uniform, her shoes, the side of her face, her mouth and her hair, but most of all on her hands. She was supported by a policeman at each side of her. Her feet barely moved. At the bottom of the steps, a pair of attendants or paramedics tried to get her to lie down on a stretcher. She protested wildly, pushing against a restraining hand on her chest, as if she feared she might drown. But the men overpowered her. In shock, in her raving, she raised her knees and spread them, kicking, and Andy saw, up her skirt, the white flash of her underwear. He felt a shiver move through his chest. He thought then that of all the things he had witnessed that night this was something he should not have seen.

HE STANDS up to rinse out his glass. He puts it on the sideboard. He is mesmerized by the quiet. He is not sure he has ever before realized how quiet it is here, how unnerving that quiet can be. He thinks of turning on the radio but realizes the loud voice of a late-night disc jockey will be even worse. And anyway, he tells himself practically, he has got to sleep. There's that list of chores.

He turns out the lights as he goes. In his room, he makes a halfhearted attempt to remake the bed. As he bends to tuck in the top sheet at the foot, he suddenly realizes that the dream *did* get it wrong. Or if not wrong, exactly, then out of sequence. He sits on the bed and replays the dream. In his dream, he has imagined that it was the cry of a woman that first woke him—with thoughts that it might be his mother. He remembers that panic, that struggling to the surface, as if for air. And yet it can't have been a woman's voice he heard first, he thinks logically. It has to have been the voice of a man first, the voice of Mr. Close.

Surely, the woman's cry came later.

I watch you with the sight of years ago. I hear your screen door, and I see you on the driveway. When you

*walked below my window, then, did you have a thought
of me? You are a boy with arms as thin as wood. Your
hair is growing longer because soon you'll go away. I
teased you at the river, but you wouldn't touch me.
You wouldn't touch the buttons or my skin, though I
dared you to, and others had already. Which you knew.
And when I made you look, your face was calm, though
your hands trembled. And you said . . .*

*I see your collarbone beneath a plaid shirt. Your
cuffs are rolled. There's a shimmer on the water.*

*She said your mother died, though I knew before she
told me. She is waiting for you to go away.*

*I hear your car come in the driveway. It purrs before
you turn it off, like a cat. I hear your feet on the gravel
and I see you with your hair grown longer over your
ears, and I know that soon you'll go away. I hear your
footsteps to the road and see you looking over the
cornfields. I am forgetting colors, but not the shape of
your eyes. I remember how you smell.*

TWO

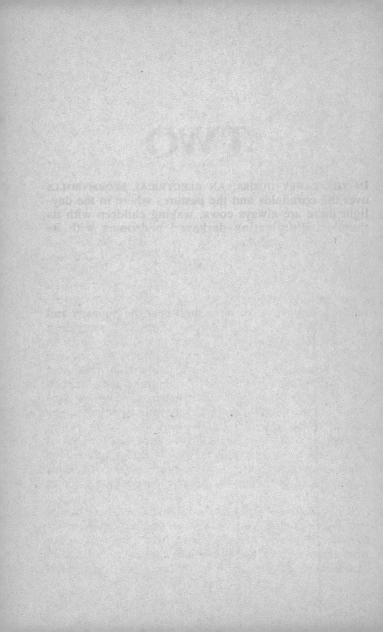

IN THE EARLY HOURS, AN ELECTRICAL STORM ROLLS over the cornfields and the pastures where in the daylight there are always cows, waking children with its thunder, illuminating darkened bedrooms with its flashes of lightning and causing even those who do not wake, like Andrew, to stir in their sleep and alter the course of their dreams. The rain drums against the shingles and tin of the farmhouses and along the smooth cedar shakes of the high ranches closer to town, against the long low flat roof of the mall near the highway and against the windows of the few shops still struggling in the village: the white stucco gas station, built in 1930; the luncheonette across the street, now owned by a Vietnamese couple; the old barbershop that once again gives crew cuts to boys; the small shop next to the barber's, where the TV repairman's sign is; and now, new to Andrew, a mini-superette next to the gas station. After the rain, near dawn, the storm moves out, leaving in its wake a chill wash of air, the first in more than a week, and in the palely lit bedrooms, the relief is palpable. Men and women, some with their children still in their beds, sleep their deepest sleep in days.

When Andrew was a boy, the town, no more than a patchwork of dairy farms with an undistinguished village at its center, was distinctly rural, devoted to the production of milk and butter and cheese and ice cream at Miller's Dairy. The men of the town, descended

from Poles, Irish, Italians and migrating Yankees,
tended livestock and cornfields, or they worked for the
dairy. Their women hovered somewhere between
farmers' wives and suburban matrons, and their children, like Andrew, grew up for a time thinking the
universe was cornfields and cows and men who woke
before dawn, until they were eleven or fourteen or seventeen and began to feel the first stirrings of a desire
to get away, or the first flutter of fear that they might
not have the courage to.

For Andrew, who knew for a certainty from an early
age that he would go away to college (his parents, with
no working farm to leave to him, were united in this
goal), the town lost its menace before it had had time
even to register, and when he was away, at school, or
in the city, he felt, if not consciously thought of, his
childhood years in the town as unencumbered by the
ethics of a more sophisticated urban life. So much so
that he often failed to notice on his visits home, these
visits growing less frequent with each passing year,
how much the town was changing.

But on this visit home he has observed, with more
clarity than he has had before, that the town is not as
it used to be. There is a highway now and the mall.
There are subdivisions where once there were just
farms. In the next town, six miles away, beyond the
mall and the biggest subdivision, there is a large insurance company that employs more people than the
dairy ever did and a factory that makes cassettes and
videotapes. The old dairy itself, so shiny and new
when Andrew's father was a foreman, seems hobbled
now by time.

Sometimes when Andrew dreams, he sees the town
as it once was—the street corners and playing fields
and cornfields and railroad tracks that made up the
landscape of his childhood. But there will be in the
dream an anachronistic conversation, or a person not
encountered until years after he left the town, or an

object not invented yet when he was living there. And though he will wake from these dreams confused or, more likely, bemused, the dreams, more than his memories, resemble the truth.

Andrew wakes and doesn't want his clothes from the city; in fact, he needs work clothes, although he has brought none with him. He finds, though, a pair of faded jeans, ironed and neatly folded over a hanger in his closet. The cloth is as soft as velvet, and he can see the faint line where years ago his mother let the hem out. When he has put them on, the bell-bottom cuffs look silly and hopelessly old-fashioned, but since he has nothing else suitable to wear, he is glad his mother saved them all these years.

In the kitchen he has a cup of instant coffee and a piece of chocolate cake someone from the Ladies Guild has brought to the house. When he finishes this, he walks out into the yard, letting the screen door slap smartly behind him. He puts his hands in his back pockets and inhales; the air tastes of mint and sage from the tangle of herbs by the back stoop. He can see that the lawn, which badly needs cutting, has shrunk, yielding its borders up, year by year, to the thicket of bracken and fern, of blackberries and wild apple and dogwood marching toward the house—as if soon they will swallow the white clapboards. How quickly a house wants to sink back into the land, he is thinking, to give up the struggle against the grasses and the rain and the sun. He feels inappropriately fine. He circles the house, the grass soaking his old canvas sneakers in a matter of seconds. Perhaps his mother had been ill for some time, he speculates, surveying with more clarity than he's had in days the disrepair of the property he must now offer to strangers. A small bed of badly overgrown zinnias, dahlias and flowers with spindly stems and unattractive red blossoms is a mass of weeds and seems to have no distinct outline. The south wall of the house, he observes, is peeling badly.

The shrubs and the hedge need a savage pruning, and there's the falling gutter that must be put right. He notices, with an unreasonable cheerfulness, a screen with an ugly gash that will need replacing.

He can offer the house as it is, he knows, and return to the city and his job—it is not as if he needs the few extra thousand that the fixing and mending will bring—but he finds the thought of the physical labor, the mental list of tasks, oddly appealing. It has been years since he has had such a list of chores. Even when he had a home of his own, in Saddle River with his wife and child, someone else did the work, such as there was, in that new, immaculate structure: a cabinet-maker, a plumber, a lawn service to tend to the shrubs and bushes there. He doubts that anyone in his home-town would ever contemplate buying such a service, just as the women here, he knows, clean their own houses. At best, like the Closes, they might hire a boy to mow. There were always plenty of boys who needed the money.

He should return to the office, of course. He looks at his watch. At this hour he would already be at his desk in a summer suit. There would be a pile of pink phone messages, and some would seem urgent. He would have about him an air of earnestness leavened by an unobtrusive wit he has learned to cultivate, fielding the puns that his boss, like a college sophomore, is so fond of. And he would feel a small pressure, around his shoulders and along the back of his neck, because there would be a deadline and surrounding it a manufactured sense of importance. Though he would not be able to escape, as he hasn't for some time now, a growing certainty that all the efforts of all the men, like him, in offices are merely an elaborate bit of theater, in which the principal actors have so long and so thoroughly played their parts (like the actors in a long-running television series) that they are known to each other—and perhaps even to themselves—only as this character or that.

He remembers, with a slight shudder, how narrowly he escaped accepting, from a woman in his office, an offer of a house in the Hamptons. He can think of practically no worse way to spend a vacation than with strangers in a town nearly as crowded as the city—or so it seems to him from here. He had thought of taking Billy camping in Nova Scotia, but Martha was being unaccountably difficult this summer, insisting that Billy not miss any of his expensive day camp and announcing that when camp was over she was taking him to visit her parents on Nantucket. Andrew likes his in-laws and thinks that Billy should visit them, and it was becoming too complicated to sort out when his mother had suddenly died and inadvertently solved the problem.

He looks north over the cornfields and finds he wants to say the word *beautiful*. The word is strange on his tongue. It is a word he has not said in a long time, and it is all the more strange spoken beside this ruined house—this house, once loved, falling into disrepair. Both houses are now shabby in the sunlight, the back steps of the other nearly rotted out, the privet climbing wild over the sills. He sees a large crack in a kitchen window—from a branch or a bird? he wonders; not now, surely, from a child—and that a shutter has been blown from an upstairs window.

Two women, two widows, living far from town, neighbors with a lifetime of history, but not women who liked each other much, he thinks, not women who called upon each other much for warmth or for talk. He sees now what he has been too preoccupied to see before—the obvious disintegration of two houses that have no men in them, houses patched up as best they can be by women of a certain generation who were never taught how to putty a window and who do not know the names of tools. They make their kitchens gleam, he knows, but if a shutter falls from an upstairs window, it is carried to the cellar and left to stand there.

He will begin with the scraping and the sanding, he decides. The grass cannot be cut until it dries out, and that won't be until late afternoon at the earliest— although he should take a look at the lawn mower before then to see what kind of condition it's in. An oriole darts from among the thick foliage of the hydrangea tree. He wonders if the scrapers are still kept in the same black metal drawer in the garage.

HE HAS been scraping for an hour, and his arm is already sore, when she comes out the back door, gingerly making her way down the rotted stoop. Reflexively he looks at his watch. Quarter to. He knows she works four hours a day, from ten to two, seven days a week, at a nursing home nearby. It was a detail among many in a letter or a phone call from his mother that he'd read or heard quickly, but now the detail comes back to him, and his mother's expression of bewilderment at anyone's willingness never to have a day off. ''She even worked Christmas,'' he remembers his mother saying or writing.

He calls to her when she is at the bottom of the stoop. She looks at her car and then turns to look at him. Delicately, she brings a thin hand to the side of her brow to shade her eyes, for the sun is behind him, and he must be to her a black silhouette against a brilliant sky. But he can see her clearly, as he couldn't yesterday: a pinkish-gray dress, an upturned face, her skin as soft as chamois. Perhaps she forgot that he would be there, but she shows no surprise. He towers over her, and she has to squint to see him. Her hair is ashen, where once it was the color of her bracelets, and is still worn long, drawn back in an intricate knot at the nape of her neck. She has on a strand of pearls— incongruous on a summer morning, driving in a Plymouth to a nursing home, but so in keeping with how he has remembered her that even the greater incongruity of her careful grooming against the ugly ruined farmhouse barely registers on his consciousness.

She walks toward him, each foot grating slightly on the gravel.

"Mrs. Close," he says, and instantly regrets the childish greeting, when he knows her name is Edith and he ought to call her that now, at thirty-six; but he feels diminished in her presence, as if he were a boy again and she'd come out to give instructions. He begins to back down the ladder.

He sees that there are folds beside her mouth where her skin has fallen and that her eyelids are hooded now. And below her eyes, there are smudges indicating that she hasn't slept well; the smudges match the color of her dress. He wants to break free of his image of himself as a boy, but when he says, too loudly for just the two of them, "I thought I'd tackle your lawn too, Edith, while I'm at this one later," his voice seems uncharacteristically boorish and rude.

She looks around at the tall grass and the wild privet, a look of weariness passing over her face.

Again he feels the boyish compunction to please, the awkwardness he has always felt with her.

She doesn't answer him directly. "A fine morning," she says.

How strange that they are speaking to each other in just the same tones of voice, using the same polite vocabulary, as they might have twenty-five years ago— as if nothing had intervened or changed in all those years, as if there had not been all that death and the birth of his own son.

She nods, and there is something in the tilt of her head or the angle of her profile that gives him a sharp memory of the younger woman he remembers her to have been. He sees a woman's hand on a man's wrist, pulling him up the steps and inside, even though the laundry basket under the clothesline is still half full of wet sheets. He remembers knocking on the back door one afternoon when he was eight, carrying a basket of tomatoes from his mother's garden, bountiful that year, and Edith opening the door, flustered, a red blush staining her throat and chest where he could see it, her hair loose and damp at the temples. She was fingering the top of her dress, where the last two buttons were still undone, and he understood, if not entirely comprehended, that Jim was in the house somewhere, home early, and that they had been doing together something secretive and thrilling.

The knowledge had come before he had even known what it was or what it meant—the suggestion that there might be between a man and a woman something that set them apart, something that could not be shared by others and ought not to be seen from the outside.

And after that day, he would watch her carefully, as if important information could be had by examining her. For other boys in the town, boys who liked to climb onto the high leather seat in the dairy truck or boys he knew from the hockey rink or in the cold tiled corridors of the junior high school, the knowledge had come differently, more predictably, from girls seen naked on a dare in woodsheds or from pictures found in magazines. Sean O'Brien, who was the goalie when Andy and he were in ninth grade, and who would be killed only three short years later, had once told of finding lurid and wonderful pictures of men and women together in a drawer marked "Hinges" in his father's cellar; and later Andrew, when he had grown and had his own house, would sometimes have a fleeting and sad image of a middle-aged TV repairman retreating to the bowels of his house for furtive pleasure.

He was aware that she was different from his mother and from the other mothers—an awareness that was inadvertently encouraged by his mother's disapproval of her neighbor, which hovered somewhere between quiet outrage and thinly disguised envy.

"Edith is not discreet," his mother would pronounce, having caught sight of her across the yard, or remembering a gesture or a remark her neighbor had made that day. "Edith is sometimes quite careless," she would say, and his father would wisely just nod, although Andy sometimes thought he smiled. And one evening his father volunteered, "Well, at least they're well matched," and his mother had said, "Shush," indicating that the boy was in the room. Her tone alerted Andy to a sentence that otherwise might have gone unremembered, and caused him to save it, as children do, until he was old enough to understand it.

He understood also, with a child's unerring antennae, that the woman his mother envied loved only the one person and that she was indifferent to the world outside her door, as if she knew she must be careful not to squander her reserves. She had seemed, for example, always to be spectacularly indifferent to Andy, thinking of him only, he felt, as the neighbor's boy and then later as the fellow who helped with odd jobs around the house to earn money for college. He sometimes thought, in fact, that she didn't actually *see* him in the yard as he trimmed a blackberry bush or raked the leaves from the flower bed. He'd say hello and nod; yet she might just pass silently by, lost in her own vision, unaware of his presence.

She waves once just before she gets into the Plymouth, and Andrew climbs back up the ladder.

Jim, though, Andrew thinks to himself, did notice him as a boy. He never passed Andy without a greeting or a question or even a piece of gum for the boy in his pocket. When the adults were in the yard, absorbed in each other, it would be Jim who would break away and take him by the hand—or even play a game of catch with him.

Scraping and painting the side of the house, as his

own father did every five years, Andrew remembers
the way Jim would watch his father when he worked—
hands in his pockets, restless, but feeling no urgency
to tackle his own chores. Jim was a man who started
things but never finished them—unlike the steady, slow
progress of Andy's father. And Andrew can remember
being asked each August to tidy up a vegetable garden
Jim had left too long to the weeds. In the spring, Jim
would begin with enthusiasm, having bought exotic
seeds from the catalogues and coming home each Saturday morning from the nursery with a shiny new tool
or a bag of peat moss. But as the spring wove into
summer, Andy would see him on the back stoop,
smoking, drinking a beer and listening to the radio as
if he had forgotten entirely that there was anything in
the yard at all.

He was a tall man, a genial alcoholic, a man whose
charm and smile made people say he was good-
looking—though he was not, with his long face and its
flat planes, a truly handsome man. It was understood
that he had appetites—most obviously for women and
for drink—though he didn't look the part. He was said
to be irresistible to women, and as a teenager, Andy
sometimes wondered if his mother's envy of her neighbor didn't spring from an unspoken and unacknowl-
edged attraction to her neighbor's husband. He
remembers that sometimes Jim would goose his mother
in the yard, and she would, as she twisted away from
him, giggle and look girlish.

He was attractive to Andy too, though differently,
and primarily because he was not a dairyman, like
Andy's father and most of the other fathers Andy knew,
but a salesman. That he only sold metal parts for farm
machinery didn't bother Andy; it was the fact that Jim
frequently left home for other places that seemed so
grand. He was the first man Andy ever knew who routinely traded in what seemed to be barely used cars
for new models every year—always a Buick and usu-

ally black, sitting gloriously in the gravel drive, making his own father's old Fords look like dusty country cousins. It was the traveling, he thinks now, that made Edith panicky in the mornings when Jim left her, sliding his hand down the curve of her narrow hip before he swung open the door of the Buick. He would lay his arm along the rim of the leather seat and back the Buick out the drive, waving cheerfully when he hit the road as if he were the only happy man in town.

And instantly she would be preoccupied, standing in the gravel drive long after he'd gone—as though he'd taken her with him. She would appear surprised and distracted if Andy's mother called to her—which Andy sometimes thought his mother did just for spite—and nearly deaf if he himself had to ask her a question about a chore or the whereabouts of a tool.

The worst, though, was her indifference to Eden. Even when Eden was small and her mother held her on her hip, Edith would seem for long seconds or even minutes to be oblivious to the child's entreaties—Eden, who seemed to have dimension and life in Edith's eyes only when Jim returned from wherever he had been.

HE REMEMBERS it as clearly as a just-told story, or he thinks he remembers it; it is hard now to sort out what he actually remembers on his own—this, his first true memory with a story and a plot—and what he might have been told later by his mother or his father or by Eden herself and then sketched into the picture he sees in his mind.

It was summer then too, he remembers, though earlier, fresher, June perhaps. A fine day, the morning, because his father was at work. And Jim, too, was traveling, because Andy's mother that night, using the phone, found him in a motel near Buffalo and called him home. Andy was in the garden with his mother. He remembers the scent of the soil, an evocative aroma he has not smelled for years, and a row of radishes, the fat red globes pushing up from the black earth. He was happy and rather proud, because his mother had said he could pick them. He remembers that he was wearing brown leather shoes and white socks and that the gap between the shoes and the socks was filling up with black dirt.

Edith came across the yard and stood by the gate in the wire fence. She was holding a bundle, wrapped in a yellow towel, in her arms. He knew at once, by the way she cradled it, that it was a baby—though possibly (the thought crossed his mind) it was the Closes' cat, sick somehow. The fact that she might just appear on a random morning with a baby didn't strike him as odd at all; friends of his mother's often just appeared at their door with new babies. It was much odder that the cat might be sick; after all, Andy had just seen it that morning, and it had seemed fine. It wasn't until he saw his neighbor's face, and then felt the way his mother got up from her knees to go to her at the gate, that he knew something was terribly wrong. It was a baby, but perhaps a sick baby, he thought.

"Edith," said his mother. He knew in the name there was a large question.

"I was vacuuming in the kitchen. And when I stopped, I heard a sound," said Edith Close. "It was a strange sound. I thought it was the cat, whining. Or a hurt bird. It was out front somewhere, and I wanted it to stop."

She was wearing, he remembers, the kind of dress she always wore—a dress with a narrow waist and a top like a shirt, with sleeves she rolled to the elbow. Her forearms were narrow, and she had on gold bracelets. Her hair was parted in the middle and hung straight behind her shoulders, as she often combed it, in a style that would become fashionable years later with younger women. He remembers the bright red lipstick on her mouth, and that her face was white.

"And when I went to the door and opened it, there

was . . . there was this cardboard box, out near the road but just inside the privet hedge. It said Oxydol on the side, and I thought someone had thrown their garbage onto the lawn like they sometimes do with the beer bottles. And then I heard the sound again, and I was angry because I thought someone had left us a litter of kittens, and I knew how hard it would be to get rid of them. . . . So I went to look, and the box was open and filled with towels, and this was in it, crying. . . .''

Andy's mother leaned across the wire fence and pulled a bit of the material away from her neighbor's arms.

''Jesus God,'' said his mother, stepping back quickly as if she'd seen something deformed.

The two women stood looking at each other for a moment and didn't speak.

''What is it?'' his mother asked finally.

The other woman didn't understand the question. ''What is it . . . ?''

''A boy or a girl?''

Edith looked momentarily stunned. Then she tilted her head back and closed her eyes. ''Oh God, I wish Jim were here,'' she suddenly cried. ''I don't know. I don't know.'' She looked as though she were about to fall, with the bundle in her arms.

''We'll go inside,'' said his mother quickly, clicking into gear in that way she had when there was a crisis or when he had fallen and hurt himself. ''We'll look at the baby and make sure it's all right and call the police. Then we'll find Jim.''

She turned to look at Andy, crouched in the dirt. Her face was unusually cross. She spoke in the voice she used when she ''meant business,'' and pointed her finger at him.

''You are not to leave this garden under any circumstances. Do you understand me?'' It was not a question. ''You stay here and you don't move until I come back for you. I have to go next door with Mrs. Close.''

Chastened and frightened, for she had never left him alone with no adults around, he watched them walk toward the other house and disappear inside the back door.

THAT WAS the first intruder, he thinks suddenly to himself, not the man who came in the August night, but the person who brought and left a child on a June morning fourteen years earlier. A parent himself, he tries to imagine what he has never thought of before: a woman stopping her car, the swift movement around the hedge. Had she hesitated, wept, bitten her lip for courage? Had a man or a boy brought her and insisted that she do this? Was she a young girl, a child herself, or an older woman with too many children to feed? Why that house and not another? Had she been driving up and down the road, searching for hours for the perfect doorstep? How had she been certain there was someone at the house to care for the baby?

''It might have been us,'' his father said that night at supper. His voice was unusually quiet. ''It could so easily have been us.''

And but for the accident of the other house facing the road, and theirs, seventy feet back, facing north, he came to understand, he might have had a sister, and that the fate of the child who would be called Eden had been determined by geography. And as he grew older and heard the story often repeated, it was hard for him not to think of her as a near sibling, someone who might have been called Ruth or Debbie, as his mother planned to call the daughter who never came, and that she might have been his and theirs.

BUT BEFORE the day was out, she was not anyone's but Jim's. Andy's mother heard it in his voice on the telephone from Buffalo.

"How did he take it?" asked Andy's father when his mother put down the phone.

"He's coming right away. He sounded . . . well, he just sounded very excited. And he asked the queerest questions," she said. "For a man."

"What questions?" said his father.

"He wanted to know . . . well, he wanted to know how much it weighed and how old it was, and what it looked like, and what the doctor had said, in all the details," she said, smoothing her hands along the front of her apron. "Like a woman," she added, but, of course, not like the woman who ought to have asked those questions, her voice implied.

And then his mother shook her head and sighed: "Poor man." For they all knew that the baby would be taken away as soon as the police could arrange for a place in an orphanage or a foster home. When the police had come that morning, accompanied by Dr. Ryder, who examined the child, they had asked Mrs. Close if she would keep the baby until the matter was settled, and she had said yes but had not suggested that she herself wanted it. And yet it was common knowledge, as Andy's mother had reminded his father (and had later incorporated into the oft-told tale of Eden's arrival), that Jim especially wanted a child and that they had been trying for years to conceive one, despite Dr. Ryder's pronouncement that the environment of Mrs. Close's womb was "hostile" to Jim's seed. An irony not lost on anyone.

THE MUSCLES in Andrew's right shoulder are screaming when he sees a red Honda Prelude pull smartly into the gravel driveway. It can't, at that speed, he thinks, be another chocolate cake from the Ladies Guild. A man unfolds himself from the driver's seat and snaps the door to as neatly as a soldier. He wears a tan summer suit and a pair of dark aviator sunglasses. His hair, which Andrew last remembers seeing unwashed and wild behind his ears, is short and trim. The man puts his hands in his pants pockets and grins.

"Andy-boy."

"T.J."

Andrew begins to back down the ladder. Tom Jackson lowers the sunglasses along the bridge of his nose and peers at Andrew. "Nifty," he says.

Andrew looks down at the anachronistic bell-bottoms. "They were in the closet," he says, and shrugs.

"Hey, listen," said T.J., losing the smile and advancing toward Andrew with his hand outstretched. "I'm really sorry about your mother. I just heard this morning. A client said . . ."

The two men shake hands. "It was mercifully quick," Andrew says inanely, parroting the words of Dr. Ryder. He realizes suddenly that the job of the bereaved is to allay the embarrassment of those who come to offer solace.

"Yeah, quick, that's the way to go," says T.J. He takes the sunglasses off and hangs them by a stem from his jacket pocket. "You're looking good, Andy-boy," he says, lightly punching Andrew's arm. "You workin' out?"

Andrew has not been working out, but he knows from the way T.J. has said it and the square look of him that *he* has and that he devotes some time to it. When they were boys, it was always T.J. who would arrive early for practice.

"No," says Andrew apologetically. "I was running for a while, but I moved and I lost it."

"You gotta have discipline," says T.J., the fastest skater Andrew has ever seen, a skater who seemed to hover effortlessly over the ice. "You gotta make it a habit. Every day, no matter what. You gotta stay in shape. Hey, man, forty's just around the corner."

Andrew has not thought of forty quite that way be-

fore, if, indeed, he has thought of it at all; but the
soreness in his shoulders is telling him that he is not
as young as he thought he was.

"Want a beer?" he asks. Andrew's memory of the
landscape of his refrigerator is vague, but he thinks
there may be the remnants of a six-pack he bought the
day before at the mini-superette.

"Sure," says T.J. He turns with a flourish to let
Andrew know that he is examining the black BMW in
the driveway. He whistles appreciatively. "You must
be doin' OK," he says. "Hey, I thought *I* was doing
good, but a BMW. Whadda they go for now—twenty,
thirty?"

Actually Andrew is embarrassed by his car and has
been since arriving at the farmhouse. It sits in the drive
looking as out of place as a woman in a mink at a
garage sale. It also makes him anxious in a way he
can't precisely define.

"To tell you the truth, I'd rather have your Prelude," says Andrew, lying graciously, since he would
not for one minute own a bright red car. "The BMW's
too temperamental," he adds, compounding the lie;
the understated black vehicle runs as smoothly as a
panther.

He leads the way up the back stoop and into the
kitchen. With relief he sees that there are three Hei-
nekens on the top shelf of the fridge. T.J. takes the
tan jacket off and drapes it carefully over the back of
a white kitchen chair. He rolls his neck, squares his
shoulders and leans against the sink. He pops open his
beer. Despite his lack of interest in working out, Andrew is impressed by T.J.'s flat stomach.

"So what's it been? Ten years?" asks T.J., taking
a long swallow.

Andrew, leaning against the fridge, calculates. "I
think it's more like fifteen or sixteen," he says. "I
think the last time we got together was seventy-one or

seventy-two. We went to see Tom Rush over Christmas break. I think.''

''Sixteen years!'' says T.J., exclaiming. ''Jesus H. Christ. It sounds like something my old man used to say.'' He shakes his head. ''Holy shit.''

He runs his fingers up and down the beer can, making patterns in the condensation. ''So whadda you do now?'' T.J. asks. ''You in business or what?''

''I'm with a pharmaceutical firm in the city,'' Andrew says. ''I'm vice-president in charge of marketing and advertising.'' In this farmhouse kitchen, his job description sounds absurdly pretentious, but T.J. nods his approval.

''You were gonna be a writer,'' T.J. says.

''And you were going to be a musician. Keyboards.''

''Yeah.''

''One thing leads to another,'' says Andrew, for something to add. He doesn't particularly want to go into the specifics, however, of how smoothly he was ''led'' into moving to New York and taking his first job with the pharmaceutical firm. Nor into the specifics of how quick Martha was to see, in that move, certain financial possibilities.

''Yeah,'' says T.J. ''Right to the bank.''

The two men laugh.

''To money,'' says T.J., raising what's left of his beer in Andrew's direction.

Andrew raises his can in response.

''You married?'' asks T.J.

Andrew shakes his head, ''I was. We were separated about a year ago. I have a son, Billy. He's seven.''

''Hey, man, I'm sorry,'' says T.J. ''About the split, I mean. That's rough. Your idea or hers?''

Andrew reflects that this is the second time in ten minutes T.J. has said he is sorry for Andrew—three if you count the scolding over not working out.

"I guess it was mutual, the way those things are," he answers evasively.

"Yeah, right," says T.J., draining the last of the beer. He puts the can on the counter.

"Have another," offers Andrew.

"No. Can't. Thanks anyway. I got a corporation this afternoon wants to see the Gunther farm. For condos. Could be a fantastic deal."

"You're in real estate," says Andrew.

"For now," says T.J. "But developing is where it's at. The old farts are selling their land—the kids don't want to farm anymore. So what else is new, right? It's condos now—working couples, retirees, they don't want to have to mow the lawn. I had a deal about a month ago—a developer who bought the Gorzynski place and is putting in a country club with condos, a golf course, a pool, the whole nine yards."

T.J. picks up the empty beer can. He puts it back on the counter. "You gonna be around awhile?" he asks. "I'd like to get you out to the house to meet the kids. I married Didi Hanson, by the way."

"My mother wrote me that," says Andrew. He has an image of Didi Hanson's perfect teeth, a blond flip, and matching sweaters and skirts, long after the girls he knew were wearing jeans. He also remembers that Didi was a cheerleader and that she took it seriously, like a course.

"We've got two boys ourselves. Tom junior's fourteen now, a handful. Ellis, the little one, is nine going on two, if you know what I mean."

Andrew isn't sure he does, but he nods. "I'd planned to stay a week," he answers, "fixing up the place before I put it on the market."

As soon as he says the word *market,* an unwelcome suspicion enters his thoughts. Has T.J. sniffed a potential sale and come looking for a client? Do real estate salesmen routinely read death notices in the papers? Or, to give his friend the benefit of the doubt,

did T.J. really hear of Andrew's mother's death only
this morning from a client? He can imagine the conversation: *I'm sorry to hear that,* T.J. would have said,
immediately calculating how to get the edge, the same
quality that, in another era, had made him the best
hockey player the county had ever seen. *Her son, Andy,
and I used to be real close friends.*

"You selling?" asks T.J., too casually, bending
down and peering out the kitchen window, as if something out there had caught his attention.

"I guess," says Andrew.

"Really," T.J. says, standing up but not quite
meeting Andrew's gaze. "Well, shit, you need a
hand, I'd be glad to help out—for old times' sake,
like. To be perfectly frank, I don't really handle such
small layouts these days, but seeing as how we're old
friends . . ." He looks around the kitchen as if eyeing it afresh, but Andrew has the sudden and distinct
impression he's been taking inventory since he walked
in the door.

"Whadda you want for it?" T.J. asks.

Andrew shrugs. "I've no idea. What do you think?"

"It's in pretty bad shape," says T.J., "and pretty
isolated except for the Close house, and that's not an
asset, if you follow me. . . . I dunno, maybe a hundred. One twenty-five."

Andrew nods. He is certain that T.J. has made these
calculations earlier in the day. They fall from his
tongue too quickly.

But since Andrew hasn't committed himself to any
other real estate agent, and because he wants only to
make the transaction as painless as possible, he begins
to see the arrival of T.J. as remarkably fortuitous, if
not entirely coincidental. He wonders if T.J. feels the
same awkward distance from their friendship as he
himself does—or if he even cares.

"Be my guest," he says.

T.J. shakes his hand. "Excellent," he says, smiling

and giving himself away completely. "I'll be speaking to you later about the details, and as soon as I talk to Didi, we'll have you around. I'd pick a date now, but I have to ask Didi—you know how women are."

Andrew winces inwardly. He doesn't know how women are any more than he suspects T.J. does, but there is something in the use of the cliché that tells Andrew that his friend's marriage isn't good. The knowledge surprises him—and then he wonders if perhaps he's mistaken, if the marriage is only not good that day, that week, that morning. If T.J. had come by last week, he wonders, would Andrew have sensed a different marriage? One more intimate, more hopeful? He knows that for most of his own marriage, its character often changed from one day to the next, depending sometimes on circumstances, sometimes on whether or not he and Martha had made love that morning.

"So," says T.J., shifting his weight against the sink.

Now that business, in its own way, has been conducted, Andrew can smell T.J.'s need to be moving on. It's human nature. Andrew has done it countless times himself.

T.J. picks up his jacket and puts it on. Andrew notices that there are beads of perspiration on T.J.'s upper lip. They move toward the door, open it and stand together on the stoop. They are both looking out at the other house.

"You seen Eden yet?" asks T.J.

"No, I haven't."

"I don't think I've seen her six times in ten years," says T.J. "And each time she was in a car with her mother. Pretty isolated out here. Of course, she was away for so long in that place upstate. . . . Everybody kinda goes his own way, you know what I mean. Sometimes I feel bad I never just drove over and knocked on the door after she got back, but I never knew what I'd say really."

"Yes," says Andrew.

"She was one fantastic-looking girl. You remember?"

"I remember."

"A real knockout. She was—what, fourteen?"

"About."

"A mess, if you ask me."

T.J. squares his shoulders and looks down the drive toward the cornfields on the other side of the road. "I always figured he buried the gun in the cornfields somewhere, but I don't know," he says. "You'd think it woulda been plowed up by now."

"You would think so," says Andrew.

The sun glints sharply off a silver Mazda that speeds along the road, intercepting their view of the fields. Above the fields, a flock of crows makes a half-moon arc.

And as they had done for weeks after the shooting, silently, not wanting anyone to know of their preoccupation, Andrew realizes that once again they are drawing diagrams in their heads of how the unthinkable could have taken place: The father walking into the house, hearing the muffled sounds upstairs, opening the door to his daughter's room, the horror of what he sees there, the frenzied shouts. A hand, reaching for a gun. Eden with a sheet clutched to her breast, moving toward her father. . . . The mother's footsteps on the stairs.

He remembers the terrible sound of the crying.

"You ever see Sean's parents?" asks Andrew.

T.J. makes a movement with his shoulders, as if to shake himself loose from his speculation. "His father's still got the TV repair shop in town, but he's usually pretty far gone by afternoon. The mother died a few years back. Cancer. Bad news, that story. About Sean, I mean."

"Yeah," says Andrew.

"So," says T.J. He grabs Andrew's hand. "So listen, take it easy,'' he says, moving away and sideways along the driveway, toward his car, reaching in his pocket for his keys.

Andrew watches him from the stoop. With the same economy of movement that made him the most fluid skater in the county, T.J. slips his long body into the Prelude. Andrew is about to wave, when T.J. sticks his head out of the window.

''And for Christ's sake, Andy-boy,'' he says, turning the key in the ignition, ''go buy yourself a decent pair of jeans.''

Andrew smiles and shrugs. He wonders how certain qualities in a boy can turn out so strangely in a man. And yet who is he to criticize? Has he not himself, in business, made the same dismal moves?

The beer on an empty stomach has left him light-headed. He goes back up the stairs into the kitchen.

As he opens the screen door, he has an image of Eden naked under a flower-print sheet—and the image startles him.

Why think of that now? He wonders if T.J. knows about this fact. Did he, years ago, tell that detail to his friend?

AFTER JIM had held the baby, there was no thought of ever letting her go. She was his before he even arrived at the farmhouse. Andy's mother was in the Closes' kitchen, waiting, with her neighbor, when Jim flung open the door and let his sample case fall from his hands. She watched the way he bent to the child—his eagerness for the child seeming to be a natural extension of his largesse—and how he held her aloft as gracefully as a baby nurse, as if he'd been practicing in his dreams for years.

And she saw, even in the confusion, the face of Edith Close, who put herself forward to be kissed before giving over the child, but who was not kissed or touched until much later in the night and who sat watching numbly at the kitchen table as her husband danced with his warm bundle over the worn linoleum floor. And Andy's mother saw, too, her struggle to compose her face, to realign her features to match her husband's new expression, to feign a joy she knew she must display so as not to fall behind.

She knew at once not to protest, nor to bring up even one objection—though, said Andy's mother later, there were plenty of them for a practical woman to consider: a distraught mother might, with second thoughts, return; the baby might not be right in some as yet undetermined way; she might herself wake up pregnant any day now, creating two babies to care for (this last objection would immediately be seen as transparent, however, as it had all but been ruled out by the all-knowing Dr. Ryder).

"Eden," said Jim, dreamily skating between the sink and the stove. "We shall call her Eden."

Edith looked up at him; she seemed to be about to protest.

"The Garden of Eden come to us in a basket," he rhapsodized, exposing. Andy's mother was to say later, a hitherto unrecognized and not altogether welcome strain of sentiment, seeing as how the child had actually arrived in an Oxydol box; and creating in that instant a lifetime of confusion by giving the infant a name that sounded so like the adoptive mother's. ("Edith's had stitches?" Andy's father would say distractedly from the dinner table, having half heard a story his wife was telling. "No, *Eden's* had stitches," she would reply, in endless exasperation.)

And Eden she became, as Andy's mother sat watching her neighbor's face—and saw upon it the struggle give way to the swift sharp knowledge that something irrevocable had happened in her life and that the exact shape of what she'd had before was, in an instant, gone. The hand that had been propping up her chin slipped silently into her lap. Her mouth opened

slightly, and Andy's mother could hear beside her a
long, slow intake of air.

ANDREW RUBS his sore shoulder and bends down to
survey the dismaying contents of his mother's refrigerator. He observes that it seems to contain random
pieces of a number of different puzzles—nothing add-
ing up to a satisfying whole. He has never been fond
of Edith Close (primarily, he supposes, because she
so ignored him—but more, he'd prefer to think, because of Eden), but despite this dislike he cannot help
but feel for her the fundamental unfairness of it all:
the neat and terrible symmetry of the two intruders—
the one on a fresh June morning, a foretaste of what
could be lost; the other on a humid August night, taking everything.

AND WHEN the police came the next day, with a social
worker, there was Jim at the door. He announced they
were keeping the child. If they had to be merely foster
parents for a while, that was fine, said Jim. But even-
tually, he was sure, the child would legally be theirs.
The police, unprepared for this, had papers stating
otherwise, but these were of no consequence to Jim,
who calmly went where he was told, signed where he
was bidden, showered his irresistible charm on women
who knew shortcuts through the bureaucratic maze,
and in that way slipped through the miles of red tape
that might have daunted another man.

  With motherhood rudely thrust upon her, her hor-
mones ill-prepared for the job, Edith Close performed
the tasks required of her as if directed by remote control—a poor connection that might short-circuit at any
time and often did. With Jim around, the infant had,
at least, a playmate—though Edith's nascent jealousy,
a subtle mist through which she floated and which had
not yet created the sharp tongue that would come later,
often demanded that Jim put the baby down "so the

poor child can sleep.'' But with Jim away, Eden ceased to exist in any tangible way at all—the tree falling in the forest with no one to hear.

Andrew, who has settled for a casserole left by the Ladies Guild, which looks more or less like goulash, remembers the afternoon Edith Close left the baby outside in the carriage without the net and went upstairs to lie down. The Closes' honey-colored cat—whose jealousy, unlike his mistress's, was uninhibited—leapt silently into the carriage and was about to do away with the usurper when the baby's screams brought Andy's mother running from the kitchen. She scooped up the child, giving the sullen cat a remarkably deft kick—thinking the row would alert her neighbor. But even when she went to the back door and called for Edith—rather crossly, Andy thought—it was some minutes before the dazed woman arrived at the door. It was Andrew's mother's impression, as she told his father at dinner that night, that Edith had simply *forgotten* the child altogether.

Andrew doubts, as did his mother, that their neighbor willfully meant to harm the baby. It was rather, as he has thought before, a case of faulty connections: a matter of her fear of losing Jim (who for years had gone off in his black Buick to other rooms in other towns, and about whom rumors of other women often circulated). A child who developed, as luck would have it, an astonishing head of blond curls, several shades lighter than the hair of her adoptive mother. Though she was not a fat child, she had plump cheeks, an appealing pink coloring and remarkably dark lashes for so fair a skin type. Her eyes were blue, like Edith's, causing the women of the town to comment how like the mother the child was (a remark that must have filled Edith with ambivalence), but a more vivid blue, a greenish blue, which on an older girl or a young woman today you'd say was enhanced with contact lenses. She was a child whose beauty was indestructible: You could forget to wash her face or comb her hair, as Edith often did; you could put her in a pair of dull hand-me-downs from the rummage sale—and yet, passing by the playground at the school, it would be she whom you noticed first among the other faces and small bodies on the swings or on the jungle gym.

The more Edith ignored the child, the more Jim spoiled her, as if to redress the deficit—or perhaps it was the other way around: Edith meant unconsciously to temper his excess. But his love being the more passionate and less ambivalent of the two emotional forces in the household, Eden grew up more spoiled than ignored—spoiled ''rotten,'' his mother sometimes said, a phrase that has always suggested to Andrew bruised and softened fruit, a picture distinctly at odds with the beguiling, if willful, child who was growing fast into puberty next door.

Eating the congealed goulash, Andrew remembers scenes he has long forgotten. Jim arrives home from a trip and opens the door of the black Buick. He in his shirtsleeves, with his tie still knotted. There are packages in his hands. He sees Eden on the new swing set he has ordered from Sears, the one Andy's father had to pour the cement for when Jim could not (or would not) figure out the directions. Eden spies Jim, squeals with delight and looks for the present she knows will be there. Then there is Edith at the screen, peering out, patting her hair. She runs down the steps to her husband. She is wearing a new sweater that Andy, who is playing with an old toy car on his own back stoop and who is wishing Jim would look his way with a stick of gum, has never seen before—a soft white furry sweater with a low jeweled neck. Sometimes she says the name *Jim*. Sometimes she puts her arm around his waist. Then, when he has greeted his wife with a kiss, Edith bends to the child, and in an animated voice neither Eden nor Andy has heard in three days, says how pretty the dress is that Jim has brought her and touches the child for the first time since Jim went away. In the beginning, when she is very small, Eden is happy to have her mother hug her at last. Later she will just be confused. Then she will learn to smirk. And finally she will shrug her mother off with a rude word or a gesture that Edith will publicly ascribe to Eden's "difficult phase."

Andrew, giving up on the goulash and scraping his plate, now understands these domestic jealousies in a way that was impossible for him as a child. Jealousy was there, even in his own house, he realizes, on his father's face, when Andy, with a fever or a scraped knee, would choose his mother's embrace instead of his; and he has felt it himself, more recently, watching a flicker of hesitation pass over his son's features when Billy leaves his mother to come away with Andrew for an evening or a weekend.

But, in an instant, as he grasps Billy's hand or ruffles his hair, the hurt is gone, healed, as quickly as it came. While for Edith Close, there seemed to be no healing, no respite from her own imagination.

THEY WERE FRIENDS, good friends, for a year, possibly two. He was fourteen and Eden was eleven. Before that time, she'd been uninteresting as a playmate, though she'd always possessed the inherent fascination of a celebrity by dint of her arrival. And before she was eleven she whined a lot, having learned early that the thin grating sound was the only one that seemed to penetrate the thickening fog of preoccupation that surrounded her mother, and that it worked miraculously with Jim, who couldn't bear to see his daughter unhappy, no matter how absurd the cause. But by the age of eleven, she'd seen, looking across the yard, that Andy and his friends were considerably more interesting as potential companions than her distant mother and her too attentive father or the girls at school, who had never quite been friendly. And being clever, not to say manipulative, she was quick to intuit that acceptance by these older boys required radical surgery. Thus Eden became, for a brief and happy period in her life, a tomboy.

He remembers vividly the day she first came to them. He and Sean and T.J. were fiddling with their fishing rods by Andrew's back stoop, getting ready to head out to the pond to catch some catfish before supper. It was September or October, Andrew thinks, a school night, because he'd had to finish his homework before he could go. But early in the year, before hockey practice had started. It was muggy; they were in T-shirts, enjoying the last taste of summer and summer pleasures before the cold set in in earnest.

T.J., who was always the quickest of the three, had his rig ready to go, leaning against the side of the house, and was executing an idle tap dance in the dirt by the stoop, his sneakers raising puffs of dust around his feet.

"Come on, you guys," he said impatiently. "It'll be dark soon, and anyway I gotta be home by supper or my old man'll cream me."

"Take it easy," said Andy lightly, threading his line through the guides. "We've still got two hours."

But it was Sean who was having trouble that day, his line hopelessly tangled in a knot he'd been working on with no results for twenty minutes. His brow was knit into a furrow, and his face was nearly as red as his hair from his frustration. T.J. and Andy were both waiting for him to blow, Andy more than a little worried that Sean would suddenly yell *Shit,* with Andy's mother chopping vegetables right beyond the screen. And then that night at the supper table, there would be the lecture about bad language and comments about the company Andy kept. Though his parents liked T.J., who had, even at an early age, the gift of charm and who had developed a talent for salesmanship, mostly of himself, they were nervous about Sean.

Sean's parents were well known in the town. Both
were heavy drinkers, but their reputation had been
earned because of their fights: legendary sharp-
tongued battles heard through the open window of the
apartment they lived in with their three children over
the TV repair shop; bitter tirades in the shop itself
while embarrassed customers pretended to be studying
the contours of a picture tube; or silent, ugly tableaux
seen through the rolled-up windows of the family Pon-
tiac, Sean's mother's lined and dead-white face turned
toward her husband, who would, like his son, grow
red from his fury.

As a boy, Sean was visibly chagrined by his parents'
displays of temper, even though, as he grew into his
teens, his own temper would betray him when he least
wanted it to. But T.J. and Andy accepted this embarrassment and his parents' volatility as a given, much
in the same way they unconsciously acknowledged that
Andy's mother was too fat and T.J.'s mother was a
social climber—these facts intruding upon their childhood, sometimes even causing them a moment's pain
or awkwardness, but ultimately easily dismissed as not
being pivotal to their lives. The weather was pivotal.
And the condition of the ice or the fishing. Or a stolen
baseball glove or the offer of a driving lesson or a
chance at the playoffs. Their parents, however, seemed
more like obstacles to be negotiated than central fig-
ures in the daily drama.

(Yet Andrew thinks now how wrong they were to be
so complacent. For that legacy of volatility, or perhaps
it was the alcohol, ultimately would destroy Sean; and
is not T.J., Andrew wonders, just as socially ambitious as his mother?)

Andy didn't notice Eden until T.J. said, by way of
a greeting, "Hey."

She was wearing a plaid cotton shirt and a pair of
white shorts. She was barefoot, he remembers, and

her hair, still long then, was pulled off her face in a low ponytail.

Although she'd sometimes come over when Andy was alone, she'd never approached him when he was with other boys, and Andy was waiting for a message or a summons from Edith or Jim about some task that needed attending to. But she stood there, her hands in her pockets of her shorts, and said, redundantly, "What are you doing?"

It all happened, Andrew thinks now, in a matter of seconds—a deft dance of questions and positions, each one finding, in the space of a few sentences and a look here and there, a role to take on. Sean looked up, the anger draining from his face, replaced by confusion. T.J. shoved his hands into his pockets and said, *Fishing*. Andy, not getting it yet, waited for the summons. Eden smiled, a deliberate smile that made them all stare at their feet, but when they looked up, the smile was gone.

"Can I come too?" she asks quite seriously.

T.J. whirled in a circle on his heel. Andy fumbled with an answer. "I don't know," he said unthinkingly. "You haven't got a rod."

T.J. hooted and punched the air. Andy, realizing the pun, rolled his eyes. Eden stood her ground.

"So?" she said, challenging them.

T.J. put an arm around Eden's shoulder, something Andy had never done. He was sure he himself had never touched her, and T.J.'s touch startled him, caught him off guard, so that he felt in succession annoyed with T.J. and then confused, as he sometimes felt when he was in a room with his friends and his parents and had no idea what to say or whom to be.

"You want to watch the big boys fish?" asked T.J., winking at Andy. "It's a thrill."

Eden shrugged—careful not to appear too eager now that she had made her move.

T.J. put his hands back in his pockets. Andy said,

unsure just what it was he was committing himself to, *OK by me*.

Sean, looking first at Eden, then at T.J., then back to Eden, screwed his face into a squint. He peered at Eden as if she were a species unwelcome at the best of times.

"Jesus H.," he said aloud.

As A TOMBOY, Eden was brilliant. She learned to be tough and savvy as if taking on a foreign language, and in doing so discovered an aptitude for it. After an initial period of disbelief, Andy and T.J. and Sean grudgingly found this new character acceptable, and they were more than a little awed by a tenacity in her that none of them could quite match. No matter how hard they tried in the beginning to shake her off, she stuck, like a stray. She made her mother cut her hair, though Jim had forbidden it; she took to wearing dungarees and white Keds. Though she was inches shorter than Andy or T.J. or Sean, she matched them stride for stride as they walked the tracks, her hands stuffed like theirs into the pockets of a maroon and gold junior high school jacket that was several sizes too big for her, a black knit cap, like the ones they wore, all but covering her bright gold fringe.

It was the year T.J.'s father let him have a BB gun to shoot squirrels with, and after she had wheedled a turn, Eden showed an enthusiasm for tracking and shooting small animals that surprised them—especially Andy, who even at fourteen was hard-pressed to understand why killing animals was fun. In winter, when every afternoon was spent with a hockey stick on the pond behind the cornfields, Eden watched the others at first, hunched in her school jacket, stomping her feet on the ground, both to keep warm and in irritation. "I want to skate, you assholes," she cried, employing the word that was at the farthest edge of their vocabularies that month. And in the end, she bullied

Andy into teaching her. Though she was small, she was, like her demeanor, fast and headstrong. And when she was hit with the puck—on the shin through her dungarees, at the side of her cheekbone, drawing blood, causing a scar that might have been permanent had that particular mark not been obliterated three years later—she, like them, did not cry but rather held her breath and stood perfectly still and let her face go white with the pain.

They played at the pond from early December until late in March. He remembers the way the toes went first, and then the ears, because they'd been bitten by the cold years earlier one day when you hadn't noticed. He remembers the way the ice felt when it was refrozen and bumpy and the sinking in the stomach when you'd caught an edge and knew you were going down on your kneecaps. In early December, after a cold snap, the ice was black and gorgeous, but for most of the season, in the late afternoon, it was snowy with streaks and ruts and graceful arcs, with the sun blinking red-gold behind the lacy silhouettes of the bare tree limbs, the sky already turning navy blue.

He remembers they'd been sitting one afternoon in the snowbank at the edge of the pond, unlacing their skates, timing it so they'd emerge from the cornfields just as it turned pitch, calling each other "shithead" and "fink" in a confusion of vocabularies, trying out words they'd heard at school or from their parents. It was just after Christmas, because Andy and Eden had new skates. He remembers that his fingers were stiff with the intense cold and that he couldn't get the wet knots undone. And then suddenly, raising his head in frustration, in the thickening dusk, he saw it.

She drew from her pocket a pack of Old Golds—casually, as if the pack, wrapped in cellophane, were merely sticks of gum. He can see it still: the pleasure and triumph in her eyes at being the first to have them, thus cementing for herself, with this single gesture, a place among the elect.

One by one they stopped what they were doing to watch her as she expertly opened the cellophane and shook one cigarette from the pack. She lit it. She inhaled deeply, as none of them had ever done, and Andy realized she'd been practicing, possibly for days, watching and waiting for the precise moment to make her move. Sean, his nose running from the cold, tried to disparage the gesture, breaking the silence by saying that she had the only parent who smoked, implying she had an access denied the others, but the moment belonged to Eden, and she knew it. She held out the pack, and they each took one, holding it between their fingers the way, years later, they would learn to cradle joints. She tossed the matches to Andy, fixing him with her eyes. And with this look, she dared him to inhale as she had, though he could hardly breathe from the cold and his earlier exertions on the ice.

They had all smoked the one cigarette, and then they'd had another, till they were nothing but four embers glowing in the dark. And at the edge of the cornfield, as they were about to disperse—T.J. and Sean still with the long hike back toward town, their skates knotted and slung over their shoulders, their heads spinning and their stomachs rising—it was Eden who'd produced the roll of peppermint Life Savers, instructing them each on the importance of masking their breath. And if she had not already truly become one of them earlier when she offered them the cigarettes, she would have done so then—for though they all "caught shit," as T.J. put it, when they arrived home later than they ever had for dinner, none of them yet had to face the shouts and heated lectures that would come months later when smoking among them was already commonplace and they'd grown careless.

* * *

BY MIDWINTER they were no longer a threesome but a foursome, a mismatched quartet (seen from behind as they walked the tracks with hockey sticks parked on their shoulders) of three tall, reedy clarinets and one short piccolo. Indeed, Eden had become so much a part of them that they minded when she wasn't there.

"So where is she?" T.J. said one afternoon when Andy and Sean got to the pond. T.J. already had his skates on, having arrived first, and was carving impatient circles in the bumpy ice near the shoreline.

Andy, aware that his friends looked to him as a source of information about Eden, his status enhanced by this circumstantial intimacy, knew she was at the dentist and said so, registering as he did a flicker of disappointment in the way T.J. stabbed the ice with his stick. At the very least, it was easier to play a game with four.

Sean, yanking at a lace, was still pretending then that Eden wasn't much more than a pain in the neck and clicked his tongue in disgust; but when he said, with almost too much of a complaint in his voice, "This was the day I was supposed to show her how to do an eagle," Andy thought that he, too, had come to expect her presence.

For a brief time, their days together were a satisfying blur spent on the ice, at the baseball diamond or in the cornfields, looking up at a summer sky that floated too quickly past them. It seems that then he and Eden were always together—sometimes in the larger group, often alone. He supposes now that you could say they were best friends, though if you'd said it to him then, he'd have bristled at the thought, however unfeminine she was. Perhaps it was the circumstance of long summer nights spent tossing a ball after dinner, or the quiet of the fields where they hid to smoke, but when they had things to say then, they said them to each other.

"Edith doesn't like me," he remembers her saying

one night as they lay on their backs in the path through
the cornfields, just out of sight of the houses. They
were eating Fudgsicles; he recalls that a bit of chocolate had melted and had dribbled onto her neck. The
ice cream man passed the houses every night after dinner that summer and made a point of parking his truck
at the end of the drive and ringing his bell on his way
to the next town. Andy and Eden would buy something
for themselves, and often Andy would get something
for his mother as well. (What a wonderful mix, he
thinks now—the innocence of the Fudgsicles and the
secret acrid thrill of the Old Gold cigarettes they
smoked afterward.) She was wearing a T-shirt and a
pair of shorts, as he was, and they smelled of 6–12;
the mosquitoes in the cornfields were ferocious on humid summer nights.

"Sure she does," said Andy. "You just think she
doesn't. Everyone thinks that once in a while."

"I think it all the time."

Andy could not remember a scene he had witnessed
lately that would prove Eden wrong, though he found
it nearly incomprehensible, in the abstract, to imagine
a mother not liking her child.

"What are we doing tomorrow?" she asked.

"I don't know," Andy said. "T.J.'s gotta do the
lawn for his father, and I don't know about Sean."

"Why don't just you and me do something?"

"Like what?"

"Like take our bikes and ride to a town we've never
been to before and have a picnic."

"We could. . . ."

The idea appealed to Andy. He tried to remember
if he, too, was supposed to do something for his father
in the morning.

"We could discover a new lake, go fishing," she
said.

"Bring the poles on the bikes, you mean?"

"Sure. I bet it could be done."

Andy pondered the logistics.

"I think I'm going to die young," she said, licking the last of the chocolate off the wooden stick.

"Don't be stupid. Why do you say that?" It was one of the things Andy didn't like about girls, this tendency toward melodrama. He tried to quash it in Eden whenever he thought it was surfacing.

"Because I can't picture myself doing anything as an adult."

"Huh?"

"I can't see myself as a housewife, and I can't see myself as a schoolteacher or a secretary or an actress or anything. So I must be going to die young."

Apart from a vague image of himself going off to school somewhere, and a feverish wish to become a major league baseball player, Andy could not picture himself doing anything either.

"Well, neither can I, and I don't think I'm going to die young," he said.

"Sean doesn't like me very much, does he?" she said.

"Sean's a jerk, and besides, I think he likes you as good as he likes any of the rest of us."

"But you like me," she said.

He sat up, swatted at a cloud of no-see-ums that were hovering about his forehead.

"You're all right," he said, unable to commit himself out loud any further, for the truth was he'd come to prefer her company to that of T.J. or Sean. He turned to look at her lying on the grass.

"But don't let it go to your head," he said, shoving her in the shoulder. She sat up quickly, catapulted a Fudgsicle stick with expert skill. It landed on his ear. He tried to zing one at her and missed.

"I think my real father must have been a jock," she said.

Andy knew that Eden had been told at an early age that she was adopted—even the story, which Jim managed to make charming, like that of a princess in a fairy tale, of her arrival in a cardboard box. According to Andy's own father, Jim was smart to have done this, because it would have been impossible to keep the tale from her once she'd entered school. Indeed, when she did encounter the children of the town, whose parents regarded Eden as a curiosity if not something of a living legend (her arrival itself a historical event in the unofficial town record), she was sometimes the butt of childish and cruel teasing: "The girl in the box! The girl in the box!" the boys in her class would call across the playground.

"He might have been," said Andy.

And then the two of them lay back on the dirt and dried grasses and smoked the cigarettes she stole from Jim (how can the man have failed to notice the two or three packs a week they were putting away then? he wonders now) and thought about these questions and other, more pressing matters, such as whether or not Andy's father would carry through with his threat to keep him off the hockey team if he didn't pass French in the fall. Or whether T.J.'s father was going to get the pool built before the summer was over. Or, failing that, the best way to talk yourself through the gate at the town pool, above which Eden swore she could actually see the chlorine shimmer.

THEY WERE together that first year, through the summer and well into the spring of his junior year. By then he had long ceased to think of her as an anomaly among his friends. She was simply Eden, his friend too, though if pressed, he'd have said that he worried more about Eden, looked out for her in a way that was never necessary with T.J. or Sean—or perhaps with Sean when Andy and T.J. would have to cool him off to avoid a penalty on the ice.

But when he thinks of the summer Eden turned thirteen (the summer he was waiting for his senior year in high school to begin, the summer inaugurated, it seems now to him, by that fateful day on the baseball diamond), it is as if a wave were pulling away from him then with the force of a powerful undertow.

They had let her play third base that spring for their unofficial sandlot team. She was a so-so hitter, but fast and accurate in the infield. He remembers their team was losing narrowly that day. She was on the bench beside him, hunched over as he was, her elbows on her knees. It had rained earlier in the day, but the sun had cleared the mist, leaving only puddles in the depressions in the field behind the school. He saw her sit up, put an arm across her abdomen. He thought her face was especially white, whiter than it ought to have been. She was wearing her cap backward, with the brim pointing down her back. She moaned slightly, almost too faintly to be heard, but he had, and he asked her if she was all right. She looked at him but didn't answer. And then T.J. hit a home run, and they were on their feet, for this brought in two runs, and they were tied.

He sat down on the bench. Eden was still standing. And then he saw it, the dark red stain.

At first he was scared. She'd been hit, injured somehow, and hadn't told anyone. That would be like her, he thought. But then, in the second instant, it came to him.

"Eden?" he said quietly.

She turned to look at him, and when she saw his face, she sat down.

"Don't get up," he said.

He looked down the bench and saw a jacket on the other side of Sean. Leaning behind his friend, he jerked the jacket off the bench, casually laid it on his lap, and then he slipped it to Eden.

She tied it around her waist, knotting the arms in front.

"Hey, look," Andy said to Sean, who was absorbed in the game. "Eden's sick to her stomach." He was surprised how easily the lie came to him. "I'm taking her home. Put Warren in for me, OK? He's been dying to play first." Sean nodded absently without looking at Andy.

Andy turned to Eden. He hesitated. Then he said: "You know what's going on?"

She shrugged. "I guess."

They walked home the two miles from the playground diamond, each carrying a glove, Eden with the jacket tied around her waist. He punched his glove repeatedly, sometimes arced his arm in a pantomine of a pitch. Neither spoke of the reason why they were walking home before the game was finished. Neither mentioned that Andy needn't have come with her. Indeed, Eden hardly said a word. He thought she must be embarrassed, so he tried to talk of other things, tried for a tone just this side of flippant, but there were long pauses in his monologue.

When he thinks about that walk now—now, twenty years later—it is not embarrassment he feels (he smiles to think of their awkwardness and of her delicacy); rather it is sadness that overtakes him. For though she was young and tongue-tied, though she was barely able to negotiate this strange and bewildering matter, he has no doubt now that it was, for Eden, her last pure day of childhood.

THAT SUMMER she quit the team, quit playing sports. She gave no explanation save that she found them "boring"—an explanation that puzzled Andy. For though he, too, was reaching puberty—with his broken voice and faint mustache—he felt himself to be essentially unchanged, still passionate about hockey and baseball, still tied to his friends like a brother. He was busy days with his first summer job—at the dairy, unloading the trucks as they came in, setting up the bottles for the washer. In the evenings, after supper, in this second summer they had together, he and Eden

sometimes played catch or escaped from doing the
dishes into the fields. But they bickered for the first
time. He said he thought her newly pierced ears were
barbaric; she stubbed out a cigarette and called him
"an infant." She teased him when he couldn't name
the Top Ten, and he accused her of doing nothing all
day but lying in her plastic chaise longue in the backyard, listening to the radio. That was not all she did,
she said, and showed him earrings and rings she'd
shoplifted from the Woolworth's in the next town. She
got on the bus in the mornings, she said, and got off
when she felt like it. She said she'd try for a Timex
for him next time, and he said, irritably, "Don't
bother." In truth, he was horrified. Stealing frightened him. Finding a ten-dollar bill on the floor of a
truck he was emptying just the week before, he'd
sought out the driver at once; simply holding the ten
had made him feel guilty.

She wore shorts and halter tops and was developing
a backyard tan. She curled her legs under her when
she talked, and when she smoked, she sometimes ab-
sentmindedly ran the tips of her fingers along her arm
up to her shoulder and back again. The gesture mesmerized him. She was letting her hair grow out, and
she had painted her nails.

By September, the transformation was complete. He
remembers the first day of school that year, waiting
for the bus. She was late. He could see the vehicle, a
yellow dot in the distance, making its way along the
straight road from town. He turned and cupped his
hands around his mouth and shouted toward her house:
Eden.

She came around the corner from the back stoop;
not running as she would have in the spring, but sway-
ing lightly from side to side, adjusting the strap of a
pocketbook on her shoulder. Before she met his eyes,
he saw a slow smile crawl across her face. She was
enjoying his bewilderment. Out of her mother's sight,

she opened her pocketbook and took out a tube of lipstick. She parted her lips slightly and removed a speck at the corner of her mouth. He had never seen her wear lipstick before. Her hair was combed to the side and hung in a long curve across one eye. She was wearing a straight tight black skirt, but it was her blouse that plunged him momentarily into the red heat of confusion. It was a white short-sleeved shirt with a collar—a schoolgirl's blouse or a shirt you'd wear to camp—except that the cotton was thin and he could see that beneath the shirt she was wearing a bra. Her breasts had sprouted overnight, it seemed, too fast for her small frame; they pushed against the fabric. The bus came lumbering to a stop. Quickly, he climbed the steps, walked past several boys he knew and sat on an empty seat close to the window. Too late, he realized his mistake.

In the spring, she'd have sat down beside him, with more of a thwack than you'd have thought possible from her tiny body, and would have said, through the clicking of her gum, where the fuck did he get that wimpy shirt, and he'd have shrugged and felt OK, for it *was* wimpy—a thin white shirt with shiny stripes on it—and he was wearing it only this once, to please his mother, who had bought it the week before.

Instead he watched the leer of the driver and the astonishment of the other boys as this creature he felt he no longer knew at all made her way down the aisle, holding her own as the bus lurched forward, grasping with her fingers the metal bars above the leather seats. Then he saw a brief flash of painted nails and heard the swish of her skirt sliding on the leather seat behind him. He stared out the window, furious with her.

He felt in his mouth, for the first time in his life, the metallic taste of betrayal and longing. With it came the knowledge that the shape of things you had known and trusted as certain could be twisted, overnight, out of recognition.

* * *

I think you know. I think, of all of them, you're the only one who knows. You talk like you don't know, but I think you do.

I hear you scraping, scraping, and then you move the ladder. My window is always open. My world is what I hear. I can tell you exactly what time of day it is just by the sounds outside the window.

My life is nothing but this.

She washes my hair. She bends my head back in the sink. Her hands are rough. I am like an old person she has to care for.

I listen to your voice and T.J.'s. His is full of lies. You can hear them when he laughs. He once was in a car with me, and I let him touch my breasts. I opened my blouse, and there were other boys with him. I bet he never told you that.

There was a shimmer on the water. You sat on the ground with you knees up. Your arms were on your knees. You were growing your hair long to go away to school, you said. I made you look at me.

I said, Afraid?

You shook your head.

You said I might have been your sister.

THREE

THE WALK IS SHORT, SEVENTY FEET. THE LAWN IS DRY-ing, and he could even now be mowing it. He thinks: *In an hour, I'll be doing that.*

He has washed, changed into a pair of khaki pants and a dress shirt, rolled to the elbows. He walks with his hands in his pockets, a walk he made unthinkingly a thousand times in his youth. He heard her car in the drive when he was washing up in the bathroom, and the faint clatter of a screen door; like clockwork, she is home at two-fifteen each day. A dozen large rosy-brown hydrangea blossoms are strewn along the top of the long grass by the drive; the small tree, he notes again, took a beating during the electrical storm in the night. He can't imagine it will last much longer now. His mother planted it the year she and his father bought the house, forty years ago at least, and he has always associated it with his mother, its lush growth with her well-being. Now it seems to him its foliage has grown too dense for its spindly trunk and must soon topple over.

His heart is beating too fast when he reaches the back stoop. Annoyed, he takes a deep breath and squares his shoulders. When he puts his foot on the first step, he feels it give—as if it had accustomed itself all these years only to her weight and could not bear a pound more. It has been nineteen years since he entered this house—and he is aware, as he raps quickly on the frame of the screen door, that he is stepping again into a scene from the past, even though he knows, from the encounters of the last several days, that it won't feel at all as he has remembered it.

She comes to the door at once, wary, then alarmed. Their eyes involuntarily flicker away from each other, in the manner of people who do not like each other much but feel compelled to be polite.

"Andy," she says, not opening the door.

"I came to say hello to Eden," he says almost too brightly, and with this greeting, he opens the door and steps up into the kitchen. Edith backs away from him.

"Eden's asleep," she says quickly.

She is still wearing the pinkish-gray silk dress she had on earlier, a color that immediately begins to fade as he follows her away from the bright sunlight of the doorway into the kitchen. The shades are drawn over the sink and over the window facing the drive, a detail he has not noticed before, coming and going in his car. The effect is of a kitchen shut up for a season, waiting for the summer people or the new tenants to enter. He has a powerful urge to raise the shades with a snap, to see her kitchen and her face in the sunlight.

"I keep them closed to shut out the heat," she says, noticing his glance toward the window. "It's cooler that way."

He stands in the center of the linoleum floor, waiting for his eyes to adjust to the interior dusk, waiting for a cue, but she gives none.

"May I sit down?" he asks.

With an odd nervous movement of her hands, she indicates the chair. She offers to make him a glass of iced tea. She is at the sink and then the refrigerator, getting ice, her back to him still.

"Thank you for everything you did for my mother," he says, although he is not entirely sure exactly what was done.

"I feel badly about your mother," she says, turning now with two tall glasses in her hands. "I ought to have seen it coming on. She did say once she had headaches. And in June, I was in the market when Carol—you remember Carol Turner—Carol said your mother had nearly fainted in the store just the day before. But I thought it was the heat, not a spell.''

A *spell*. He hasn't heard the word used this way since he lived at home and his mother spoke of his grandmother—to make him understand why she was sick and couldn't see him. *She has these spells, Andy,* his mother said. And so had his own mother, only there'd been no one at the house to know.

''We see them in the patients at the nursing home,'' she says. ''They're small strokes, and there's medication that can be given. And I should have realized . . .''

''It's not your fault,'' says Andrew. He takes a sip of iced tea. It has been made from a powdered mix. It has sugar in it, which he doesn't like. Now that his eyes are adjusting, the color is coming up on the walls: a pale green he remembers now, a green of hospitals or of government buildings. He recalls that this particular shade of green, reflecting off the walls, changed the color of your skin. Or was it his mother who said that, shaking her head critically, and he noticed it himself later, coming for Eden or to collect his weekly money? A sickly green, he thinks now, though the effect is muted without the light.

The kitchen is like his mother's in its layout, and both have the same rounded Magic Chef stoves, but there is otherwise little resemblance. There are no signs on the counters or on the table to indicate that anyone ever cooks here, or ever comes here—not a crusted sugar bowl, not a toaster oven with crumbs on the bottom tray, not a misshapen potholder made by a child. On the wall beside the fridge, where in his mother's kitchen there is a framed collage of snapshots—most of them Billy as a baby—there is only a plastic wall clock. And most disconcerting of all, though perhaps troubling only to Andrew, who has missed the intervening nineteen years of the evolution of this house, there is no sign that Jim was ever here—not a trace. Always, he remembers, there were coats and felt hats on the hooks at the back of the door, a row of heavy leather shoes by the stove, a pile of magazines on the table—*Life, Reader's Digest, Popular Mechanics* (this last a family joke in his own house)—and Jim's bowl of fruit, ready to be peeled, never empty. Not only is there now no fruit in the room; there is not a hint of anything edible at all. Perhaps it's different in the bedroom upstairs. He thinks of his father's dresser in his own mother's bedroom, kept intact, as though any minute his father might come back and need the items on the linen runner. The windows, he notices, have no curtains on them—just the shades. He tries to recall if this was always true.

"You'll be selling, then," she says. She takes a sip of iced tea. He remembers this trait of hers: how she is able to conduct entire conversations without ever once looking at you. He forces himself to study her face, and in doing so sees again, in the dim light, as has been happening of late, the woman she used to be, the profile more defined, superimposed over the face across the table.

"Well, I'll have to sell," he says, knowing his steady gaze is making her uncomfortable. "There's no reason now to keep it."

"No," she says, touching her hair at the nape of her neck. "No, I suppose not. Though with new people coming . . ."

She doesn't finish her thought. Andrew repeats what he has said earlier. "I'm doing some things to tidy up the place—not much; just cosmetic, really. It's no trouble to lend a hand here too, while I'm at it. The grass, of course. And your back stoop needs fixing. It's dangerous. You could break your leg on it. And I could put back that shutter that's fallen from the upstairs window."

"Oh," she says, taken aback. "No. Not the shutter. I . . . I haven't got it. And it's not necessary. The steps, if you like, yes. I'll pay you, of course."

"I couldn't—"

"I'll pay you," she says, cutting him off.

Her face, her aged one, comes clearly into focus. Beneath a faint dusting of powder, he sees a delicate calligraphy of lines around her eyes. Her eyes are hard to look at, but he would say, in telling someone about her (which he thinks he may never have done), that she is still quite handsome. It is not simply that she has aged well (she seems not to have the deep scoring that so changed his mother's face these last several years); it is, rather, a particular something she holds in reserve—her shoulders held back—that something patient and waiting. He thinks, too, about all the longing there was inside her, so intriguing for a boy, from a distance, to observe. Where does it all go to, he wonders, when the person you long for dies?

He turns his gaze away from her. Despite the years, despite his discomfort here, he has a strangely familiar sense of this room. Sometimes when he dreams, this kitchen is the setting. The characters are ones who don't belong here: his boss at work; Billy; a woman he has seen that day turning a corner. They gather in this kitchen; or there will be, in the middle of another dream, a shift in place, so that he is here with them, unfolding a plot begun elsewhere.

"How is Eden?" he asks suddenly. His voice is louder than he has intended.

She looks at the sink. "Eden is not well. She tires easily." The sentence sounds rehearsed, or oft repeated.

"I'd like to see her," he says recklessly.

She shakes her head. "It would upset her."

"I wouldn't upset her. I would just . . ." He searches for a word. "Visit."

"Well, not today." She rattles the cubes in her glass, and her mouth tightens. She raises her chin.

"Why not?"

"She's sleeping. And I've found that memories from the past upset her," she says. "I have to contend with that for days." She brushes an imaginary strand of hair from her forehead.

"But does she see anyone?" he asks. (His persistence surprises him. Why is he being so rude? But he is in it now and cannot stop.) "Does she go anywhere? There must be programs, centers for the blind."

She stands up and rinses her glass at the sink. "I'm a *nurse*," she says, with emphasis on the last word, as if that should settle the matter. As if trying to make him again the neighbor's child. "As you must know, Eden *was* away for several years in the beginning, but we've found she does better with me here. We have a quiet life, and it suits her."

He is about to quiz her once more, when above him he hears a sound, like that of a chair leg scraping against the floor. Or he imagines that he hears a sound. Edith Close says nothing; he examines her to see if she, too, has heard anything. Then he hears another sound, the weight on the floorboards of footsteps moving from one side of the room to the other. Eden's room, in the corner, is above the kitchen. Or does she have another room now?

Edith Close walks to Andrew and holds her hand out for his glass. "Will five dollars an hour be enough?" she asks.

He looks up at her. He sees no point in protesting. He knows she won't let him do the work without an arrangement of some kind. He says, *Fine.* He gives her the glass, which is still nearly full. "And there will be lumber for the steps," she adds. "Shall I give you some money now?"

He shakes his head. He knows she wants him to go. He stands up, and as he does so, he hears music from a radio. He freezes and listens. It is definitely a radio. She hears it too; he sees her shoulders hunch almost imperceptibly, as if wishing to ward off the sound. He thinks he hears a phrase of "Glory Days," then silence, then the voice of a disc jockey. He looks at the ceiling.

She touches him, a hand on his elbow, and the touch startles him. Her fingers are cold on his skin.

"I have to see a patient," she says, guiding him toward the door.

And though he knows this can't be true, and though he wants to say that Eden must now be awake, her touch—that cold, unwelcome touch—makes him feel as if he *were* a boy again, eager to get away, to be gone from the dark kitchen.

She walks him to the door. The radio voice follows them, seems distinctly louder, in fact.

"Thanks for the iced tea," he mumbles.

He backs down the steps with something like a wave, and she quickly closes the door. He forgets the rotting stoop, and with his weight, the bottom step cracks. He nearly falls backward onto the gravel, awkwardly catching himself on the railing. When he turns, his hands are shaking. He thrusts his fists into his pockets to collect himself.

He is almost to his own back stoop when he feels a prickling at the back of his neck. He stops and turns quickly. One, two. He sees first, at the edge of a shade in the kitchen, a swift settling; and then, in the upstairs window, a gentler movement, a slow blur of a turn, a faint afterimage of a blue dress and a thin white arm.

The image is gone in a second. But he stands straining after the open window, willing it to come back, unable to move away.

She can't have come to the window to see me, he is thinking. *She must have come to be seen.*

* * *

HE FILLS the mower with gasoline and checks the oil. He has no idea how old the oil is, or when the machine was last used, but he is too impatient to make another trip out to the gas station. Bending to the pull cord for the fifth time, he gives it everything he's got, more in frustration than with any common sense, and against the odds, the machine belches into life. The sound is harsh and satisfying, shattering the silence. He hopes the loud noise is irritating to the woman behind the drawn shades. He takes a deep calming breath. The noise soothes him. It is a sound that feels good, that he can understand—even though, ironically, it's been years since he has mowed a lawn, anyone's lawn.

The work, he thinks, is equally satisfying. You push the mower down a straight and even path, you look behind you and you see a neat swath, though he is only taking off the top two or three inches this pass— the mower set high, so as not to clog the blade with the damp clippings. He is throwing the grass out to the side; but later on, he'll put the bag on and go over the lawn again, trimming it shorter, picking up the clippings.

The sun is hot and dry on his face. He can feel the tension leaving his body, even as his arms vibrate from the machine. The trick, he thinks, is to keep moving, to move inside the noise, to let the noise drown out the thoughts in his head and the images behind his eyes, until they fade into something distant and manageable. He wants to shut his eyes altogether, but, of course, that isn't possible. He wouldn't mind, though, he thinks, standing just for a second inside the roar, his eyes shut, his face tilted toward the sun.

She was one fantastic-looking girl. You remember?
    I remember.
    Sometimes he felt as if he hardly knew her then, though he saw her every day. But he heard what was

said about her. And he knew the stories. He watched her—as you'd watch a house you once lived in become transformed by new owners.

He saw her on the bus on the way to and from school; in the backyard, meeting in the driveway; in a corridor, stopping for a drink of water from the fountain. She liked to tease him, and he let her. He didn't know how to make her stop. Confronting her, as he did at first when her growing reputation alarmed him, made it worse; he lost the verbal battles. His best defense, he decided, was to ignore her—though she persisted, drawling his name in a husky voice that seemed to have blossomed overnight with her anatomy and that, unhappily, carried the length of the school bus or across a room. And he sometimes wondered, when he was being honest with himself, if he didn't enjoy the odd status that her attention conferred upon him.

She's hot for you.

She is not. I've known her since she was practically born.

She's giving it away, man. Perillo felt her up at the drive-in four times in August. He says her boobs are—

She's only thirteen, for Christ's sake.

She's been doin' it since school started. A chick wants it, she wants it.

Why don't you guys leave her alone?

Leave her alone? Hey, you sure you're not getting any?

IT WAS as if she were changing to suit her body, was somehow growing into the body that was developing too fast for her. He had no other explanation. Or rather, he thought, the basic traits were still there— her nerve, her brazenness—but they'd veered off in a new direction so that she used her talents not to *be* one of the boys but to have power over them.

Sometimes, sitting on the back stoop, pretending to study his French, he would see her across the grass and gravel and wonder about what it would be like to be in a car with her at a drive-in. He couldn't keep from thinking about it: the idea was in the air and in his blood. But the thoughts made him uncomfortable, nearly in the same way that thinking about his parents doing it did. And sometimes he felt guilty, as if he were supposed to have taken better care of her some-how—though that, *he knew,* was crazy. She was beyond his care, or anyone's, for that matter.

And sitting on the stoop, he would sometimes hear raised voices in the Close kitchen, a mother and a daughter scratching at each other like cats: words thrown whining and bickering through the screens. The fighting had come on gradually during that summer and the school year following that awkward day on the baseball diamond, Eden beginning it (seemingly de-manding it), taunting her mother with her outrageous dress and behavior, until Edith Close, a novice at this combat, began to learn from her daughter, raising her voice to a new shrillness—born, he imagined, out of bewilderment. You cannot, he thought, remain indif-ferent to a stinging bee.

In the beginning, he and his parents had been mildly alarmed by the raised voices next door. His own par-ents rarely yelled at each other or at him. But then, as the weeks and months passed and the bickering voices seemed to find no truce, he began to grow accustomed to the nightly battles—like the rattling of a scheduled train—as though these, too, were part of an evolving landscape.

And sometimes the screen door would slam, and Eden, her eyes inflamed, roughly pushing her hair off her face, would spot him on the stoop. She might put a fist on a cocked hip and narrow her eyes at him. Or she might, with dizzying speed, change her stance and her expression entirely, sashaying across the yard to meet him, a smile skimming her lips as she clutched a pack of Old Golds or Winstons. She would smoke after these battles, in full view of her mother, prolonging, by this gesture, their animosity. (He couldn't conceive of smoking in front of his parents; indeed, he was thinking of giving it up altogether.) She would reach the steps where he was sitting, lean against the rail and shake a cigarette from the pack, deliberately offering him one. She kept her matches in the cellophane. Sometimes, maddeningly, she would ruffle his hair, and he would toss his head sharply to shake her off.

"Enjoyin' the entertainment tonight?" she would say.

When Jim was home, there was no fighting. It was not so much that Jim kept order in his household; it was that in his presence, Edith would not criticize their adopted daughter, nor rise to the bait if Eden dangled it, by wearing a too tight sweater, or by missing supper entirely, or by coming home at eleven o'clock, an hour after her nominal curfew.

"Sweetie," Jim would say, coming out onto the steps on these late nights, intercepting Eden before she entered the house.

"Daddy," Eden would say, though out of earshot she referred to her parents as Jim and Edith, and Andrew had never heard Eden address Edith as "Mother" or "Mom" at all.

"Sweetie, your mother is upset. You should have told us where you were going. We waited supper for you."

And Eden, brilliantly contrite, would tilt her head ever so slightly and murmur, "Sorry, Daddy," in a voice Andy seldom heard, the voice, he thought, of a regular fourteen-year-old girl.

Jim, instantly mollified, poised to be charmed by what he imagined to be his daughter's sweetness, would kiss the top of her blond curls.

"Sickening," his own mother would say of Jim's

inability to discipline his daughter, as she witnessed the scene from their kitchen window.

ONE AFTERNOON that last spring, he remembers, he was changing the oil in the car for his father when he heard a sudden and particularly loud spate of bickering, followed almost immediately by the sound of splintering glass. It was Sunday, and Jim had been away for days. There'd been no buildup of voices, no warning of a coming storm. Until the fighting, Andy hadn't even known Eden was home.

The caliber of the bickering was different than he'd heard before, and while normally he would simply register the sound and then go back to what he was doing, this time he slid out from underneath the car and sat up. His father, working that afternoon on the plumbing under the sink, came to the back door.

"What the . . . ," said his father.

But the shouting had stopped by then, and his father turned away from the door. Andy was about to go back under the car, when Edith Close came out of the house, her coat on, her purse over her arm, her mouth set in a thin line. Without acknowledging Andy, she turned down the drive, made a right on the road and walked to the tree where the county bus regularly stopped.

Andy sat on the gravel. His hands were smeared with grease. He stood up and walked to the other house, hesitating below the steps, out of sight of Edith at the bus stop. He wiped the palms of his hands on his jeans. He listened, heard nothing and then climbed the steps. It was April, he remembers; he had on two old flannel shirts of his father's. Edith, in her haste, hadn't closed the door. He put his face to the screen, put his hand up to shade his eyes.

Eden was sitting on a chair by the table. She was wearing a long nightgown and a bathrobe. Her hair was disheveled, uncombed, as if she'd just woken up. She was crying. He didn't think he had ever seen her cry before. She brought her hand up and touched the corner of her mouth. He remembers thinking how small she looked in the chair. He remembers wanting to go in and sit beside her. He wanted to knock, but he didn't.

BY MAY of his senior year, the spring before the shooting, Eden seemed to have settled, in a fairly deliberate way, and in a manner that surprised everyone, on Sean. Andy was never to know what it was exactly that drew Eden to his old friend, if, indeed, she could actually be said to have been drawn at all. For he sometimes wondered, then and later, if it wasn't in keeping with the perverse, self-destructive course she'd been on for almost a year to choose a boy known for his volatile temper and, more to the point and perhaps for Andy's benefit, to strike so close to home.

Andy was sitting on a bench in the locker room when T.J. told him. It was after a baseball game, and Andy, with a towel around his waist, was trying to untangle his underpants, when T.J. said, his back to Andy, "You know about Sean."

"Sean?"

T.J. opened his locker and hunted for a sock.

"And Eden," he said.

"Sean and Eden?" Andy didn't get it yet. Had they had a fight? Got caught smoking on school premises?

"They're like a thing," T.J. said. He looked quickly at Andy and then away. He began to whistle between his teeth.

"You mean they're going out?" asked Andy. He said the words *going out* distinctly, as if they could not possibly apply to the present situation.

T.J. scratched his chest. "Yeah. Like that."

Andy shook his head. There had to be some mistake. "That's impossible," he said. "Are you sure? I'd know if it were true."

"Oh yeah?" said T.J. "And how is that?"

''I'd have seen them together at the house or something.''

''No you wouldn't. Her father won't let her bring any boy home. So they hang out in Sean's car. . . .'' T.J. stopped, not wanting to lay out the graphic details to his friend.

''But Sean never really liked Eden,'' protested Andy. ''Of the three of us—''

T.J. snapped around. ''You know, Andy-boy, half the time, I swear to God, you're livin' in a dream world, you know that? You don't see what's goin' on right under your nose.''

''I don't know what you're talking about,'' said Andy, stung by T.J.'s sudden attack.

''I'm talking about Eden,'' said T.J. with exasperation.

''What about Eden?''

''Anybody with two eyes could see that it's always been you she liked best, and you're either blind or you're more of an asshole than I thought you were.''

''You must be crazy,'' said Andy defensively. ''She's only fourteen. She was one of the guys. She was like a sister. . . .'' He stopped, aware that he was contradicting himself.

''Oh really?'' said T.J., buttoning his top button and picking up his gym bag. ''Well, that's history now, isn't it.''

T.J. slung his gym bag over his shoulder and headed for the door. He didn't wait for Andy, and he didn't say goodbye.

Andy sat on the bench, his underpants balled in his fist. He was trying to imagine Sean and Eden in a car together, she laughing, Sean reaching over to finger the collar of her blouse, but something inside him wouldn't let the image coalesce. He threw the underpants into the bottom of the locker. He slammed the door shut with his feet.

''Fuck it,'' he said, and pulled his pants on.

* * *

AFTER THAT DAY, without appearing to do so, he looked for signs of them together. And he concluded that T.J. had been right: he *was* blind, for how could he have failed to miss the way Sean was always dressed first after a game and out to his car, or the way Sean sidled past him with a greeting but had not really had a conversation with him for weeks? Or the way Sean and Eden sat on the steps behind the gym and smoked during third period, their shoulders touching? And as the days passed, there were more overt signs: Eden missing the afternoon school bus day after day, arriving late for dinner, saying she'd walked home from school, though Andy knew Sean was dropping her off a quarter mile short of the house. And once Andy came around a corner into an empty corridor by the music room at school and saw Sean pressing Eden into the brick wall with his body. They were kissing, and Andy was caught. He couldn't turn around, couldn't retreat. He tried to saunter past them, tried to appear intensely absorbed in the cover of his math book. Eden pulled away just as Andy passed.

"Andy-boy," said Sean, breathless.

"Sean," said Andy, moving past them.

"Hi, Andy," drawled Eden.

He heard giggling behind him.

HE NOW AVOIDED Eden as best he could, stopping short at the screen door if he saw her emerge from her house and cajoling T.J. to pick him up and drop him off for the couple of weeks left before school ended. Sean brought Eden to the graduation party, but Andy had his own date and aggressively pretended to be having a better time than he actually was. After he took his date home, he and T.J. drove for hours in T.J.'s car and got so drunk they had to park by the side of a deserted road before they both passed out. When he got home, well after six in the morning, expecting the wrath of his father to greet him at the door, his father took one look at Andy, shook his head sadly and went upstairs to bed.

ONLY ONCE, in the weeks before the shooting, was he alone with Eden for any length of time. It was a Monday afternoon, he remembers, his day off from the Texaco station. That summer he was working long hours, and his parents let him do what he wanted on his day off, an indulgence that pleased him since it seemed to suggest that he was a man now—a workingman with days off and privileges. He had slept late that morning, and when he came down to the kitchen, his mother was already dressed, already halfway into her day. It was the summer he was reading *No Exit* and *The Stranger* to get ready to go to college in Massachusetts, and he had a book with him at the table. Out in the backyard there was an aluminum reclining chair on which his mother sometimes dozed in the afternoons with *Family Circle* on her lap; and so after breakfast he went outside and lay back on it, shielding his eyes from the sun with the paperback held over his face. It was after twelve, and the sun that day, he remembers, was ferocious. Almost immediately, he unbuttoned his shirt, fanning himself with the cloth.

He was asleep when he felt a large insect crawling over his stomach. He sat up with a jolt, flailing at his chest, trying to brush it off. And then he heard her laugh—a laugh that sounded unpleasant and grating through the fog of his sleep and the pounding of his heart. He fell back against the chair. Her face was over his, too close to his own, blocking out the sun as the book had done.

"Lazybones, get out of bed. The sun is up, the witch is dead."

"What?"

"Andy, it's almost one o'clock."

"*You* should talk."

"Want to go for a swim?"

She was wearing a pair of tight white shorts and a blue sleeveless blouse. Her arms were tanned, and when she moved away from his face, he noticed that her chest, where he could see it, was tanned too. His eyes strayed to her breasts and away again. He hoped she hadn't seen. It was a powerful reflex he was trying to cure himself of—the way, when looking at a girl, his eyes went immediately to the breasts rather than to the face. Instinctively, he began buttoning his own shirt.

"No," he said. "I'm reading."

She laughed. "Right," she said. She picked up his book, which had slipped onto the grass, and squinted at the title: *The Myth of Sisyphus.*

"Jesus Christ, Andy. You're turning into such a fink, you know that? Anyway, you haven't been swimming in weeks. I happen to know that for a fact. It's summer, in case you haven't noticed."

She sat on the edge of the chair. "I'm not leaving until you say yes. I'm bored sick, and I want company."

"Where's Sean?" he asked, the name catching in his throat. They had never spoken of Sean.

"Oh, him," she said too casually. "How should I know?"

"You should get a job," he said, "if you're so bored."

"I'm only *fourteen,*" she whined. "And anyway, what's it to you?"

"*I* worked when I was fourteen," he said, instantly regretting it.

"Well, la-di-da. You sound like an asshole sometimes, Andy, you know that?"

"All right, all right," he said, capitulating. "Where?"

"The pond," she said. "The pool is *totally* revolting. I swear to God there's half an inch of scum on the water."

"All right," he said again, grudgingly. "I'll get my suit. You go get yours."

"I'm wearing mine," she said.

He checked his eyes just in time, but his visual memory was flawless. That couldn't be true, he thought, but he couldn't very well challenge her.

"Listen, I'll tell you what," he said. "Compromise. OK? I'll walk you down to the pond, and you can swim. I'll keep you company, but I don't think I want to swim myself." Actually what he didn't want was to go through the hassle of looking for his suit and the even greater hassle of explaining to his mother where he was going and with whom.

She shrugged and stood up. "Suit yourself," she said.

"That's good," he said, appreciative of the pun.

She looked blankly up at him.

THEY WALKED through the cornfields, the sun baking their heads, their feet following a path so familiar he was sure he could have found his way blindfolded. Almost at once, away from the shade of any trees or houses, he wished he'd bothered to get his suit. He'd be dying for a swim by the time they got there. Well, what the hell, he'd go in with his clothes on. They'd dry in the sun on the way home anyway.

She walked in front of him, and it was impossible not to notice the way she moved—her narrow hips twitching from side to side in her white shorts. Her hair was in a ponytail, and it, too, swayed back and forth. He thought, fleetingly, of what was said about her. Of what was said about her and Sean. Phrases came into his mind, and he worked to push them away.

He *hadn't* been to the pond in weeks, not since before school let out, and he was surprised by the lush growth there: tall scarlet lilies and Queen Anne's lace and old grape vines. There were trees here at least. He sat on the grass under the shade of one, and to his surprise, she sat down beside him.

"I thought you wanted to go swimming," he said, looking at her.

"So?" She stretched her legs out on the grass and crossed them. She kicked off her sneakers. He looked at her legs. They were tanned, golden, all the way to her shorts. She had lost the bruises of the year before. Now all he saw was the long, smooth shape of her legs and the red polish on her toes. He tore his gaze away.

There was a sparkle on the water. He had learned to swim in this pond when he was a boy, no more than five. His father had taught him, patiently, over many days. Though Andy sometimes suspected his father had subtly planted the notion that there were leeches in the pond—thus hastening the process. He'd been so terrified of touching bottom that he'd learned to float the first day. It wasn't true, though, about the leeches. The pond was crystal clear, even if the color of the water was brassy from the minerals in the soil. He was thinking that any minute he'd just make a run and a flying leap, and the cool water would close in over him.

"Oooh," she said. "Ants." She twisted her body to flick something off her thigh and in doing so brushed his bare arm with her own. The touch was electric, galvanizing, and instinctively he pulled away from her.

"What's this for?" he asked suddenly.

"What's what for?" she said noncommittally.

"This," he said, gesturing to include the space that surrounded them.

"I don't know what you're talking about."

"You don't?"

Maybe he was wrong, he thought. Maybe she did just want a swim. But if so, why was she sitting so close to him? The sun glinted painfully off the water.

"Andy," she said. There was a question in her voice.

"Let's hit the water," he said quickly. He bent forward, as if to get up.

"Andy, do you ever wonder what it would be like?"

There was a ringing in his ears. "What *what* would be like?"

"You know."

"No, I don't," he said irritably. "You *said* you wanted to swim."

He knew that all he had to do was stand up and begin heading for the water, and that would be that, but instead he waited for what she would say next. He wanted to hear what she would say next. Despite himself. Because of himself.

"I think about it," she said in an oddly quiet voice.

"Think about *what?"* he said, trying for a tone of exasperation.

"Us."

The word fell like a leaf to the grass and lay there in front of them—him with his body still poised to stand; her with her legs crossed in front of her. There was a sparkle on the water, so bright it hurt his eyes like a headache. Around them insects buzzed and whined in the heat. The pond always seemed smaller in the summer, he thought, hemmed in by the vegetation. Looking at it, he couldn't imagine playing a hockey game on it.

She moved around in front of him, on her knees, blocking his path to the water.

"Eden," he said.

"You can touch me if you want," she said. "You can touch my blouse."

He looked at her blouse. The longing inside him was so deep and so tight it made his throat dry. He could see the pressure of her breasts against the cloth. He could tell that she wasn't wearing a bathing suit or anything else beneath her blouse. He had never touched a girl's breasts, though he wanted to and he dreamed of it—he had sometimes dreamed of touching hers. He dreamed now of touching the buttons, undoing them slowly, one by one. He looked up at her face. Her eyes, blue-green, were locked on his.

He turned his face away from her. He saw nothing—only a shimmering blur. The color was rising to his face, but there wasn't anything he could do to stop it. His hardened his fists against the grass.

"Eden," he said again.

There was a movement of her hands. He knew what she was doing, and he froze, pretending not to know. He wanted her to do it. He knew what she was doing, and he wanted it.

"Look at me," she said after a time.

And slowly he let himself turn and look at her. He made his face stay calm. It was a test of some kind, and he would make his face stay calm no matter what, though he longed to hide his face in her skin. Her breasts were very white, and the whiteness held him. He could see the tan line of her bathing suit. He brought his hand to his forehead to brush the hair from his face. He kept his face calm, but his hand gave him away.

She said, "Afraid?"

He shook his head, but he was lying. He felt dizzy—loose and big and floating. He knew that all he had to do was touch her.

He raised his face and looked up at the sky. There was a corona around the sun. She was kneeling there, in front of him, waiting. A minute longer, he knew, and they'd both be lost.

He stood up, not gracefully. "I'm going for a swim," he said. His voice was deep, unfamiliar to him. He walked to the water's edge. He bent down to untie his sneakers. He stood up and knifed through the surface of the pond and swam as if his life depended on it, though you could reach the other side in fifty strokes. And when he did, he turned and swam back again, repeating the course over and over until he could barely raise his arm above the water. And then he swam some more, treading water, really, until he knew it was safe to get out.

When he climbed onto the grass, shaking the water out of his ear, Eden was sitting with her knees up.

She had buttoned her blouse. Her face was closed, and she wouldn't look at him. He knew then, watching her, that he had not done the right thing. She looked small and lonely, a fourteen-year-old girl with no-where to go. He wanted now to touch her skin, to tell her that, yes, he had dreamed of her, had wanted her, that he did often think of them together, that he felt for her something he had been afraid to say even to himself—but he didn't know how.

"You could have been my sister," he said instead.

She said nothing.

They walked back in silence. She was in front of him. His shirt was sticking to his chest, drying some. His hair was plastered in rivulets to his forehead.

When they drew closer to the houses, he jerked his arm forward and tried to take her hand. There was something he wanted to tell her—he *would* tell her now—but she chose that moment, unaware that he was reaching for her, to sprint the rest of the way to the houses. He tilted as if to run after her, but then he stopped himself. He wouldn't catch her. He remembered that she could run as fast as he could.

THE FOLLOWING WEEK, T.J. reported to Andy that Eden had suddenly dropped Sean. It was rumored, said T.J., that Jim had found the pair one night in Sean's car about one hundred yards short of the house and had strenuously forbidden Eden ever to see Sean again, but T.J. thought it unlikely, and Andy agreed. Although Jim's drinking had grown worse over the years—and particularly so in the last year—sometimes

causing him to accost Andy's father and harangue him
for hours on some arcane subject, or to sit mute on
his own back stoop, beer in hand, waiting for Eden to
come home for supper, Andy thought it virtually impossible that Jim could be capable of so decisive an
act of discipline. Rather it seemed more plausible that
Sean had concocted the story to salvage his pride. For
from all appearances, Eden had simply tired of Sean.
He had served an uncertain purpose for a time and
was now no longer very interesting to her—a fate that
threw Sean into a frenzy. At first he besieged Eden
with pleas and questions, but when his entreaties would
not move her, his fury ignited and was boundless.

"I'll get that bitch," he said, to anyone who would
listen, his anger growing with each passing day. "I'll
kill that bitch," he shouted, his temper ricocheting
around the interior of his car. T.J. told him to calm
down and get a grip on himself. Then later, when T.J.
had wearied of Sean's relentless tirades, he told him
to "grow up."

But Sean, enraged and bereft, would not let up. At
2 A.M. on the last day of July, he totaled his car on the
road leading from town to Eden's house and was ar-
rested for speeding and for drunken driving. On a
morning in the first week of August, a summer care-
taker at the high school found two windows smashed
to bits in the east wing, near the music room. By the
middle of August, Jim had called the police station
twice to lodge a complaint against Sean, who had been
standing across the road for days, waiting for Eden to
leave the house to walk to the bus stop.

But that was not the worst of it, T.J. said to Andy
one August evening after work when the two of them
were going to a movie. The worst of it was this: When
Sean had first told T.J. that Eden wouldn't see him
anymore, Sean had gripped the steering wheel in his
car so tightly that his fingers had turned white. And

then he'd gulped once as if for air and had cried like a baby.

WHEN HE shuts the mower off, he hears the phone ringing. It's his own, inside the kitchen. He begins to run, leaping over the back stoop, letting the screen door slam, reaching it in three rings.

"Hello?" he says, breathless.

"You're outta shape, Andy-boy. Maybe you should take up jogging."

"T.J."

Andrew puts his hand on his chest, as if to slow his looping heart.

"What were you doin' anyway?"

"I was moving the lawn," says Andrew. "I ran for the phone."

"You should get a cordless. We got a cordless in the backyard."

"Oh," says Andrew. Is it worth the effort to remind T.J. that he has no plans to stay in this house and to tell him of the cordless phone he and Martha had in Saddle River?

"So listen. I spoke to Didi. Can you come over Friday night?"

Andrew calculates. "What day is it?" he asks.

"It's Tuesday." There is a pause. "You all right?" asks T.J.

"I'm fine," says Andrew, thinking how easy it is to lose track of the time when there is no office to go to. "I'll still be around then. I'd planned to be."

"Excellent," says T.J. "Remember the Conroy place?"

Andrew has a memory of an alfalfa farm about two miles east of town, a blue crop undulating like a rolling sea, a tall glistening white silo, a ship, rising from the expanse of unbroken color. "The alfalfa farm, right?"

"Yeah. It's houses now. Kind of an upscale subdivision. Water's Edge, it's called. We're on Tudor Lane, the second left, number twelve.''

''OK.''

''We'll talk about selling your house when you come,'' says T.J.

''OK.''

There is another pause. ''You sure you're all right?''

''I'm *fine*,'' says Andrew.

''All right, all right, I believe you. See you about seven, then, OK?''

Andrew puts his hands on his hips, feels his heart jogging back to normal. It irks him, but T.J. is right: He *is* out of shape. He pours himself a glass of water and sits down on a kitchen chair, his legs spread out in front of him. He is trying to imagine how the Conroy place could now be houses—what did they do with that immense white silo?—when the phone rings again. He thinks it must be T.J., that he has told him the wrong time, and so he answers, casually, ''Yeah,'' but it is a female voice on the other end.

''Andrew?''

''Jayne,'' he says with some surprise.

''How are you?'' his secretary asks. ''How are you feeling?''

''I'm fine,'' he says for the third time in five minutes. ''And thank you for the flowers,'' he adds. ''Thank everyone for me, though I know it was your doing.''

''We've all been thinking of you,'' she says. ''We've all been wondering how you were. We hadn't heard from you, and we . . .'' He can see Jayne in her gray suit with the white silk blouse, her salt-and-pepper hair cut short. Her desk will be impeccably neat. She has a gift, he has often thought, for absorbing the chaos of the office and transforming it into neat, simple packets of common sense and order.

''I'm sorry,'' says Andrew. ''I should have called. They couldn't do the funeral Sunday, and so we had it yesterday, and I've been tied up with details here. I have to sell the house, see to my parents' things. There's no one else, really, to do it.'' He stops. His voice sounds unconvincing, even to him.

''Geoffrey has asked me to tell you to take all the time you need, but he was just wondering . . . if you should happen to know when you might be coming back. Apparently, there's some trouble with the agency . . . but not to hurry, says Geoffrey.'' Andrew thinks he can hear some slight embarrassment in Jayne's voice. *See if you can find out when he's coming back,* Geoffrey, his boss, will have said, passing on this onerous task. *See if you can't light a fire under him.*

Andrew runs his fingers through his hair and looks out the window. The patch of grass that he can see looks good—short and trim. He could say, definitely, *I'll be in the office Friday morning,* but he doesn't want to. He could make it by Friday easy, he is thinking; there's no pressing need to stay. T.J. would handle everything if Andrew asked him to.

''I'll try for early next week,'' he says, waffling.

''I'm sure there must be . . . a great deal to do,'' she says, ''and you must be feeling drained. I'll tell Geoffrey that you have . . . things to attend to.''

''Yes.''

''Shall I say Monday or Tuesday?'' she asks after a moment.

''You can say . . . Jayne?''

''Yes?''

''I need some time,'' he says in an apologetic rush. ''It's hard to explain. A few days. Tell Geoffrey Monday. But it might not be Monday. You understand?''

She misses only one beat. ''Perfectly,'' she says.

He rolls his eyes to the ceiling. He loves his secretary. Although she has been stern with him when he has delayed overlong in returning important phone calls, she has run interference for him more times than he can count.

"You're great, Jayne," he says.

"I think you deserve a rest," she says. He knows that she is smiling. "And don't worry; I'll take care of Geoffrey."

WHEN ANDREW hangs up the phone, he is smiling too. He snaps a bongo beat on the Formica countertop and rolls his shoulders, unkinking his muscles. Another week. He feels, unreasonably, as if he'd won a prize.

Just a week ago, he was overseeing a project that was giving him sleepless nights, an unwieldy ad campaign for a pain reliever that had been his bailiwick— worse, his idea. He thinks he should be worried about the faltering project, from habit if from nothing else, but it seems too remote to fully grasp, as if the mileage alone had sufficiently distanced him from his office. He feels as if he is playing hooky—fishing when he should be taking a physics exam.

And yet, realistically, he knows there is practically nothing he can do to damage his reputation, to change his character in the ongoing soap opera at the office. He has been the unassuming protégé for years—a role he has found easy enough to play, requiring only that he do his work and appear to be committed. He is not sure why he has been so successful, because he has always been aware in himself of a certain lack of an edge to his ambition; rather, he thinks, it has been a consequence of a fairly passive journey through open doors. Martha used to say that it was because Andrew did not appear to be overtly hungry that so many had been moved to open the door *for* him—as indeed (she often reminded him) she had done.

He finishes his glass of water, sets it down on the table, and is halfway out the door when the phone rings again.

"Jesus," he says aloud cheerfully.

* * *

"I'VE BEEN calling all afternoon," Martha says at once. "Where have you been?"

It is as inevitable as night falling. No matter how often he has promised himself he will remain immune, the sound of Martha's voice over the telephone sets up a chemical reaction in his blood, which goes immediately to his voice box. His voice withers, sounds hollow, dies.

"Martha."

"I called four times at least. I thought you were supposed to be sorting stuff out."

"I was mowing the lawn," he says quietly. He knows, as surely as he knows the effect of her on himself, that she sounds petulant in this way only with him. It is one of the things they have done to each other.

"Oh. Well, we're on Nantucket," she says.

"You said you might be."

"I called to see how it went."

"It went fine," he says.

"That's all? It went fine?"

"There's nothing to it," he says. "You say a few words, you put someone in the ground, you have a cup of coffee, and before you know it, it's over."

There is a pause. "It sounds to me like you're not dealing with it."

"I'm dealing with it. Where's Billy?"

"He's right here. Want to talk to him?"

"You know I do."

He leans against the fridge and waits for the sound of his son's voice.

"Daddy?"

It hits his stomach like a strong drink, the warmth spreading.

"Hi, Billy. What are you doing now?"

"I'm talking to you."

Andrew smiles and nods his head. "I know that,

Billy. What were you doing before you were talking to me?''

"Me and Mommy and Nana were getting mussels. But . . . um . . . not the kind of muscles you have on your arms. The kind . . . Do you know what mussels are?"

"They have blackish shells, and they're stuck to rocks in the water?" says Andrew.

"Yeah. That's them. And they're hard to get off. You should see my fingers. And Nana is going to show me how to steam them, and we're going to eat them with melted butter.''

"That sounds yummy," says Andrew.

"I don't know," says Billy skeptically. "I might not like them. They look yucky.''

"I miss you," Andrew says, trying to keep his voice even.

"I miss you too, Daddy. Where are you?"

"I'm at Grandma's."

There is a silence.

"Billy?"

"Mommy said Grandma's in heaven."

Andrew is surprised by this, since Martha despises religion. Or does she now? Or was it simply the easiest explanation of death to give a seven-year-old? "That's right, Billy. She is. But I'm at her house, packing away her things.''

"Oh," says Billy. "Daddy?"

"What, Billy?"

"Don't pack away the car."

He knows that Billy means the wooden go-cart that Andrew's father built for Andrew when he was a boy and that Andrew's mother saved for the time when Andrew himself had a child. During a visit to his mother when Billy was five, he took his son to the high school parking lot and taught him to steer.

"No, I won't. It's safe and sound in the garage."

"Mommy wants to talk to you."

"Billy?"

"What, Daddy?"

"I love you."

"I love you too."

Andrew can hear the squelchy sound of Billy kissing the telephone mouthpiece. He bends to do the same, but the small voice is too quickly gone. He hears a shuffling of the phone, Martha asking her mother to take Billy outside. Andrew braces himself.

"So," she says. He hears a faint sigh. Fatigue? Irritation? Then there is a quick drag and exhale of cigarette smoke. He can see her as clearly as if she were standing next to him. Jeans, a white shirt, a sweater tied around her neck, sandals, her feet tanned. There will be a frown of impatience on her brow. Her head will be slightly inclined because she wears her shoulder-length brown hair parted to one side now, and often there is a wave of hair that wants to fall across her face.

"He sounds . . ." Andrew takes a quick breath of air. "He sounds good."

"He's great," Martha says. "Great. He wanted to talk to you. He was upset when I told him about your mother. But he's better now." Drag and exhale.

Holding her cigarette between her fingers, she will push the hair off her face. He has seen her on the phone a thousand times.

"I'm relieved," says Andrew.

"So listen," says Martha. "You sure you're OK?"

"I'm OK."

"How long are you going to stay there?"

"Another week."

"Oh. . . . I guess there isn't anything I can say."

"No. Probably not."

"You'll come get Billy when we get back?"

"You know I will."

"Well, then."

There is a pause.

"Andrew?"

"What?"

"It's strange, isn't it?" she says.

"What is?"

"You doing this alone."

A PERSON walks into a room and says hello, and your life takes a course for which you are not prepared. It's a tiny moment (almost—but not quite—unremarkable), the beginning of a hundred thousand tiny moments and some larger ones. A random sperm meets a random egg and becomes your child, whom you love more than life itself. Yet the meeting, that infinitesimal beginning, is no more astonishing than the division of a cell.

He had met Martha at an antiwar rally their senior year at college. Not a memorable meeting—she had asked him merely to hand out leaflets in front of the ROTC building—but he had found himself attracted to her, despite, or perhaps because of, her total preoccupation. It was her anger that he noticed, a clear blue anger, so purely defined by the effort to stop the war— an anger that gave high color to her cheeks even as it lent her speech, with its broad *A*'s and its other New England idiosyncrasies, an articulate speed. At first he was content merely to observe her—she was ferocious without being strident in the meetings he attended— but as the year progressed he found himself more and more often paired with her on political projects. Years later, when he would be forced to examine the reasons they had come together, as if puzzling over an insolvable calculus problem, he reflected that it wasn't that the pairing had ignited a passion between them but rather that it had allowed them to drift toward a future that was as much determined by circumstance as it was by desire or will. If they, for instance, had met their junior year in school or later, in graduate school, and had not had to face together the milestone of leaving

dormitories and finding another place to live, would
they have been impelled to take an apartment they
could share together?

Not that he didn't love her. He did, or thought he
might, though she, with the admirable bristles and
spikes of her anger, was not always easy to love. They
were married by then, living in a one-bedroom third-
floor walk-up on Fayette Street in Cambridge. The tub
was in the kitchen. Martha studied on the bed. He took
a table by a window in the living room. At night, when
he was finished studying, he'd go into the bedroom.
She would be asleep, sitting up, with a book on her
lap. Gently, so as not to wake her, he would carefully
remove all the papers and books to a table beside the
bed and would ease her down under the covers.

And sometimes, having done that, he would watch
her, beginning to formulate the calculus problem that
would be their marriage. For even by then her anger
was starting to become unfocused, more diffuse. The
war had ended; it was harder now to find a cause.
She was often dissatisfied, discontent. He thought then
it was courageous of her, her willingness always to live
at the edge, but later he came reluctantly to see that
she was this way not by choice but because the anger
was herself.

He thinks now how slow he was to understand this,
and how often he was impatient with this thing in her
she had not wished upon herself, could not control.
When they were in New York and living on the East
Side, he thought her anger the result of having been
uprooted from her home territory and of not being
able to find a better job than teaching English in a
private school. But by the time Billy had arrived and
they had moved to Saddle River, the anger had focused
on himself, or, more specifically, on the marriage, or,
more specifically still, on the state of being married
at that particular place and time. And by then the anger had become contagious, so that he had developed

in her presence bristles and spikes, though he would never be as concise or as articulate in an argument as she, and so more often than not lost the verbal battles.

He used to think it was the move that had destroyed them. It had happened coincidentally: a door had opened just when he had wished it to, and so he had walked through it. It was on an afternoon in their last year of graduate school—both of them waiting to hear of jobs for the next year—when he had had an epiphany of sorts following a stultifying session of a freshman course he had taught. He had seen, that day, standing in the classroom after the students had left, a future stretch before him of endless similar afternoons, of dusty books and chalk-filled rooms and freshman themes, and he had realized that this was not what he'd had in mind at all. Yet it wasn't until Geoffrey called, some weeks later, asking Andrew to come and work for him at the pharmaceutical firm, that a plan had taken shape. Geoffrey had been his professor in an American Studies seminar; Andrew had been his favorite pupil—indeed, the two had often finished the seminar with beers at a local bar. *It needn't be forever,* Geoffrey had said on the phone, knowing Andrew would be reluctant after so long an investment to turn his back on academia. *Just come down and give it a try.* And so he had, and the company had offered him so much money that even Martha had been, for once, speechless.

When he tries to think of himself and Martha in Saddle River before they separated, he remembers too much and not enough. The memories flood in upon him like rain, but like rain, they fall through his fingers before he can grasp them. He used to think he could not remember because his memory was failing him, but now he thinks the forgetting is a trick of his mind to protect him. His mind protects him from the good memories, which are painful now to contemplate, and from the bad memories, which make him embarrassed for them both.

When their nights were very bad, he was incapable of remembering the good ones. Or if he did, they were like childhood stories that no longer had meaning or resonance. Yet when there were good times, sparse though they were near the end, he could absolutely not remember the silences or the bitterness or the emptiness that had followed their fights just a week earlier. Or the fear—a persistent image—that the tiny family he had made was coming apart at the roots. He would sometimes not even be able to remember any of the words of a fight they had had just the day before.

They were growing out of love, as if the love itself had always had a finite and predictable life, like childhood. And if they'd been told of this in the beginning, they might have chosen not to marry and have a child, though Andrew could not conceive of ever having made a decision that would lead to a world without Billy. And so they stayed together well past the time when the love had ended, pretending and hoping the hiatus was only temporary, fearful of the future. Until one day when the gulf between them had grown so deep that Martha, having more courage than he and fearing less that she would lose Billy, went to stay with her mother until Andrew was able to move out. He found that night, when he returned home from work, a sad note that, though it offered him a certain kind of relief, nearly drove him mad to read.

And yet weren't those the best years of all—with Billy as an infant, a toddler, a little boy standing up in his crib with his arms wide to greet his father who had come home late from work? A tiny boy with a glove two sizes too big for him, cheerfully missing each ball thrown to him, happy simply to be playing with his father, as indeed the father was happy simply to be playing with him.

Andrew marvels at this conundrum, and he wonders

often if this happened only to him, or if it happens all the time, to everyone who marries.

AND HOW MUCH, through all this, did he think of Eden? Did she not rise and bubble to the surface in his dreams?

In the beginning, when he was first at school, he felt uneasy when he met a girl. Pursuing pleasure, when Eden was so damaged, felt to him like an act of disloyalty. On visits home the first few years, he'd pester his mother with questions, but she was oddly reticent, changing the subject, as though she wished to protect him from the facts of the sordid and tragic business next door, perhaps believing the facts might distract him from what she thought was a more important matter—his education. When Martha began making the journey north with him, he found it awkward to ask of Eden, except in the most casual way. And by the time they'd moved to New York (and the journeys north had become even more infrequent), he had news of Eden only when he had a letter from home—in that era of ten-hour days at the office and of Billy's birth.

And yet it seems to him now that Eden was always there, a presence hovering at the edge of his dreams, a fragment of a life not entirely left behind. He would think of her at odd moments, at a hockey game with his son, or when he saw a girl with a head of blond curls on a street corner. Sometimes, when he thought of Eden and himself, the image that came to mind was of two trains on parallel tracks hurtling forward with abandon, until one had stopped short, derailed, while the other, his own, had gone on and on.

AND DID HE NOT, through all this, think often of Sean as well?

The afternoon after the shooting, Sean left town—whether from grief or guilt no one ever was able ac-

curately to say. Nor did anyone know where he had
gone, for he had left no note. But T.J., realizing by
evening that Sean was missing, told Andy in confidence over the phone that he thought Sean had gone
south, toward New York City.

As it happened, this was a shrewd guess, confirmed
on the second day after the shooting when a state
trooper called at the apartment over the TV repair shop
a little after supper to inform Sean's parents that their
son had been killed in a hit-and-run accident as he was
attempting to cross 178th Street in Washington
Heights. The boy had had too much to drink in an
Irish bar on the corner, said the trooper, and had, according to witnesses, walked across the street as
though blind. It was never known what Sean was doing
on the periphery of Manhattan—whether he had got
off the bus at the George Washington Bridge by mistake (not realizing there was another leg down into the
center of the city, with a stop at Forty-second Street),
or whether he had met someone on the bus who had
enticed him into the neighborhood. But if there was
someone, he or she never came forward. Indeed, none
of the witnesses had ever seen Sean before.

After that day and later, Andrew was to think often
about that ill-fated bus ride, to imagine what Sean had
been thinking on the thruway south to the city and to
wonder where it was that Sean had slept that night and
why. Even today, when driving north on the Henry
Hudson, he catches sight of the George Washington
Bridge, or when he crosses the bridge from New Jersey, he never fails to think of Sean—blind drunk and
lost in Washington Heights.

The town reeled from the news of the two events
(there hadn't been a murder in the village in forty-two
years; never a report of a hit-and-run) and waited for
Eden to wake up, hoping she would put the pieces of
the puzzle into place. And so it was that when Eden
came out of the coma that had kept her a silent sleep-

ing prisoner in her hospital bed for ten days and said
(her mother vigilant beside her) the single name—one
time, never again to confirm or deny it—no one was
surprised.

IN THE MORNING, he surveys the gutter. It has come
away from the house at one end and sags, as if at any
minute the entire trough will break loose. It must be
put right, though he has no certain idea how to do it.
Walking back and forth along the southern face of the
house, he tries to think about the problem logically.
He will inspect the supports that are still holding, see
how they're fastened, then reproduce that system along
the length of the gutter. It isn't as though he has never
done repair work before. He has, and still retains a
vestigial memory of fixing things with his father in his
boyhood. It's that he is, for reasons he can't bring into
focus, edgy this morning, his nearly bucolic calm of
yesterday morning badly ruffled.

He assumes it is because he slept so fitfully during
the night. When he awoke at 5 A.M., having nearly
asphyxiated himself with the loose top sheet and wanting, inexplicably, to drink a beer, he had been dream-
ing of a blue dress in a window. He looks over at the
other house. The window, with its four vertical rectangular panes, is bare and lifeless, as if what he saw
there *had* been only a dream and not a tangible image.

He gets the ladder and lays it against the house,
careful not to dislodge the gutter further. When he
climbs up, he sees to his dismay that it is nearly im-
pacted with gunk—a mix of caked silt and petrified
leaves. Now is when he could use his father to tell him
which task to do first: clear the gutter or refasten it?
He may not be able to fasten the trough to the house
with the added weight and detritus; on the other hand,
any pressure in cleaning it could rip away the entire
structure.

The work is irritating and annoying, unlike the pleasure of mowing the lawn yesterday. The payoff is not as immediate, not as showy. No one but him will even know the gutter has been fixed. The wood is rotted out where the nails should go; one entire board should be replaced, but he thinks that if he moves the supports, he may just be able to get away with using the wood that's there. It's not the way his father would have done it, he knows; not the way he himself was taught. But his patience is thin today. Especially thin when the only trowel he can find to clean the gutter (after nearly fifteen minutes of searching for any trowel at all) is too wide to fit into the trough.

He is returning from the garage with a chisel when he sees her open the door of the Plymouth and slip in. She pretends not to have seen him, and he doesn't wave. He wonders how she got herself past the now broken step; he must definitely fix that today. He stops to watch her. She puts the Plymouth in reverse, angles out the drive. It will be quarter to ten; he doesn't need to check his watch. He looks again up at the window in the corner. He waits for a blur of blue to come and disappear, but there is no movement at all, no sign of life anywhere inside that house.

By noon, he has got the gutter three quarters clean. His fingers are scraped raw, and the heat, shimmering up from the tar shingles, has given him a ferocious headache. Periodically, he puts his forehead against the lip of the gutter to rest his eyes, but he doesn't leave it there long. He's nearly done now and is impatient to be finished.

He moves the ladder another two feet along the side of the house. He climbs up the rungs, inclining his head in such a way as to stop the throbbing. Perhaps he should eat something, take a couple of aspirin. What does she do all day? he wonders, unable to rid himself of the vision in the window. He examines his memory closely to see if there are details he has missed, details that might tell him something important—though what

details he cannot imagine, since he sees nothing beyond an indefinite shape and an afterimage of color.
He tastes the beer he had for breakfast, a beer he suspects is the real reason for the headache, exacerbated
by the relentlessly bright sun overhead.

He digs the chisel into the gunk, barking his knuck-
les again. Wincing, he digs it in again and gets an
unexpected purchase. Six inches of gunk comes away
effortlessly, throwing him off balance. Panicky, he
reaches for the roof, but his hand scrapes and slides
to the gutter. He grabs for the gutter, which stops his
fall but in doing so comes loose from its supports and
pulls away from the house, taking the downspout with
it. In the mishap, Andrew has slipped two rungs on
the ladder.

He curses and throws the chisel to the ground, where
it lands straight up as if he had aimed it. Shaking, he
descends the ladder and gives the wrenched downspout a kick. He puts his hands on his hips and
breathes deeply. He feels an urge to move fast in his
car, to get away, for an hour or two, from the houses.

He'll have lunch in town, he decides, at the luncheonette.

ANOTHER SCREEN DOOR, slapping faintly behind him,
and he has never left. The same orange Formica
counter with the pencil-line pattern of white and blue
boomerangs, the same tall metal revolving stools with
their red vinyl seats, stools he and Sean and T.J. spun
on endlessly, thinking, talking, cooling down after
practice—the kind of soda fountain stool Billy would
die for now. The same white Buffalo china mugs, the
Kellogg's cereal boxes next to the coffee, the bubble
gum machine—providing his first tedious lessons in
the fickleness of inanimate objects, mysteriously gob-
bling nickels and refusing to release the five hard round
colored gum balls he'd paid for. Remarkable, he
thinks, but it *is* the same machine, still five for a

nickel, perhaps the last uninflated buy in America. If Billy were with him now, they'd give it a try.

But, of course, it's not the same place at all. The Vietnamese woman behind the counter nods politely but without recognition. When he came here as a boy, the luncheonette was Bud's, they called it that, *See you at Bud's,* and through the years it has evolved from Bud's to Bill's to other names and now, enigmatically, to Al's—though that cannot be a real Vietnamese name, he is thinking. The place is cleaner than he remembers it ever being—a feeling more than a valid comparison, for it wasn't anything he paid attention to as a boy. But even the old ceiling fan, he sees, has been polished shiny.

The specials are on the blackboard: Beefeater Sandwich Served With Fries/Turkey Health Club With Sprouts And Avocado—this last the only real clue, besides the new owners, to the passage of time. He slides onto a stool near one end of the counter. The Vietnamese woman nods, and he nods back. He orders the Turkey Health Club and a Pepsi.

There is a rustle at the other end of the counter. An older man in a gray jogging suit picks up his sandwich and his glass of milk, walks to the stool next to Andrew and lays his lunch on the counter.

"Andy?"

Andrew begins to rise. He shakes the man's outstretched hand. "Chief DeSalvo."

"Not anymore. Retired six years. Art. Call me Art. Mind if I join you? I'm here every day. Same time, same station. I get bored of my own company."

"Not at all. Please."

The Vietnamese woman brings Andrew a tall glass of Pepsi filled to within a millimeter of the rim. There is no ice in the glass. Andrew and DeSalvo look at the Pepsi.

"Some things just don't translate," says DeSalvo, and Andrew laughs.

"Sorry about your mother," says DeSalvo. "A lot of memories."

"Thank you."

"You in town long?"

"No. A few more days. Just to pack away some things. Fix up the house."

"You sellin'?"

Andrew nods. DeSalvo's hair is steely gray, clipped short, like a Roman's. A fine gray stubble covers his cheeks, hiding some of the pockmarks on his jowls, but his eyebrows are still thick and unruly and black. Beneath the jogging suit, his body is round and shapeless, what they used to call a barrel chest gone to fat. There's a wheeze in DeSalvo's voice, though the eyes are still a surprising blue and hard.

"My boy was ahead of you—what, three, four years?"

Andrew nods. "Nicky. How's he doing?"

"I dunno," DeSalvo says wearily. "Kids. They're a heartache. You got kids?"

"I have a son. Billy. He's seven."

"Great age. Terrific age. It's later they break your balls. Nicky, he's had a bitch of a time with drugs. Lost his job. His wife and kids left him. Hey, I don't blame her one bit. He's clean now, but big fucking deal. The ball game's over, and he didn't even get to suit up."

"People can change their lives," Andrew says cautiously.

"Yeah, tell me about it. My wife, she cries herself to sleep every night: her grandchildren are in California. Your boy skate?"

"Not really," says Andrew. "He lives in New Jersey. The ponds don't freeze for very long in the winter. Hockey's not the passion there it is up here."

The Vietnamese woman brings Andrew his sandwich, which is stuffed with sprouts and looks surprisingly appetizing.

"He lives in New Jersey, and you don't?"

"I live in New York City."

"You divorced or what?"

Andrew nods.

DeSalvo shakes his head. "I always say to my wife, 'You got your health, you got your family, the rest is bullshit.' "

Andrew nods again, feeling vaguely chastised.

"Anyway," says DeSalvo, "you look like you're doin' good. I seen your car. You're lookin' good. You workin' out?"

Andrew smiles. "No," he says.

DeSalvo turns and examines him. "You haven't changed much. Last time I saw you, musta been—what, ten, fifteen years?"

"More like twenty. The last time I saw you probably would have been the night of the, you know, shooting."

"Did you go to the inquest?"

"No," says Andrew. "Since my mother and I had been together the whole time, they used her testimony instead."

"Yeah, I remember now. Long time."

The Vietnamese woman appears with a cup of coffee for DeSalvo.

"Bothers me, that case," says DeSalvo. "Bothers the fuck outta me, if you want to know the truth. I'll tell you straight out, we blew that one. There was procedures we coulda done sooner—we lost ten, fifteen minutes. It makes a hell of a difference. And we shoulda gone straight for the O'Brien kid. Questioned him at the very least, had him in custody so he couldn't leave town. It had the marks of a hot-tempered son of a bitch like O'Brien—you know, some kid she turned down and he'd gotten pissed. Then he panicked and shot the father. So when she said, you know, that one time to the nurse, it was him, we were ready for it.

And, of course, by then, he was already dead, so where was the problem?''

He takes a sip of coffee. He puts his cup down.

''You seen the girl?''

''Eden?''

''Yeah.''

''I'm not sure. I might have seen her yesterday in a window.''

''Hell of a story, that one. Caught the edge of the shower of the buckshot. They say a piece of it damaged something important behind her eyes. I forget exactly. I always felt sorry for her, even before. Well, she was a little bit of a pain in the ass too, if you want to know the truth, and she coulda gone wild, real wild. I had her in for shoplifting a coupla times. But she had spunk, and I liked her. She had a screw loose somewhere was all. What a waste.''

DeSalvo bends his head forward and massages the back of his neck. ''This is when I could kill for a cigarette,'' he says. ''Had to give 'em up a year ago. I tell you, though, what really bothers me. You want a cup of coffee?''

Andrew nods. DeSalvo signals the Vietnamese woman and mimes a coffee for Andrew.

''What?'' asks Andrew.

''You tell me why she was completely naked,'' says DeSalvo. ''A fellow rapes a girl, he don't wait for her to undress. Take it from me, and I seen some rapes.''

''But surely, at midnight, she only had on pajamas or a nightgown,'' says Andrew.

''We found a long summer nightgown, a pair of underpants and a book in a heap by the side of the bed. She'd been reading.''

''Reading?''

''Yeah. A real egghead book. Reardon knew it. She'd stolen it from the library, by the way. Lemme think. . . . *The Myth of Vesuvius,* or something like that. Mean anything to you?''

The Myth of Sisyphus? Andrew looks sharply up at
DeSalvo. He doesn't know which detail he finds more
unnerving—the book or the modesty of the underpants.

"He could have made her undress at gunpoint,"
Andrew says, testing this notion, for he, too, has been
subliminally thinking of Eden naked under the sheet.

"Yeah. He could have. But she don't remember that.
She don't remember anything, in fact. Wouldn't say a
word then and won't now, far as I know. But you think
about that. I been thinking about it nineteen years."

THE CONVERSATION with DeSalvo is making beads of
sweat break out on Andrew's forehead and between his
shoulder blades. For a second or two, he feels the same
way he sometimes does when he knows he's going to
be sick. The fan makes slow revolutions above his
head, while beside him, beyond DeSalvo, he hears the
clinking of spoons and knives on china. Men eating,
a midday break from the job or the house, maybe the
highlight of the day, looking forward to the slice of
blueberry pie, homemade, now in season, like an
earned reward. He has on the slacks and the shirt he
wore yesterday to visit Edith, and he can feel the shirt
growing wet at the back and under his armpits. He
looks at the clock next to the blackboard with the specials, a round face set into a fake copper kettle. It
reads five to two. But it might be wrong. He checks
his watch. The same. Five to two.

Is it possible?

He has to try.

He stands up abruptly and reaches in his pants
pocket. He pulls out his checkbook, a wad of cash,
some loose change. The smallest bill he has is a ten.
He puts it on the counter. "Cancel the coffee," he
says to the Vietnamese woman. He has to say it loudly,
because she is at the other end of the counter. One or

two of the men glance up, and DeSalvo suddenly looks at him.

"What's the . . . ?"

"I just saw the time. Jesus, I'm an idiot. I'm supposed to be at the house for a conference call from my office at two," says Andrew, improvising wildly. "I'll be screwed."

"You'll make it in that car," says DeSalvo. "But just between you and me, Matheson's got a speed trap going by the Gansvoort place. I can take care of the ticket, but getting pinched will slow you down."

"Thanks for the tip."

Andrew gives a kind of wave and walks out the door. He jogs across the street to where his car is parked. His body wants to bolt, but he fights to keep himself moving steadily and easily toward his car, as if it were only a conference call he was trying to make.

When he slips behind the wheel, however, he can barely restrain himself. He is not thinking *why*; it is only getting there that matters. He has to make it. He puts the car in gear, guns it, makes an illegal U-turn in front of the luncheonette and, like a kid who's just learned to drive, leaves rubber on the quiet road. He checks his watch. One fifty-eight. On this straight and narrow stretch from town, it can be done in two, three minutes. He knows this from one harrowing race with Sean when they were seniors, the two of them abreast at midnight, himself in his father's car praying there wouldn't be a dog or something larger on the road.

He lets his mind become the racing engine, because he knows that if he allows himself to think about what he is doing, if he can see himself doing it in his mind's eye, he will begin to doubt, and once he doubts, he will be lost. He slows to an irritating thirty-five at the Gansvoort farm, peering out the passenger window to see if he can spot a cop car in the forest of old and rusted '55 Chevys that Gansvoort has been collecting for years, but he sees nothing. A quarter mile past the farm, he brings the car up to sixty. To sixty-five. To seventy.

He's doing nearly eighty when he sees the houses in the distance. He checks his watch. Two-oh-two. He skids into the drive, throwing bullets of gravel as he does so. The Plymouth isn't back yet. He has known it wouldn't be.

He hurls himself from the car. He leaps over the broken step and tries the kitchen door. It opens. Only now does it occur to him that it might have been locked.

He is blinded by the gloom in the kitchen, by the abrupt change from bright sunlight to darkness. He moves, more by instinct and childhood memory than by sight, making his way through a shrouded dining room, through the living room, where he barks his shin on a low table, to the front of the house, where he knows there will be a hallway and the stairs to the second floor.

Memory serves him well. Ricocheting through the rooms, he reaches the front hall and turns the corner. He stands at the foot of the stairs. He looks up.

She is there, waiting, on the landing at the top.

"It's Andrew," he says.

"I know," she says.

THERE IS a shaft of light from a raised shade to one side of her. His heart, which has been beating so fast he is sure he will have a heart attack, thumps loudly against his breastbone. Her hair is long, nearly to her waist, falling in tangles from her shoulders. The blond that he has remembered is now darkened to a dull brass—by time, by neglect. She is wearing a white sleeveless jersey and a pair of blue shorts that are too big for her. There seem to be smudges of gray, like paint, or something else, on her hands. The skin of her bare arms and legs is bone white, flawless, the unblemished white of Buffalo china, or so it seems to him, seeing the long white of her legs from the foot of the stairs.

She turns her head, or inclines it, as if to catch a sound. A bit of light from the window falls on her face as she does so. Her eyes, though sightless and seeming to stare at a point somewhere over his right shoulder, are still the same vivid blue-green, an unsettling color. She moves her hand to push a tangle of hair behind her shoulder, and the movement reveals a delicate haze of small white scars near the temple beside one eye. He sees now that this eye has more of an almond shape than the other, the hood of the eyelid slightly elongated into a slant.

"She'll be coming," Eden says.

Her voice is odd, atonal, as if she seldom uses it.

"I know. I'll be back," Andrew says.

He puts his foot on the bottom step, but she shakes her head. She is fourteen and thirty-three and, towering above him, as insubstantial as a dream, more beautiful than any woman he has ever seen.

He wants to climb the stairs, to see her face more clearly. He wants to peer at her scars and her eyes. He wants to touch the white skin of her arm.

"There isn't time," she says, and backs away.

The car was swimming fast along the road, and then I heard the gravel.

When I tell you nothing, you will go away from me.

You broke the shimmer on the water, and I thought that you would drown. I prayed that you would drown. Your shirt is wet and sticking to your skin.

Your weight is on the step. Have you finally come for me?

Your voice is through a fog, but I know your voice, and I have heard it all these years. You will be as I have dreamed you.

I heard you take the car slowly to its place. You

*stood there looking at my window. You are a boy with
arms as thin as wood. Then I heard her car along the
road. You didn't go inside. You watched her leave her
car, but you didn't speak to her.*

This room is very long and empty.

Your father was a brave but foolish man.

FOUR

IT IS RAINING, A HOT FAT RAIN THAT WILL END SOON and bring the worms to the surface, so that when he emerges from the house later and stands on the grass or the gravel, the earth will smell of them. Last night, he went finally to the A & P near the mall, and this morning he had his first decent breakfast in nearly a week—cereal, toast, juice, coffee—the meal reminding him of his normal routines, his regular life. The rain drums and splashes against the panes in his mother's room, and too late he sees that he has left a window open during the night. He wipes the wet sill dry with a towel from the bathroom. His mother's papers are on the bed, a random, chaotic spill of papers found finally, after supper last night, under the bed, in a box meant usually for storing winter woolens. She had not known or even guessed she might die, he is sure, for there is no order to the papers, no series of little notes explaining about the insurance or the mortgage or where the key to the safety-deposit box is.

He stands in front of her bureau, with his hands on the brass pulls of the top drawer. It is an oak piece, heavy and Victorian. He has never looked in this drawer, and it has about it, for him, a sense of the forbidden, a sense of the child stealing into the secrets of the adult. His father had a similar drawer—has it still, Andrew supposes, having not yet tackled his father's bureau—which Andrew, as a boy, *did* investigate one night when his parents were at the movies.

He must have been young, no more than nine or ten, for he remembers the thrill of discovering a package of Trojans and knowing they were, in some way, connected with sex, but not understanding (not allowing his mind to compose the picture) precisely how. And certain—he laughs now to think of it—that his father was merely keeping them for someone else.

The drawer slides noiselessly open as if it had been waxed only yesterday. The contents are precise and neat, rectangles and squares of different sizes, arranged to fit in an intimate puzzle. Her spirit was not, he knows now, in her papers, which bear the mark of carelessness and neglect, but here in her top drawer— her treasures laid out as if she were saying to herself or to anyone who might open the drawer: *This is me*. There is an aging, ivory-colored satin nightgown, deftly folded in the left-hand corner, and on it a string of pearls with a diamond clasp, a gift from his father to her on their wedding night. There is a small pink quilted jewelry case behind the nightgown, and to its right a thin packet of letters, postmarked 1943 and 1944: letters from his father in France during World War II. In the right-hand corner are his own baby things: an infant's hand-embroidered playsuit, a pair of tiny brown leather shoes, a baby book with notes and photographs sticking out of it. He has seen this before. He remembers the night his mother brought it out to share with Martha when Martha was six months pregnant with Billy, and how complete he had felt then with his mother and his wife huddled together and with his child coming.

In the center of the drawer there is a cream-colored folder. It, too, is overfull and wants someone to open it, and so he does. In it there are newspaper clippings, mostly of himself in his hockey uniform, and certificates and papers marking a boy's progress through childhood: a homemade valentine for his mother, a

second-grade spelling paper with "100" on it, a letter
announcing he'd made the National Honor Society.

He puts the heels of his palms on his eyes and rubs
them. These were her treasures: a wedding night
nightgown, mementoes of her only baby, the milestones of her boy's childhood. No secret love letters
from another man; no mysterious rings with enigmatic
inscriptions; no vials of tranquilizers; no risqué underwear; no diaries giving clues to bouts of rage or
bitterness. Though she has to have had an interior
monologue he will never hear, she has put away the
tangible evidence of the simple pleasures he has imagined for her. He sits on the edge of the bed and stares
blankly at the opened drawer. What will he do with
these things? he wonders helplessly. Where will he
take them?

There is so much now he'd like to ask of and say to
his mother, so much left unsaid these last dozen years,
when his own life, his own self-centered concerns—
his work, his lapsing marriage, his fatherhood—caused
him to think of her less and less, as if she were not as
substantial as she'd been, a memory already beginning
to fade; and this house, paradoxically, receding further
and further into the distance, though you could reach
it today, on the thruway extension, an hour sooner from
the city than a decade ago.

There was a time, when he was a boy, when he used
to think that he could absolutely not survive his parents' deaths, that if they were to die together in a car
crash, he, too, would spiral into nothingness. Now it
is his son's death he cannot bear to think of or imagine, reading as he does with benumbed horror reports
of children with leukemia or falling from open windows. When Billy was five, one of his classmates was
struck and killed by a school bus while the mother
watched from her front door. The boy, who had been
taught always to walk in front of the bus, had dashed
behind it instead—no one knew why, except that he

was only five—and the driver (a youngish woman with a spotless record, a mother herself) had backed up over him. For a week, the school had hired a psychiatrist to ride the bus with Billy and the other children in the event any of them should show disturbing signs that the tragedy had affected them too deeply. But it wasn't the children who needed the shrink, Andrew thought. It was the parents, like himself, who repeated the tale to each other and to their friends and colleagues over the phone, at the office or in their kitchens for days, as if talking about it endlessly would keep it at bay.

He walks to the window, drawn there by a tease of sunlight on the floor. Though it is still raining, the clouds are moving fast overhead, allowing the sun to break through here and there. The rain will pass any minute now, he knows, and he will go outside. He loves the earth after a fresh rain, has always loved it.

She will be waiting for him.

He checks his watch. Nine-oh-five. Less than an hour to go. He could tinker some with the gutter to pass the time.

He leans his shoulder on the window, his hands in his pockets, and looks over at the other house. A wash of sunlight, like a flight of a bird, passes over the roof and is gone.

He wonders where she would be now had the shooting never happened. If the rapist had not stolen into Eden's room, and Jim, in turn, not blundered after him, who might she be? Wild, as DeSalvo suggested? A married woman, with two children, mired in a loveless marriage? A waitress? A whore? Or would she have rescued herself—or someone have rescued her—so that she might be happily married now in Boston? Or acting in Los Angeles? Or working, perhaps, in New York, like himself. Might they have met by accident on a street corner or in a bar?

As she is, he thinks, she's oddly pure—untouched, unmade.

HE WAITS by his own kitchen door out of sight, shaded by the screen. It is quarter to. Within seconds, Edith Close will open the door he is watching, make her way down the steps and enter the Plymouth. He checks his watch again, the tenth time in fifteen minutes, and as he does so, he feels faintly ridiculous. A grown man, hiding behind a screen door, unwilling to confront an aging, impotent woman.

He sees a sliver of pink cotton, a flash of gold on a wrist. Of course. Sensible woman. Edith Close has come around from the front of the house to avoid the rotted back stoop. With the sun behind her, he cannot see her face, though she seems not to glance in his direction. Eden won't have mentioned him, then. He didn't think she would. He watches Edith Close back her car carefully out the drive, as he has seen her do several times this week, as she does every day of the year, according to his mother's reports. Angled toward town, she puts the old Plymouth into first and heads south along the straight road to the nursing home.

Even though he could go now, he waits a bit behind the door. A thick peaceful hush settles over the two houses—or does he merely imagine that it does? He hears a buzzing; in the summer there is always a buzzing in the cornfields off in the distance and, closer, the continual hum and whine of insects in the weedy perennials, but this is part of the hush, the hush of two lonely houses set apart from town with only the whiz of a car or, seldom now, a human voice to rattle the quiet. He shuts his eyes and inclines his head toward the screen, listening intently, as Eden might do, this her only world, as cacophonous and distracting as the noise of the city if only he could hear as she does, if only he could tease out the differing sounds and their meanings.

Edith Close will not come back for a sweater or a forgotten purse, he decides. She hasn't done so once this week, so why today? He lets the door slam, to announce his intentions, and walks across the spongy wet grass, soaking his old sneakers. Unlike yesterday, his walk is slow and deliberate, and when he reaches the rotting stoop, he picks his way up over it with care.

He raps once lightly on the door and almost simultaneously opens it. He enters the kitchen, unhurried, again nearly blinded by the gloom. Then he sees her, an image in a photographer's tray, emerging into focus.

Later that night, lying in bed, unable to sleep, or bending to the fridge for a beer, Andrew will recall again the swift surprise of her presence, her back resting against the sink, her arms folded across her chest. It wasn't that he hadn't expected her; he had known she would be waiting for him. It was that her proximity, after all these years, was deeply unsettling, as if a fragment of a dream, a dream he'd thought he lost years ago, had indeed turned out to be real.

"HELLO," she says.

She is holding herself still, her gaze seemingly directed toward a window beside him.

"I wanted to see you," he says. He shakes his head. "To speak with you, I mean." He stands in the center of the linoleum floor, uncertain as to whether he should sit at the table, make himself at home, or not. She has not invited him to. Perhaps, he thinks, she has no sense now, as he does, of the awkwardness of a conversation conducted standing stiffly face to face. Though she cannot see him, he feels uneasy in front of her. His arms and hands are appendages that seem no longer to belong to him. He folds them across his chest in unconscious parody of her stance.

"I thought. Yes," she says elliptically.

A quick intake of air she cannot fail to hear betrays

his nervousness. "So how are you?" he asks. It is an inane question, and instantly he regrets it.

She gives the faintest of shrugs. "I am always all right," she says evenly.

He searches for the next sentence as if hunting for a trail that will lead him out of an unfamiliar wood. All his choices seem lame.

"It's been a long time," he says.

She doesn't answer him. Instead she turns her head so that she is looking at him so acutely he wonders fleetingly if perhaps he has got it wrong—and she *can* see after all. Her stare is uncompromising. He tries to imagine what it is that she "sees": his presence must be to her a voice in a vast inky sea.

"Your mother is dead," she says.

Her words startle him. The sentence is bald, unadorned. Almost unfeeling. But he realizes that he likes the frank statement. Likes not hearing an expression of sympathy, likes not hearing the words *I'm sorry* for the hundredth time. The fact is a simple one: His mother is dead, and she has said only that.

"Yes. We had the funeral. Your mother came. Did she tell you?"

"She tells me . . . some things. But you always did that."

"What?"

"Call her my mother."

"Well, she's . . ."

"Not."

He nods. He realizes she cannot see the nod. "Right," he says.

It will take some time to learn how to speak to her, he thinks. Everything must be in the voice.

"Jim died here," she says.

Another bald sentence, one that takes him by surprise. During his three brief visits to this house, Andrew has not thought of this fact, but, of course, he knows it is true. Jim died in this house, on the floor upstairs, and Andrew's father found him. He has a sudden, too vivid image of Edith Close being pressed to the ground by the ambulance attendants, of Eden with a bloodstained towel at her head, of his father with the rifle limp beside his leg.

"You have a wife and child," she says, her gaze sliding a few degrees off his face.

Perhaps it is having been alone for so long that reduces her sentences to this simplicity, he thinks. She has lost the etiquette of conversation, having had, he supposes, no experience with small talk. If it were T.J., or anyone else, the sentence would have been looser: "So I hear you're married"—something with a tone of familiarity.

"No," he explains, trying to answer her with equally honest sentences. "I have a son but no wife. We're separated. I live alone, and I see Billy, my son, on weekends."

"I won't have a son," she says.

She says it quickly, without emotion, though it brings him up short. He wants to say, too glibly, *Of course you will*, as he might to almost anyone else, but her statement rings so true he cannot form a reply.

He shifts his weight. He glances down at his feet, then looks at her again. He tries to take it in. All the years spent here. All the days inside this house while he was away; all the years, while he was in college, in the city, at his home in Saddle River. He thinks of what he has had—the grown-up toys and trinkets, the days filled with color and people and work, while she has had only this. Who can calculate, he thinks, even the accumulated weight of one single day: a hundred colors seen in a glance out a kitchen window; a dozen lives witnessed in one brisk walk through an office; the complex wealth of a meal with a wife and child. While her days seem to him, appear to him, impoverished by contrast—weightless, undistinguishable one from the other. Or is he wrong? Is there in her slow universe a life as rich as, even richer than, his own?

Yet for all his advantages, he has the distinct feeling of being at a disadvantage. There is a reality here that he is unprepared for—one seeming to have little to do with the minutiae of the life he has left behind. It is in keeping, he thinks, with the way he has been feeling lately, the way he sometimes does on vacation, the workaday world he has left on hold receding hour by hour so that it seems like something from another period of his life, so that he is no longer sure which *is* his real life, that or this. His world now, circumscribed by the two houses, far from the screening room and the noise of telephones, far from the Thai restaurant where he usually lunches and from the banter of men in offices, is this tiny piece of geography and the three women who have inhabited it for all of the nineteen years he has been gone.

He examines her. He is a voyeur, seeing what she cannot see. She is taller, he observes, but not very tall at all—perhaps five feet four or five feet five. Her arms and legs are slender, her abdomen nonexistent, like a girl's. Meeting her on the street, one would find it impossible to guess her age.

With her hair tangled behind her, her arms folded across her chest, she might be a young housewife, he thinks, barefoot, in old clothes, turning from the dishes in the sink to confront a husband across the room, her children playing in the backyard, seen through the window. He notices again the gray substance on her hands. She is, in some ways, astonishingly ordinary. What had he expected? Someone retarded? Deformed? A character in a dream? Rapunzel in a tower?

And yet she is not ordinary at all. It is in her speech, in the way she tilts her head as if to catch a clue in the silence. Her speech is off—too direct and then too enigmatic, as if rehearsed but never spoken. He thinks

of the way he sometimes rehearses in his mind whole
dialogues he never actually has.

"What do you look like now?" she asks.

He lets out a small laugh, more a release of tension
than because the question is amusing. He puts his
hands on his hips.

"Well," he says, "pretty much the same, though
older and more decrepit." He smiles. Can she remember what he used to look like, after all these years of
darkness, of nothingness? Can she remember what any
human face looks like?

"Wrinkled here and there," he continues. "A few
gray hairs. T.J. says I'm out of shape, and doubtless
he's right."

When he says T.J.'s name, she flinches almost imperceptibly, but he is certain he is not mistaken.

"Are you looking at me?" she asks.

"Yes," he says.

"What do I look like now?"

"Oh," he says. Is it possible she does not know?
Of course it's possible, he thinks. Unless she can see
herself by touch, or unless Edith has patiently described her features. But he cannot imagine Edith doing this. And would Edith tell the truth?

"You've grown some," he begins, "but you look
younger than most women your age. You're slender.
Your face is much as I remember it, except for the,
ah, eye and the color of your face, which is pale. Your
skin is very white. Uncommonly white."

It is this whiteness that makes him cautious, he realizes, that reminds him he is an intruder—as if he'd
dived too deeply toward the ocean floor and found in
a sea cave a creature not meant to see the light or to
be seen. He takes a step closer to her—he wants to see
her face more clearly—and a floorboard under the linoleum creaks under his weight.

"Tell me about the eye," she says.

"It's . . ." He swallows. "It's somewhat elongated,

shaped more like an almond than your other. And beside it there is a bit of skin that is smoother than the rest. And there seems to be a small patch of very slight depressions. It looks . . . OK,'' he says, stammering. ''I mean that. It looks not exactly normal, but it's not . . . unattractive either. I am trying to be accurate.''

''Thank you,'' she says.

''Does that seem like how you see yourself? Think of yourself, I mean?''

''I didn't know my skin was white,'' she says. ''I can't really imagine that.''

''No,'' he says.

She moves her weight against the sink. She crosses her ankles. Her bones are small and delicate. It surprises him to think of her as delicate: in his mind she was always tough and sturdy, though he supposes she created this impression by her demeanor.

''Perhaps I didn't say exactly what I meant,'' he says. ''You're really very beautiful.''

He thinks he sees a smile skimming across her lips, and when it is quickly gone, he finds himself disappointed. He wants, he realizes, a real smile.

The possibility, however, seems remote. The visit is proving more difficult than he had imagined. Reunions are always fraught with awkward tensions—the necessity to account for oneself; the attempt to find, through memories, an ember of the old emotions—but this one has no rules. What memory could he dredge up now without fear of hurting her? *Memories from the past upset her,* Edith said. Is this true?

''So what do you do all day?'' he blurts out, unable for a moment to endure the silence, her poise.

''What do *you* do all day?'' she retorts quickly.

''Right,'' he says, and nods. He smiles again. This is better.

He brings his hand up, rubs his cheek with his palm. He has an idea. ''Do you ever . . . ?'' he asks. ''I've heard, or read, about it and was wondering . . . Would you like, would it help, to touch my face?''

He is thankful she cannot see him just now. It is one of a thousand deceits the sighted can practice on the blind. Or do they, he wonders, have ways of deceiving the sighted? Hearing things we did not know we said? He wonders if she will be able to feel the heat in his face.

She shrugs.

The silence in the kitchen is so complete he can hear the refrigerator whining.

He walks to the sink, pauses a moment, and then reaches for her hand. Her fingers are cool, and when he touches her, the touch is so private he feels he might lose his balance, and he nearly withdraws his own hand. But instead he pulls her hand from where it is wrapped tightly around her elbow. She doesn't resist. He brings her hand to his face, to his cheek, in an unnatural gesture. He has the weight of her hand in his, but when he lets his own go, she leaves her fingers on his skin.

At first she seems paralyzed, and he is about to reach up, when she moves her fingers slowly across his cheekbone to the bridge of his nose. He closes his eyes. He feels her touch move toward his brow. The touch is very slow, very light, very tentative. She traces his hairline down one side, pauses, moves up again to the brow and down the other side. She seems about to pull away then, but doesn't. She moves her hand up toward the eyebrows, and delicately she brushes her fingers against his eyelids. Her touch is cool air moving across his face. She skims down along the bones of his nose to his mouth. She outlines his lips, smooths her fingers across them, then dips under his chin to his throat, causing in him a deep internal shiver. He knows that she must feel his shiver, but she gives no sign of recognition. She fingers the collar of his shirt, trails her hand along the bridge of his shoulders and lets it drift away.

When he opens his eyes, she has her head turned from him, her arms again crossed in front of her.

He takes a long slow breath.

"Do I look the way you imagined me?" he asks.

"No," she says.

He puts his hand at the side of her head and turns her so that she is facing him.

"What?" she says.

"Don't move," he says.

He shuts his eyes. He begins on the cheek, as she did, and traces the exact journey she has taken. It is a map he will always remember perfectly, one he knows he will be able to recall in all its detail years from now. Her skin is smooth and dry. He feels the tightness of the almond eyelid, the silky skin directly beside it, with its tiny dots. Her mouth is warm and moist, and when he touches it, she bites her lower lip. He tries to "see" her face in this way, to form a picture with clues only from his hands. The image is different, he thinks, than the one his eyes see. Her skin feels fuller, her lips plumper. He lets his hand trail under her chin to her throat, lets his fingers rest in the hollow there. He traces the line of her shoulders.

He turns and walks toward the table. He sits down and runs his hand along the sticky oilcloth surface.

"What can I get for you?" he asks, changing the subject, knowing the question is condescending, even as he asks it. "There must be something that you need."

"Don't," she says.

"Don't what?"

"Don't bring me anything."

"Why?"

"She'll know you've come, then," she says.

"And if she knew?"

She shrugs again, not answering him. ''What do *you* want?'' she asks.

He looks at her. ''I want nothing at all, except to talk to you,'' he says.

''T.J. and Sean and others, many others, they always want something. But not you?''

''Sean is dead,'' he says. ''And T.J.?'' He shakes his head. If she is talking about what he thinks she is talking about, she cannot mean T.J., surely. Andrew is positive of this.

''There are lies in T.J.'s voice,'' she says. ''I can hear them when he laughs.''

He is confused. Her leapfrogging from present to past makes him light-headed with the effort of trying to understand her. It is as if, deprived of time, past, present and future intermingle without context, a day twenty years ago as vivid and as all-consuming as the worries of the morning, or of tomorrow morning.

''What do you mean, T.J. lies? Lies about what?'' he asks.

''He lies about himself,'' she says.

He studies her. ''When you asked me how you looked now . . . ,'' he says.

''Yes?''

''There is something else I meant to say and didn't.'' She lifts her head slightly but says nothing.

''Your hair is very tangled.''

She turns away, resting her hands on the sink.

He walks to where she is standing. He touches the back of her hair. ''I could brush it for you. Now, I mean.''

She shakes her head.

But that's all right, because he has another idea.

FILLED WITH PURPOSE, he is competent, the kitchen no longer strange to him, merely a mirror image of his own.

She comes into the kitchen with two towels, a comb,

a washcloth and the shampoo, as he has told her to. She puts them on the table. When he asked her to fetch them, she protested, and when she left the room, she was gone so long he thought she might not be coming back. She stands at the table, as if she were examining him. His hands are not steady—from false bravado? feigned confidence?—and he is again glad she cannot see him. To still his hands, he lifts the dishes out of the sink and scrubs it with Ajax until it is gleaming. He lays one of the towels over the lip, making a soft cushion, and puts the shampoo and the washcloth on the drainboard. He tests the water. When he has it as he wants it, he walks to where she is.

"I'm good at this," he says. It is, of course, an untested statement. He has never washed anyone's hair but Billy's, a boy's short crop. He leads her to a chair that he has turned sideways against the sink and guides her into a sitting position. Slowly, against her resistance, he pushes her shoulders back, so that her neck is resting on the towel at the lip of the old porcelain sink. He can feel the tension in her shoulders, a tension that invades his fingers, his palms.

"Relax," he says. "Just try to relax."

Her neck is arched, and he follows with his eye the long white curve of her throat to where her blouse is buttoned. He puts an arm under her shoulders, brushing her forehead with his chin as he does so, and lifts her up for a moment as he brings her hair over the edge. Her hair is a wild mass that fills the sink. He is at first nearly paralyzed by the sight of the tangled weave of brass and gold; it seems to him that it is something he has no right to touch. He turns on the water, lets it run through his fingers and into the hair. He sees that he cannot wet the entire head with the tap, so he hunts in the cupboards for a pitcher. He finds one and fills it with the warm water. When he pours it over her head, she winces, as though she were expecting it to be too hot or too cold. He tests it again. "Is that all right?" he asks.

She murmurs something he takes to be assent.

He pours the water slowly until her head is entirely soaked. He lifts up her hair with both hands, feels its weight. He opens the bottle of shampoo and squeezes it liberally over the crown of her head. Plunging his fingers in her hair—so thick his fingers are lost—he massages the soap into her scalp, gently at first so as not to frighten or hurt her, and, when she doesn't protest, more firmly. A faint sigh escapes her, and it is, he thinks—he hopes—a sigh of pleasure. Relieved, he sees her face begin to soften, the muscles letting go, so that, with her eyes closed, she looks nearly asleep. He lingers over the massage, not wanting to disturb her look of repose. A curl of soapsuds edges across her cheekbone, and he wipes it away with his finger. He remembers bathing Billy in the sink, cradling the infant's head with one hand while he soaped his skin with a washcloth. He remembers, later, getting into the tub with Billy when he was two and three, his own long, hairy legs stretched the length of the tub, with Billy nestled between them. Billy would squirt him with a water pistol, and the two of them would make up songs while Martha watched them from the doorway. It was always his job, bathing Billy.

It is only when he begins a succession of pours to rinse out the soap after the second wash that the tangles give way, and when he rinses it for the final time, the hair looks as though he might get a comb through it. He squeezes the excess water out gently and wraps a large towel around her head as he lifts her shoulders off the sink. Her blouse is wet all along the collar and her shoulders. Her body is heavy now, like a drowsy child's. He stands in front of her to dry her hair. Her face is inches from his stomach. He can feel her warm breath through his thin summer shirt. He has a fleeting image of pulling her head toward him so that her mouth touches his skin.

He draws up a kitchen chair next to her and begins to comb out her hair. It is a painstaking process, made more difficult because he does not want to hurt her and he is new at this. He learns to hold the hair in a tight fist above where he is combing the knots out; in that way, she won't feel the pull at her scalp. He parts it in the middle, not knowing how else to do it.

"Best to dry it in the sun," he says. His voice is husky. He clears his throat. "We'll sit on the steps. There should be a bit of sun there."

"I never go outside," she says. "And we only have twenty-five minutes."

He checks his watch. She is right. "How do you know that?" he asks.

"It's just something that I know," she says. "I hear it. Things sound different at different times of the day."

He opens the door and leads her to the back stoop. He tells her that the bottom step is broken, and she says she knows that—she heard him cursing yesterday. He laughs. They sit on the top step, side by side. He sits with his elbows on his knees. Their shoulders are almost touching.

"Why did you do this for me?" she asks.

"I don't know," he says.

They sit in silence. He wishes he could ask her what she is thinking about, but he knows he himself would mind the question, so he doesn't. Her hair begins to dry and turn to corn silk, first at the ends and then near the crown, curling around her face. It was, he thinks, an intrusive thing to have done, full of risk—a thing born not entirely of altruistic motives, were he to examine his motives, which he thinks he may not do. At the very least, it wasn't like him, though he is hard-pressed these days to know what is like him and what isn't. In all the years of his marriage, he never once even combed Martha's hair, never mind washed it.

"I'll have to go inside now, and you have to go," she says when there are only five minutes left.

She stands up, and he stands up with her.

"Eden . . ."

"She will know now," she says quickly.

"That will have to be all right, won't it?"

She doesn't answer him, instead moves toward the door.

"I'll be back," he says.

HE PARKS in front of the TV repair shop. An hour has passed since he was with Eden, and he doesn't know what made him head in this direction, but now, as he looks into the glass window of the shop, it seems to him that, yes, he meant to come here, to see O'Brien, to say hello.

The door is unlocked, but when he enters the shop, the room is so quiet, so still, that at first he thinks that Henry O'Brien is not inside. The shop seems not to have changed much in nineteen years, apart from a thickish layer of dust covering all of the TVs and radios and picture tubes and other components. Even the television sets themselves seem old—all secondhand, some portables, some larger models. He does not remember the dust from before, or this sense of deathly quiet in a hot dusty room on a summer day. As a young boy in the shop, he was fascinated by what then appeared to him as shiny, mysterious, nearly unfathomable pieces of that exciting thing called technology; and as a somewhat older boy, waiting for Sean to finish haggling with his father over a curfew or a five-dollar loan, he often felt uncomfortable in the shop, hoping only that Sean could make his escape before his father lost his temper.

"Hello," Andrew calls.

He hears a murmur, a movement in the back room. He makes his way toward the sound.

"Hello," he calls again.

He thinks he hears a greeting, peers into the open doorway. Henry O'Brien is sitting at a large gray metal desk littered with small electrical parts, white receipts, paper coffee cups, an ashtray overfull with cigarette butts and gum wrappers. Andrew can see only the top of the man's head at first—the reddish hair now paler with streaks of gray, a thinning at the crown—until the man looks up and squints his eyes to get a better look at Andrew or to place the face and body. The eyes are reddened and watery, as though with permanent tears.

"I know you," says O'Brien. "Wait a minute."

Andrew can see the progress of the man's thoughts as they pass across his face: A customer? No. A man from the town? No. Then there is the quick flicker of pain in the eyes, the moment of recognition.

"Andy."

"Yes."

"That's right. Your mother died."

"Yes."

"My wife . . ."

"I know. I'm sorry."

"You need some work done?"

There is no air-conditioning, nor even a fan in the shop, and the back room is airless, with a heavy trace of cigarette smoke. O'Brien is wearing a T-shirt with a hole in the shoulder. His skin is pinkish, blotchy, and there is several days' growth of gray stubble on his cheeks. Andrew notes, from his vantage point standing over the desk, that the coffee cup at O'Brien's elbow is filled with a clear amber liquid.

"No," says Andrew. "I just stopped by to say hello."

"That so."

It is an unexpectedly sullen response, and it takes

Andrew by surprise. Why has he come? he now wonders.

O'Brien does not invite him to sit down. He takes a long swallow from the coffee cup. He examines Andrew closely. "You done well for yourself, I know," says O'Brien, looking narrowly at Andrew.

"I guess," says Andrew.

"Better than my boy."

"Well . . ."

"They crucified him, you know. Or maybe you don't know; you went off to that fancy school. But they crucified him in this town—never mind that he was already dead. They wanted a scapegoat, they got one. Killed his mother."

"I . . ."

"The kid never got a trial."

O'Brien takes an angry swallow of liquid in the coffee cup, but it catches him the wrong way, causing him to cough once, then sending him into a spasm of uncontrollable retching. When he regains his voice, there is a tear of spittle at the side of his mouth, and indeed it seems to Andrew that the man means to spit his words.

"In this country," O'Brien says hoarsely, "you're supposed to be innocent until proven guilty, but the way people look at me in this town, you know they made up their minds a long time ago."

"I'm sure . . ."

"It's all her fault anyway," says O'Brien, wiping his mouth with the back of his hand. "I blame her."

"Who?"

"That whore. That bitch."

Andrew says nothing. He feels the heat rising along his neck behind his ears.

"She done it. She led him on, then turned on him. Made him crazy. And then naming him like that . . ."

A silence, like the cigarette smoke, hangs between the two men.

"She was only fourteen," says Andrew quietly.

"Fourteen. A hundred and fourteen. Makes no difference to me. If it weren't for her, my son'd be here now."

"Well, I'm sorry to have . . . ," Andrew begins.

"That your car?"

Andrew turns to see the tail half of the black BMW just outside the open shop door. The light outside, in contrast to the darkness inside, is so bright that it gives the car an almost surreal aura. Seen in this way, across the shabby bits of the front room, the car seems unforgivably pretentious.

"Yes," says Andrew.

O'Brien sucks his teeth.

"Well, I guess I'll be . . . ," Andrew says, turning back to look at O'Brien, who has deliberately resumed a hunched posture over a small piece of metal with many wires coming out of it. Andrew knows now that he was led to the shop by his desire to find out more about Sean, about the morning Sean left town, but he sees that he will not find the answers here.

"Yeah, you do that . . . ," says O'Brien, not looking up.

Andrew turns and walks back out through the shop. Bitterness hovers in the air like dust. Once outside, he stands for a moment on the sidewalk, letting the afternoon heat soak his head, feeling dusty and grayish and faintly guilty in the white sunshine. He looks across at the man who runs the gas station, waves. The man waves back. Even though Andrew doesn't know the man, no longer knows any of the people connected with the old gas station, the friendly wave is so reassuring that Andrew finds himself waving again.

It seems to Andrew that except for the waving, nothing in the street is moving.

THE HOUSE is now a labyrinth of cardboard boxes, some half filled, some sealed with packing tape, some empty, waiting for Andrew to decide on their contents. Tired, more tired than he has been since arriving, nearly numb with exhaustion, he wends his way through the maze of cartons, up the stairs and to his old room. It is after two in the morning. On a roll, he has been working all night, executing a kind of domestic triage, relegating some few precious items to cartons he will take with him back to the city, appointing more to be sold at auction with the larger furniture in the house, and remanding still less fortunate others to the Salvation Army. The Salvation Army and the auctioneer will come in a few days to collect everything, he has been told over the phone. He has only to transport the boxes he will keep for himself and Billy.

He turns on the light in his room and immediately shuts it off. Walking to the bed by the open window, he sits down, leans his head forward toward the screen and looks out. The night is as dark as a cave. No stars. No moon. He hears the crickets in the grass. Do the crickets live in the grass? he wonders. Across the way, there is the other house, and below his window the hydrangea tree. In the impenetrable darkness, he can't see either one.

In the darkness, he is thinking, he's as blind as she is.

THE DJ on the radio, a DJ who is too loud, too raucous, too juiced for seven o'clock in the morning, announces to Andrew as he eats his cereal that the heat is back—a fact that needs no telling. Already the inland humidity has settled on the land and entered the house like an unwelcome visitor preparing for another languid nap. In August, Andrew reflects, the heat is never far away, hovering as it does on the horizon, waiting for the brief teases of cool, clean air to dissipate and vanish.

The promise of a sweltering afternoon rearranges

his priorities. Two jobs that he has planned on tackling—tidying the herb and flower gardens and beginning the paint job on the south wall—must be done in the early morning hours. Later, after he has been to visit Eden again (the anticipated visit anchoring his day, lending his day a sense of urgency he cannot yet quite define), he will find a liquor store and buy a bottle of wine to bring to T.J.'s that evening. He wishes he had been able to think of a reasonable excuse not to have to go to the dinner tonight—though he is looking forward to finding out what T.J.'s children are like; and he is, if he thinks about it, intrigued, as he has always been, by the chance to see how someone else's life, a life he once knew nearly as well as his own, has unfolded.

He finishes his cereal and walks to the garage, where he finds a pair of ancient, dirt-encrusted garden gloves and a small hand hoe. Rummaging through the drawers there, he realizes with dismay that he will have to pack up these items as well.

He crouches in front of the herb garden and tries to read it. It is a tangled mass of differing shades of green fading to brown: some herbs, like the sage and the rosemary, are immediately recognizable: others could be oregano or summer savory or winter savory or thyme. He decides that regardless of variety, each needs the same care—a weeding, a pruning and a watering—and so he begins, working fast, hoping to get the job done quickly so that he can move on to the flower bed and the painting.

He is trimming a small plant that could conceivably be a weed, though he thinks not, when he feels a light tap between his shoulder blades. The touch is so unexpected that he starts, whirling around in a crouch, with the hoe in his hand.

"She pretends she washed it herself, which she is perfectly capable of doing, but I know you did it."

Edith Close towers over him. Ungracefully, his left

knee cracking, he stands to confront her. She has on a summer sundress, with a beige cardigan thrown over her shoulders.

He can think of no reply. It *was* a presumptuous act, and he cannot, for the moment, think of how to justify it.

"And sneaking behind my back," she says.

"I didn't sneak behind your back," he protests.

"You went when I wasn't there."

"Well, yes, but . . ."

"Well, then."

"She seemed fine to me," he says, trying to change the subject.

She has a purse on her arm. One hand is folded over the other at her waist. It is a gesture, common in older women, that he has never seen in a younger woman, a woman, say, of Martha's generation. He wonders, irrelevantly, if it is a gesture women grow into as they age.

"I'd have thought your mother would have told you more," she says.

"Told me what?"

"You know that Eden was away?"

"Yes. At a hospital, and then at a home for the blind."

She shakes her head. "Eden was badly hurt by the . . . incident."

She looks down at the strap of her pocketbook, as if contemplating it. "At first we thought it was physical," she says. "She had numerous operations. She wouldn't talk—to me or to anyone. We thought it was related to the injuries. But the injuries were . . . deeper than that."

He watches as she touches her purse—a talisman. "The injury to her head made her very sick," she says. "The place she was in wasn't, strictly speaking, a home for the blind." She looks sharply up at him, wanting to see his reaction. ''It was a mental hospital.''

He recalls Eden saying yesterday, apropos of nothing, *Jim died here.* He remembers thinking at the time that it was an odd thing to say.

''She did recover,'' Edith continues. ''Not fast, but after a time. She reached a point where I felt she could come home. It was felt, *I* felt, I could care for her just as well here.

''But she needs *quiet,''* Edith says forcefully, contracting her brow. ''She needs not to be disturbed, not to be reminded of the past. We never speak of it. I would prefer that you not speak of it. I would prefer that you not visit her at all. You remind her of the past. You may even raise her expectations, her hopes,'' she says, her voice rising, as if to emphasize her point. ''And then you will go away. And where will she be then?''

He again feels the heat seeping into his face. He wants to find her ludicrous, preposterous, but he cannot. Indeed, her speech is to him uncomfortably moving and embarrassingly accurate. For he *has* hoped to raise Eden's expectations, even if subconsciously, and he cannot deny that he will go away. And why should he have assumed that Edith cannot have changed in nineteen years? Rendered helpless, perhaps Eden immediately became more appealing to Edith. Or possibly it was the hole that Jim's death left in her life that allowed her finally to focus on her daughter. And yet, despite these sudden epiphanies, he wants to believe that visiting Eden is good for her.

''Don't you think you're overreacting?'' he says, surprising himself not only with his rudeness but also with the word itself, for it is a term he associates with psychobabble, one Martha liked to use on him, a word he normally despises. But he has never been precise in arguments. The words that come to mind in a tense exchange are not accurate enough, and thus he is often rendered inarticulate, like a child cornered by an adult.

"She is *my* daughter," Edith says, the words stapling the air around them.

The sudden flash of anger is surprising in the quiet backyard.

But in a moment it is gone. She gathers herself together in a deft sequence of subtle movements, gaining an inch as she stands more erect, and recomposing her face until it is the one he saw in her kitchen—calm, cooler and, if wary, then more in control. He watches her, fascinated.

"Andy," she says, as if weary of the effort to teach good manners to the neighbor's boy, "you must see it from my point of view. Eden and I are *family*." She exaggerates the last word. It sounds furry, her voice deep with patience. "She's all I've got now, and I'm all she has. There are aspects to this you can't possibly understand. You've been gone for nearly *twenty* years. . . ."

He is deprived (or relieved) of an opportunity to reply. The sound of a car slowing to turn into the driveway makes them both look up. A small white Toyota rolls over the gravel. DeSalvo hoists himself from the low driver's seat. Some cars, Andrew thinks, are just too small for some men.

DeSalvo waves and makes his way toward Andrew.

"You make your conference?" asks DeSalvo, short of breath, advancing slowly in the heat. "You left your checkbook on the counter."

"Jesus," says Andrew. He turns. "You know Mrs. Close."

DeSalvo casts a canny eye on Edith Close, nods. "How are you?" he asks.

"Fine. Thank you," she says.

"So all I can say is it musta been one hell of a conference call," DeSalvo says, turning to Andrew and handing him the checkbook. "You got a lotta cash in that account."

"Oh," says Andrew, embarrassed. "You looked."

"Yeah, what the hell," says DeSalvo. "I always look. I called you right away, but there was no answer. I woulda brought it by yesterday, but I hadda take my wife to the hospital. Problems with her hip. And I been tied up there with her all night. I told the luncheonette to tell you I had it, if you called."

"I hope your wife is all right," says Andrew.

DeSalvo scratches his chest. "They're gonna put a pin in, but the doctor says she'll be OK in a month or so."

"I must be getting back," says Edith Close, moving past the two men, giving them a wide berth. She walks slowly down the gravel drive toward her front door. She walks as though she knows they are watching her back.

"Piece a work," says DeSalvo.

Andrew looks at the retreating figure and nods.

By TEN FORTY-FIVE, he has been circling his kitchen floor for nearly an hour. The half-empty beer in his hand is warm; an empty is on the table. His T-shirt is damp at the back and under the armpits. Already the humidity has weight to it. His face feels gritty from lack of sleep. A shower would help, he knows, but he is reluctant to leave the kitchen, as though remaining in the kitchen for a long enough time will finally deliver an answer.

The list of chores now feels more burdensome than it did earlier this morning, but he cannot focus on it. The things of the kitchen, except for the framed collage of snapshots, which he'll keep, and the Hoosier cabinet, which will be sold at auction, are all going to the Salvation Army. A family finally dismantled. It must happen all the time, he thinks, every day, in every town and city in America.

And then who will live in this house? he wonders. A couple looking for an affordable starter home, a couple who will imagine this house to have more charm than it does, a couple who will furnish it with inauthentic country antiques? He envisions the new wife, her brown hair streaked with blond highlights, her lithe, athletic form dressed in khaki shorts and an oversized T-shirt, as she repapers the walls—as if this gesture will secure her dreams.

I should get back to work, he says aloud. He plays the phrase like an old tape that doesn't really interest him anymore but he nevertheless wants to hear again, just in case. Each day away from work makes the thought of returning there more and more foreign. He cannot this moment conceive of ever again having the inclination or the stamina to survive a ten-hour day in a thirty-story building, though he knows he must. Must return, and soon.

It's the heat and fatigue, he says to himself, though not entirely convincingly. This will pass.

He leans against the fridge, finishes the beer, moves away again. He needs a shower, needs a shave, needs a hair wash. A hair wash. His fingernails are black with soil. The knees of his jeans are green with grass stains. Grass stains don't come out, Martha said a hundred times, holding up a pair of Billy's overalls.

There's the wine to get, he reminds himself, trying to refocus on his list of chores. The south wall to paint.

I said to Eden I would be back, but what if Edith is right? he asks himself again. And then again.

He opens the back door, with no clear destination.

Then he has it. He will take the car for a spin, head north for an hour or two, return after two o'clock. He will get in the car and move, stay away. Stop by for a quick goodbye tomorrow or the next day. Leave it alone, forget about it.

Relieved to be moving forward, he hustles down the steps, walks briskly to the BMW. He puts his hand on the door. He stretches as he reaches for his keys in the front pocket of his jeans. The keys aren't there. They're on the counter in the kitchen.

I knew that, he says to himself.

"I THOUGHT you wouldn't come."

"I nearly didn't."

"She's warned you off."

"She's very concerned about you."

"You think so."

"Yes, I do."

"Then why are you here?"

"Well, I think she's concerned, but I'm not convinced she's right."

"I told her I washed it myself, but she didn't believe me. It's the part. I never get it right."

Her hair is freshly brushed, the part he made yesterday still straight.

"I want to ask you something," he says.

"What is it?" she says after a time.

"Was it very bad?" he says. "In the beginning, I mean. I never knew until today what happened, where you were."

She hesitates. "There are things about the beginning I don't remember," she says. "And what is bad? Worse than before? Worse than now?"

"You must have loved Jim very much," he says.

"He was my father."

"I know."

"No you don't."

It seems to him that she has taken some care with her appearance today. She is wearing a blue sundress with white buttons down the front, and a belt. Her feet, he observes, are still bare. When he entered the kitchen, she was sitting at the table, her body facing the door. There is a blush of pink along the bridge of her nose, across her cheekbones and on her forehead.

From the sun yesterday. It wasn't the part that gave
away his presence. It was the sun.

"You've been drinking," she says.

"A couple of beers."

"I haven't smelled that in a long time."

"I'm afraid I didn't have any time to clean up," he
lies. "I was working in the garden."

"I know. I heard her speak to you."

"I apologize if I . . ."

"Smell like you've been working hard? I don't mind.
It's interesting."

He wonders if he should offer to make her lunch.
He wonders what she eats. Yesterday neither of them
mentioned food.

"I think we should take a walk," he says.

"No." She smooths the fabric of her dress along
her thighs.

"It'll be good. Through the cornfields. Like old
times."

"There are no old times."

"Well, then, just for now."

"I almost never go outside."

"You said that yesterday. Why?"

"What is there to go outside for?"

"You don't have to be afraid. I'll hold on to you,
lead you."

"I won't," she says.

"She never takes you out, does she?"

She shrugs. "When it's necessary."

"Listen," he says.

"What?"

"We're going to do this."

ONCE OUTSIDE, it is as though, in the few short minutes he has been in the kitchen, some unseen hand
turned up the heat a few notches, leaving it just this
side of unbearable. Or perhaps it is that the gloomy
kitchen, with its drawn shades and green paint, has

had the unexpected benefit of providing a natural air-conditioning. Whatever the cause, Andrew is assaulted by both the glare and the heat as soon as he opens the door, a double assault that makes him wonder seriously if he should take her out.

Almost instantly beads of sweat form along his brow, on his upper lip and under his nipples. It is real heat, the kind that soaks a man only moments after he has put on a clean T-shirt, that drives children to seek relief under lawn sprinklers. In the luncheonette, the men will be sweating under the laboring ceiling fan. The town pool will be a mass of color and bodies, and in the backyards of the houses closer to town, old women will forfeit their dignity, choosing instead to sprawl in green and white plastic lawn chairs, their white legs, nearly entirely bare, white with purple veins, offered up to a stray breeze in the shade.

The heat makes him want to go to the pond—the body needing to slake its thirst—and this desire pushes aside caution. He holds open the screen door and reaches for her elbow, leading her out onto the stoop. Of course, he sees at once, the glare is nothing to her. Indeed, she keeps her eyes open wide, a stare into the white heat that unnerves him, with his own eyes narrowed into tight painful slits against the sun. He wishes he had a pair of sunglasses with which to cover her eyes. It is as if her gaze, so unaffected by this light, had rendered her naked, too exposed, and he is moved to shield her.

"I'm going to pick you up and lift you over the step," he says.

At her side, his left arm around her waist, he hoists her over the rotted stoop. When he puts her down he takes her hand.

"Do you remember the way to the pond?"

She shakes her head.

"Just stay by me. We'll go slowly."

"I don't want this," she says.

With an authority more assumed than convincing, he leads her along the newly mown grass south toward the edge of the cornfields. The grass is already turning brown in patches. He has cut it too short for August, too short for the heat.

She moves reluctantly, a slight resistance in his hand, a shrinking back from each step taken. Her hand in his is like that of a child who cannot keep up with, or who does not want to keep up with, an adult. He tries to convey confidence in his grasp, holding her hand firmly, not giving way to her resistance. He looks at her face. The too bright light makes it sharp in its clarity, the scar finely detailed, the blue-green eyes vivid and unflinching. He has a sense now of how strange this outing is for her, retracing a journey made in childhood, made then with the easy, unselfconscious movements of a girl, and not made in the nineteen years since. Now the journey must be to her the way a blindfolded walk through a foreign city would be to him, hazard awaiting each tentative step, a sense of complete and frightening helplessness but for the guide.

He shuts his eyes and tries to experience the walk as she must. Immediately he is aware of a sensation of tremendous heat at the top of his head and of the sullen quiet of the noon hour. He is uncomfortable, unsure in his footing, this uncertainty betraying itself through his hand, for he feels her resistance grow stronger. And when he opens his eyes—he can, he thinks, have taken only ten or fifteen steps at best—he sees that he has already veered off course.

At the edge of the cornfields, he can just make out the path to the pond. It is overgrown with wild blackberry bushes and bittersweet. Young boys seldom use it now, he imagines: perhaps the odd boy, exploring a path from the pond, coming suddenly upon the two stark farmhouses and realizing how far he had strayed.

The heat is producing a faint headache at the back

of his eyes. ''We'll have to go single file,'' he says, wiping his brow with the end of his T-shirt. ''I'll hold my hand behind me, and you take it. I'll go very slowly so you won't trip.''

''Where are we?'' she asks.

''Put your arms out,'' he says.

She does so, brushing the drying leaves of corn.

''Do you remember this?'' he asks.

She fingers a corn sheaf but doesn't answer him.

When they begin to move, her walk is even more tentative than before. Once she puts her hand on his back as if to steady herself. The journey is awkward, slow going. He wonders if they'd do better if he walked behind her, with his hand on her shoulder, guiding her.

A fly begins to buzz around his head and won't leave him alone no matter how he swats at it with his free hand. The heat in the cornfields, without any shade overhead, is oppressive. He feels the heat drain his confidence. He is afraid, for a moment, to look at her. What if Edith was right, he wonders, and this expedition is too much for her? And might the sun be harming her in some way he has not anticipated?

She answers his unspoken question with a cry. Her hand slips out of his. When he turns around, she is crouched toward the ground. He sees a shiny object near her foot. It is the pop top of a beer can, the sharp edge curved upward.

''Jesus,'' he says. ''We forgot your shoes. I should have thought. Let me look at that.''

She is sitting on the ground, massaging the ball of her foot. He takes her foot in his hand and examines the sole. He can see no blood, no puncture.

''I would like to go back now,'' she says.

He lifts her up. ''We have to get you some sneakers,'' he says. ''You have no sneakers?''

''Don't buy me any sneakers,'' she says.

''It's all right,'' he says, thinking. ''I can keep them

at my house. We can use them when I take you out.''
He says this as if it had already been decided they
would be going outside for walks together again in the
future. He says this as if sliding in sideways.

But she hears it. "Soon you will go away," she says.

"Well, not . . . not immediately.''

"If she knows that you have been again, she will
not go to work.''

He ponders this.

"I can be careful if you can," he says.

She doesn't answer him.

"I have to go to T.J.'s tonight," he says. "And I
don't want to go.''

"You don't like T.J.," she says.

The suggestion surprises him. "I don't know. He
and I are different now.''

"So are we," she says. She turns in the path. She
refuses his hand and holds her arms out instead, letting
the cornstalks guide her.

ON THE RADIO, in the car, on the way to the mall,
Andrew hears that the heat wave, expected to last for
most of the coming week, will break records for this
part of the state. This evening and through the night,
says the announcer, the temperature will remain in the
high nineties. The announcer segues into a follow-up
on the lead story, which Andrew has missed. The
thirteen-year-old girl who was found raped, sodom-
ized and beaten in her father's barn earlier this morning has died of her injuries at the county hospital.
Andrew stares at the digital readout on his radio. The
police, says the announcer, have made no arrests, but
the girl's sixteen-year-old boyfriend, who appears to
have been the last person to have seen her alive, has
been taken in for questioning.

The announcer, in a more lively voice, an advertising voice Andrew knows well, reads an ad for an
end-of-season sale on pool and garden accessories.

Andrew puts his foot on the gas, takes the car up to seventy. Before he knows it, Billy will be thirteen. Eden was fourteen. Just. But she didn't die of her injuries. A line swims up to him through the years from a book he liked when he was a junior in high school. He can't remember the line exactly. He has never been very good at precise recall of quotations. But it was something about there not being much difference between the ones at the farm and the ones in the graveyard, and how the ones in the graveyard were the lucky ones. The book was *Ethan Frome,* and he read it by his bedroom window for English homework one Sunday afternoon in January. He remembers vividly the way the world looked outside that window—a snow cover made bleak by the thin winter light of a January day— and how in keeping the earth was with the book he was reading. He imagines with an unwelcome clarity the face of the mother this morning as she was told the fate of her daughter. In New York, in the papers and on the radio, he has become accustomed, if not inured, to reports of the killing of children, the stealing of children and the sexual abuse of children, and these reports have sickened him and made him wary, and have caused him to be more protective of Billy than his own parents had to be of him. But it is this report, heard in his BMW on the way to the mall, heard not ten miles from the barn where the girl was found, heard nineteen years after Eden was raped and shot, that is the most difficult to absorb. Though he has an understanding of differing sexual proclivities, and a tolerance for tastes he does not himself share, he cannot conceive of a desire that would cause a man to sexually batter a child and then kill her. Nor can he entirely fathom, though a similar act might be said to have shaped many of his adult dreams and visions, how such a violence could take place here. It is the locale, he thinks, this deceptively inoffensive locale, that makes such a news report so incomprehensible.

He turns up the volume of his radio so that the sound of a rock song—a piece of music he has never heard before, a loud atonal piece of music with lyrics he cannot decipher—fills his ears.

ALL THE WOMEN of the county without access to a pool or to air-conditioning appear to have converged upon the mall. Inside, the temperature is regulated so that within minutes it is possible to forget the weather. Teenage girls in threes and fours, carrying packages, move en masse from one store to the next, lightly fingering merchandise, using it somehow as material for jokes, creating the mall anew as an activity to while away the long afternoon. Babies in strollers keep watch over their mothers, as the mothers sit on concrete benches along the center of the mall, eating ice cream cones and smoking cigarettes, idly giving the stroller a push now and then, thinking of what to bring home for supper so as to avoid cooking in the heat. There are almost no men in the mall, Andrew observes, and those he does see are in short-sleeved dress shirts and ties, managers, he supposes, of the various shops, or else plainclothes security personnel. He himself is still wearing his sweat-stained T-shirt and his grass-stained jeans, and his appearance seems out of place among all the clean women and babies and girls.

The mall is a long rectangle, with trees lining the center strip. On either side are the stores. He walks the length of the mall and back. There are four stores that sell shoes, not including the Sears at one end and the Caldor's at the other. There is also a store that sells greeting cards, a store that sells books, a store that sells video games and a store that sells fake country antiques. Most of the other stores sell women's clothing but not shoes.

He begins with the most promising store, one that sells athletic footgear, and at once realizes he does not know Eden's foot size. He picks up a sneaker that looks as though it had been designed for an astronaut or by an astronaut and reads the size inside: 6½. The size looks right to him. He is drawn to a rack of plain canvas sneakers in white and pink and blue, but a wiry-haired salesgirl, plucked from her afternoon stupor by the sight of a reasonably young male, steers Andrew away from the simple sneakers to an array of high-tech running shoes along the left wall.

"Jogging? No, I don't think so," says Andrew, who cannot picture the subtly toned blue and gray running shoes, with thick soles and puffy sides, on Eden. On Martha, yes, they would be perfect. His eyes stray covetously to the rack of plain canvas sneakers, but the salesgirl, piqued by his momentary inattention, launches into a discussion of the technology behind (or rather inside) a pair of white and silver "walking shoes." Lest he offend the salesgirl, who has actually stepped between him and the rack of canvas sneakers, he mumbles something about just looking and backs out of the store.

Andrew visits all of the shoe stores and the shoe departments of Sears and Caldor's. He visits some of the stores twice. He lingers over the selections, unable to come to a decision, unable to settle upon what he thinks is the perfect shoe. For he wants the shoes to be right, and he examines each display with the kind of scrutiny hitherto reserved for forays into toy stores in order to buy birthday presents for Billy. He fingers canvas shoes that have no ties, deliberates as to whether they might be a more sensible choice. He thinks of boat shoes as perhaps being more practical. He realizes, in Caldor's, throwing his head back in a gesture of disbelief at his own stupidity, that color is irrelevant. He is, for a time, seduced, despite his natural antipathy, by the endless shelves of sixty-dollar running shoes and lets himself be taught the intricacies of arch support. He passes several times by the first shoe store he entered, hoping the salesgirl there will have gone on a break. Finally, after an undetermined amount of time has passed, and after he has eaten a hamburger and a vanilla shake at Burger King, he walks purposefully into the first shoe store and makes for the rack of plain canvas sneakers. He allows the ambitious salesgirl no time to intercept him, picks out a pair of blue sneakers and says, *Size six and a half, please,* in a voice normally reserved for giving taxi drivers directions. He suspects she will outwit him by coming out of the storeroom with a smile to say they are out of stock, but perhaps she is less interested in him than he thought, for she returns in a minute with a box. He checks to see if they are indeed blue and size 6½, which they are. He pays for the sneakers and walks out with the box under his arm.

Then he begins on the sunglasses.

The quest for the sunglasses takes not quite as long, but standing in line at the register, listening to one teenage girl tell another, enigmatically, that she has burned her blue silk blouse, he looks at his watch and sees that it is already quarter to seven. He is due at T.J.'s at seven. He doesn't even have the wine. He will have to bolt, buy the wine, drop by the house, throw on a clean shirt. No time for a shower and a shave. And even so, he will be late.

He pays for the sunglasses and heads for the exit door. As soon as he opens it, the heat hits him like a thick wall. Nearly seven o'clock, and it still feels like a hundred.

He walks unhurriedly to his car. He is humming a song heard overhead in a store. He has the sneakers and the sunglasses, and tomorrow he will give them to her.

HE RINGS the bell inside T.J.'s front door, turns and glances down the street. Each house is, in its construction, identical to the one beside it. Any individuality, to the extent that characteristic exists at all, is created only by the paint or the trim or the false panes in this window or that. The sign at the entrance to the subdivision reads: "Water's Edge—Center-Hall Colonials," but the houses have little in common with the colonials Andrew knew in Massachusetts years ago. Even the driveways and the lawns and the redwood decks at the backs are clones of each other. What is to prevent a man, he wonders idly, from coming home drunk late one night, swerving into the wrong driveway and fumbling at the wrong door with his keys? Or opening an unlocked door and slipping into the wrong bed beside the wrong wife?

"Andy-boy. Pal," says T.J., opening the door and letting out clouds of frigid air. "Come in quick, before the heat gets in."

T.J. has on a white cotton sweater with the sleeves pushed up to the elbows and a pair of khaki pants with a profusion of pockets. The pants look as though they are meant to be worn on safari. Andrew proffers the bottle of wine wrapped in a paper bag. He has thrown on a clean dress shirt over his sweat-stained back. His fingernails are still black, and he has not shaved. T.J. raises an eyebrow but says nothing. The icebox sting of the air-conditioning, an air-conditioning that makes the interior of the house feel like late November, creates along Andrew's spine an instant and deep shiver.

He is too disoriented, however, to focus immediately on the cold. The two side walls of the hallway into which T.J. has ushered him are mirrored. Andrew feels as though he were floating, not anchored to firm ground. Two black stairways (or is it only one reflected in a mirror?) appear to rise without supports to an upper floor. A chandelier, in black and gold, repeats itself dizzyingly hundreds of times in the play of mirrors reflecting mirrors. A highly polished black chair is the sole item of furniture in the hallway, and even though it, too, has many copies, Andrew edges toward it for support.

"Andy-boy," says T.J.

"T.J.," says Andrew.

"So what'll you have to drink?" asks T.J. before they have even moved from the hallway.

"Drink?"

T.J. frowns. "Yeah, you know, a cocktail, a beer. You all right, pal? You look a little scruffy around the edges."

"I'm fine," says Andrew, reaching for the back of the chair. "Fine. I got waylaid, didn't have time for a shower. I didn't want to be any later than I am . . . was." The sentence trails off as he catches sight of himself and T.J. in the opposite wall. He himself looks dazed, like a prisoner brought from a darkened cell to a room where the lights are too bright.

T.J. eyes him warily. "A strawberry daiquiri OK, Andy-boy? Didi's made up a batch."

"Fine," says Andrew. "Fine."

"OK. Well. Lemme show you around, and we'll make our way into the kitchen."

T.J. reaches for a black handle in the glass and passes through a mirrored wall into what appears to be a living room. Andrew follows and is relieved to see that only one wall is mirrored here. His orientation is momentary, however, as he realizes that the floor on which he is standing is black marble, or some material that resembles marble, and that most of the furniture in the room is also black, a black-on-black effect that causes him to miss a small end table, on which he barks his shin.

The unmirrored walls are covered with a gold-flecked wallpaper. On a solid-black coffee table is an outsized gold ashtray and a gold vase. On the wall opposite is a massive console with an enormous TV screen not unlike the one in the screening room at work, and below it, like the darkened cockpit of an L-1011, an array of instruments and digital readouts.

"State of the art," says T.J., following Andrew's

glance. "We got two VCRs just in here. The kids have their own, and we got one in the bedroom. Have to, really, to keep up with all the good movies on. Fantastic picture on the tube. Wanna see?"

T.J. picks up one of three remote-control channel switchers on the coffee table and presses a button. Nothing happens.

"Hold on a minute. Must be the other one."

He picks up the second remote control and presses a button on it. Nothing happens.

"Kids musta been screwing around with these," says T.J., looking mildly flustered as he picks up the third. He presses a button. A life-size image of an evening game-show host appears on the screen.

"Great, huh?" says T.J.

"Great," says Andrew. He ponders for a lucid moment the effort, technology and expense it has taken to bring a life-size image of an evening game-show host into T.J.'s living room.

T.J. passes through an open doorway in one of the gold-speckled walls, and when Andrew follows he finds himself inside a dining room, he guesses, touching the long black-lacquered table in the center. He cannot help but see his reflection again in yet another mirrored wall on the other side. A black and gold chandelier, like the one in the hallway, hangs from the ceiling.

"We're into black and gold," says T.J.

The statement seems to call for some reply. "And mirrors," says Andrew.

"Yeah, well, mirrors are great. Make the place look so much bigger."

"Absolutely," says Andrew.

T.J. opens yet another hidden door. "Here he is!" he announces to the other side.

Andrew hears the female voice even before he sees its owner.

"Andy!"

He steps into a room of black and stainless steel, a room he takes, owing to the especially large amount of stainless steel, to be the kitchen. Didi Hanson, now Jackson, embraces him. He is aware of a white cotton sweater identical to T.J.'s and a strong scent of perfume enveloping him. She stands back and holds him at arms' length.

"Look at you!" she says.

Andrew is momentarily at a loss for words. "It's great to see you," he stammers. "Your house is . . . I think your house . . ."

"Isn't it?" she says, and whisks a frothy pink drink off a stainless-steel counter and hands it to him. He looks at the stainless-steel refrigerator in front of which Didi is standing. He, too, he thinks, once owned a refrigerator like that.

Didi's hair is still curled in a blond flip, a hairstyle he hasn't seen on a woman in years. Enormous gold earrings dangle from her earlobes. She, too, is wearing safari pants. A gold bracelet clinks when she puts her hand near the counter. He takes a sip of the strawberry froth. The deep shiver that began in the hallway takes over his body in earnest when the icy cold drink hits his stomach.

Too swiftly, before he can brace himself, Didi again envelops him, her head nuzzling under his chin. The gesture rattles Andrew's arm, and he tries to steady his drink over her back. A drop of pink froth falls on her white sweater.

"I'm so sorry about your mother," she mumbles into his shirt. They stand motionless for what feels like an uncomfortably long time. She gives a little squeeze and then lets him go.

Andrew can think of no reply. Did she even know his mother?

"So, pal," says T.J., slapping Andrew on the shoulder. "Let's go talk about your house while Didi here fixes us up a gourmet dinner."

"Well, we're just barbecuing," says Didi, smiling apologetically in Andrew's direction. The smile is identical to the smile of her youth—a dazzling display that always seemed to him part of a too vigorous performance.

"Come see where I live," says T.J., steering Andrew's shoulder to yet another doorway.

As remarkable as the black and mirrored interiors of the other rooms have been, nothing is as surprising to Andrew as the room into which T.J. leads him. It is as if, passing through the door, they had entered another era, another aesthetic, another house entirely. The room is what Andrew's mother would have called a den, a pine-paneled room with a maple "early American" sofa covered in plaid fabric. Beside the sofa are two matching reclining easy chairs. A rust-colored shaggy carpet is on the floor, and a small TV is in a corner on a wire pedestal. In another corner is a glass cabinet filled with guns.

"This is the family room," says T.J. "We hang out here."

Through a sliding glass door, Andrew can see the redwood deck on which is a gas grill, not unlike the one he and Martha had in Saddle River. Andrew wonders when, if ever, the other rooms are used.

T.J. sits on a chair, makes it recline. He takes a long sip of his drink.

"We'll go for one thirty. The furniture gone?"

Andrew stares at T.J. After a blank second, he realizes T.J. is talking about Andrew's own house.

"Nearly," he says, sitting in the other chair. "It's all arranged."

"Can you get someone in to do a good cleaning? I can recommend some people if you want."

"Sure. Whatever you say."

"I'll want to move on this by the middle of next week. You'll be gone by then, right?"

"I may," Andrew hedges. "I hope to be."

"I'd like to open it up. Get some people in quick. Think we can do a fast sale. Certainly we should get some action by early September. Come by the office Monday, we'll sort some things out."

"Sounds fine," says Andrew.

"You're fixing it up, right?"

"I'm doing some things. This heat is slowing me down." Andrew has an intense longing for the heat, looks covetously at the redwood deck. "Where are your boys?" he asks.

"They're at a friend's pool. Maybe they'll be back before you go."

"Do your boys hunt?" asks Andrew. Behind T.J.'s head is the glass gun cabinet. "I didn't know you had so many guns."

T.J. cranes his head to look at the cabinet. "Always had 'em," he says. "You remember. We used to hunt when we were kids."

"I recall only the rifle then. I don't ever remember you with shotguns."

"They were my dad's. He kept his gun cabinet in the basement. Locked. I take Tom junior hunting now and then, but he doesn't have a taste for it like I did. You never really did either, come to think of it, did you?"

"No. I guess not. I liked the skill involved, but I never liked finding the animals after we'd hit them."

"Yeah, my kid's like that. Tends toward the wimp once in a while—no offense."

Andrew is not offended. He thinks he would probably like T.J.'s son.

"You've done well for yourself," Andrew says in the silence, changing the subject.

"Can't complain. Can't complain. Course I'm mortgaged to the hilt, but aren't we all? Got a good deal on the house. Knew the developer, got in on the ground floor, so to speak. Didi's really the one with the eye, though. Made this a showplace. Fabulous taste, don't you think?''

"Remarkable," says Andrew.

"She coulda been an interior decorator easy, with her eye, but we decided she should stay home with the kids. Your wife work?''

"Martha? No, not really. But she will now. She's got a teaching job at a private school in New Jersey starting in the fall.''

"Your son's how old?''

"Seven.''

T.J. nods. "Right," he says. "Great age. You must miss him.''

"I do.''

Andrew and T.J. take simultaneous sips of their drinks. T.J. drains his glass. He leans forward as if to get up.

"Get you another?''

Andrew cradles his glass, looks into its center.

"When we were kids. . . ," he says.

There is something he wants to ask T.J., a question he must ask when Didi is not in the room. It is a question that has been hovering at the back of his mind since yesterday, but now, in T.J.'s den (or family room), the question seems too bold, too intrusive.

"When we were kids what?'' says T.J.

"When Eden was . . . was in that phase of hers before Sean . . . Did you and she . . . ? I mean, did you and she ever have anything. . . ?''

T.J. looks at Andrew with a stare as blank as Andrew's was moments ago. Then he shakes his head.

"Hey . . .'' T.J. stretches out the word so that it lasts four syllables. "Wasn't everybody?'' he says with a grin.

"You never said.''

"You never asked me.''

"That's no answer.''

"Hey, what is this, the inquisition?''

"Sorry," says Andrew. "Really, it's none of my business anyway."

"Oh, that's OK," says T.J., gesturing expansively with his glass. "You probably don't remember this, but you were pretty touchy about Eden in those days. Like an older brother. I mean, you don't go around telling some girl's older brother you're screwing his sister, even if he is your best friend. Not that we ever screwed."

"Then you didn't?"

"Well, not technically," says T.J. "And I'll tell you something else. I don't want to burst your bubble, but I wasn't the only one. Not by a long shot . . ."

T.J. leans back in the chair, brings his glass to his forehead. "The way things turned out for her, I guess it's just as well she had what she had then. Though I'll tell you something. I never really knew it then, because I was too inexperienced to know this and too—how shall I put it?—*busy* to ruminate on her state of mind, but now as I look back on it, she never really liked it. I wouldn't say she was doing it because she was horny, you follow me. It was more a kind of act. Or more like she was driven. That's the feeling I got—like she was driven, trying to burn something out of her. Course, when you're sixteen, seventeen, who cares what the chick is into, as long as she's putting out, right? But like I say, now, when I think back on it . . ."

Andrew looks at T.J. Didi, on the deck, knocks on the glass doors. She is carrying a platter of small steaks to the gas grill. She mouths the words "You watch the steaks" to T.J., puts them on the grill and disappears into the kitchen.

"Well, you remember what she was like then," says T.J., getting up. "You seen her yet?"

"No," says Andrew, lying.

An image of Eden as she is now, in her blue dress with the white buttons, her hair washed and neatly parted, fills the space between himself and T.J. He feels his glass being lifted from his hand.

"I'll freshen these up," says T.J. evenly, looking hard at Andrew.

THEY EAT dinner on trays in the family room. Andrew wonders how important one has to be to rate dinner in the mirrored dining room. He is just as happy, however, to be eating here; at least from here he can see and imagine the warmth outside. Even so, he is so cold the utensils tremble in his fingers.

Didi serves a bottle of sweet pink bubbly wine with the steaks. Andrew wonders what happened to the serviceable red he brought. Didi, he discovers, has a gift for small talk, a gift Andrew begins to cherish as the evening wears on and his own conversational skills falter. She chats amiably, in response to Andrew's polite questions, about her two sons, about the summer camp they have just finished, about the boom in new houses in the town. She volleys some polite questions of her own. What kind of a place does he have now? What's it like living in New York City? What's his job all about? T.J. embarrasses him by repeating to Didi Andrew's title and managing to make it sound more grandiose than it actually is. T.J. also manages to suggest that Andrew makes a lot of money, which appears to titillate Didi. She glances at him with what feels to him like new respect. She asks about the old house, inquires as to what he's doing with it, asks if he's seen Eden. He lies easily.

No, he says again. No, he hasn't.

"We used to call her—God, isn't this awful—we used to call her Goldilicks."

"What?"

"You know. Goldi licks." Didi blushes.

"Oh," says Andrew.

"I hear she's real deformed," says Didi with an expression on her lips that Andrew takes to be disdain.

T.J. shoots a glance at his wife. Andrew starts to speak, closes his mouth. He puts down his plate. He takes a sip of pink wine, puts the glass on the floor.

"I'm just going outside to stand on the deck for a minute," he says. "To tell you the truth, I'm freezing."

T.J. and Didi look at him as though he has suggested stepping out of an open window with a long drop below. "Sure," says T.J., recovering. "Whatever."

Andrew opens the door a crack and slips through so as not to let in any hot air. He walks to the railing at the edge of the deck. The heat envelops him like a warm bath. He puts his hands in his pockets and looks up and down the row of redwood decks behind the houses. He is struck by the silence. The grass has little of the symphony he hears outdoors at his own house. Nor are there any human voices at all—only the drone of air conditioners. The door behind him slides and clicks. T.J. is beside him, a short-sleeved T-shirt replacing the white cotton sweater.

"Sorry about that crack," says T.J. "She didn't mean anything, just remembering."

"It's nothing," says Andrew.

"She still gets under your skin, doesn't she?"

"Who?"

"You know who."

"Eden? No. That was years ago."

Next door someone lets a dog out. The dog immediately turns and whines to be let back in.

"Hot out here," says T.J.

"Yes. Sorry to have made you come out."

"You'll be going back to the city soon."

"Yes." Andrew turns, sits on the railing. He looks at T.J. "Sometimes I think I'd like to know what really happened that night, though, before I go."

"What night?"

"The night Eden was shot, the night her father was killed."

T.J. crosses his arms against his chest, looks at his feet.

"For instance," says Andrew. "I've always wondered why Sean, if he didn't do it—and let's suppose for a moment he didn't—why he left town so soon."

T.J. peers up at the hot, starless sky. He puts his hands in his pockets. He looks at Andrew. "Because maybe he thought people would pin it on him. He was always pretty impulsive, not too bright sometimes."

"But how did he know about it?"

"Everyone knew about it."

"So fast? Did you talk to Sean that morning?"

"What are you getting at?"

Andrew looks through the glass door, sees the gun cabinet in the corner.

T.J. had access to shotguns, he is thinking.

I'm losing my mind, he is thinking.

He shakes his head. "Forget it. This town is beginning to get to me. I have to go home."

"No harm done," says T.J. "You've been under a strain, your mother dying and all."

Andrew puts a foot up on the railing. "Where's the water?" he asks.

"What water?"

"Water's Edge."

"Oh, that. It's just a name. You know how these subdivisions go. Tudor Hills, Fox Run, Waverly Manor. They're trying to make it sound like we're living on an English estate."

In the silence they both hear a small plane overhead.

"Don't you miss that big white silo?" asks Andrew.

"You've seen her, haven't you?" says T.J.

Andrews hesitates, shrugs, then nods.

"You be careful," T.J. says.

"How did you know?"

"Whenever you lie, you smooth the hair over your ear. It's a dead giveaway. You always did it."

"Thanks for the tip."

"What's she like?"

Andrew glances at his old friend. "It's hard to say. In many ways, perfectly ordinary. But not really."

"What does she look like?"

"Good. She looks good. There's a scar, but she looks . . . OK. She's not deformed."

"I didn't think so. I told you I saw her a few times in a car—just a peek. She seemed OK but like she was asleep or something."

Andrew puts his foot down, stands up straight. "I'm going to go now," he says. "I'm exhausted. Tell Didi . . ."

"So soon? She probably made a dessert or something," T.J. protests, but something in Andrew's face makes him change his mind. "Yeah, OK. I'll tell her."

Andrew shakes T.J.'s hand. The two men, their hands still gripped, look at each other.

"Don't, ah . . ." T.J.'s voice trails off.

"Don't what?" says Andrew.

"You be careful," says T.J. "Go easy. You never know."

"Never know what?"

T.J. lets go of Andrew's hand. "I dunno. It's been a long time. This isn't your scene here. I can see that. You'd be better off getting back to your job, your kid. . . ."

Andrew nods. "I'll see you Monday, then," he says.

He waves as he makes his way down the redwood steps. He walks around the house to his car. Once inside, he snaps in a tape of Miles Davis and turns up the volume. As he backs into the street, another car starts up T.J.'s driveway. Two boys get out. The boys, in spiked hair and T-shirts, each holding a rolled wet towel, make their way toward the back of the house. Neither enters his home through the front door.

When he is in his own house, Andrew walks deliberately through all the rooms, opening each window as he goes, letting the night air—sultry, luxurious—into the house. Within seconds, his skin is damp. He walks to the bathroom, strips off his clothes and turns the water to hot in the shower. He steps into the steaming cubicle. Later, scrubbed clean and naked, he turns on a light in the kitchen. The kitchen has been stripped; it looks too bare in the summer night. Andrew lifts a carton off a chair, sits on the chair. He bends to open the carton. One by one, he takes each of the items out of the carton and puts it on the kitchen table. When the carton is empty, he gets a beer from the fridge. He drinks the beer slowly and with enjoyment, occasionally fingering the objects on the table.

THE STEAMY weather is bearable now, just, at five in the morning. Andrew takes a cup of coffee, goes outside to sit on the back stoop, thinking that a stray early morning breeze might come his way. The sky is pearly, with a pink wash on the horizon. He slept deeply once he went to bed, but woke too early, too alert to go back to sleep. The landscape is still, peaceful, except for the first birds. Yet Andrew knows that within the hour, it will be uncomfortably hot and humid. He thinks briefly of the chores he might do in the morning to while away the hours until the Plymouth backs out of the drive.

In the distance he hears a drone—a small plane on an early morning flight? he wonders—but when the drone draws closer, he realizes it's a machine, a vehicle. He sees it then across the road, a red tractor catching the first rays of the dawning sun, an old red tractor with its driver, MacKenzie, bathed in coral light, coming down a path between the cornfields. Andrew, with his cup of coffee, walks to the end of the drive, reaching it just as the tractor is about to make a turn onto a furrow paralleling the road. MacKenzie, who has farmed the land across from the houses ever since Andrew can remember, puts the tractor in neutral, waves at Andrew, then gestures with his arm to come across the road.

Up close, the roar of the tractor is too loud to permit conversation, so Andrew hops up beside the farmer.

"Didn't wake you, did I?" asks MacKenzie.

"No. Not at all," says Andrew.

"Have to be out early in this heat." MacKenzie half turns in the seat and holds out his hand. Andrew, switching the coffee cup to his left hand, shakes it. He looks at MacKenzie. The farmer, a tall, lean man, even in his mid-sixties, has a long, weathered face. Below his eyes, which are a watery blue, are deep pale crescents composed of tiny fine lines. MacKenzie has on a plaid short-sleeved summer shirt and a cap that says Budweiser across the front.

"Sorry about your mother."

"Thank you," says Andrew.

"I heard it was quick," says the farmer.

"Yes. It was."

"Good. That's the best." MacKenzie takes a pack of Carltons out of his shirt pocket, lights a cigarette, inhales deeply. "Actually, I was thinking about your family just yesterday," he says. "You heard about the girl?"

"The girl?"

"There was a girl they found yesterday. Thirteen . . ."

"Yes, right," says Andrew. "I heard."

"Made me think . . ."

"Yes. So did I. Awful story."

"Yeah. And the way they think it was the boyfriend," says MacKenzie. "Just like then." The farmer takes a quick drag. He holds the cigarette like a dart, between the thumb and first finger. "Course, they sure as hell tore up my fields, even so."

"How do you mean?" asks Andrew, taking a sip of his lukewarm coffee.

"They came here one morning with about six fellas at first, then a coupla tractors, and dug up half my fields before they gave up. No compensation either. You musta been gone by then."

"I must have," says Andrew. "I don't remember that."

"You working in New York City?"

"Yes."

"That all right for you?"

"It has been. How's Sam?" Andrew asks, shifting the focus onto MacKenzie's son.

MacKenzie rests his elbows on his knees, brings his folded hands to his forehead. The smoke from the cigarette in his fingers curls under the brim of the Budweiser cap.

"Gone."

Andrew at first thinks MacKenzie means that his son is dead.

"I'm sorry," he says. "I didn't know. When did it happen?" Andrew tries to remember if his mother ever mentioned the MacKenzie boy. Had he gone to Vietnam? Died there?

"No, not dead," says MacKenzie. "Just gone."

Andrew waits for MacKenzie to explain, or not to explain.

"Me and my wife woke up one morning. It was his twentieth birthday. He'd taken the cash in the desk drawer. Gave hisself a birthday present. Left no note."

Andrew tries to picture the boy he knew, a boy he always felt sorry for because he was never allowed to play sports. Instead his father made him work the farm, needed him at home.

"Do you know where . . . ?"

"Not a word. Never a word in sixteen years." MacKenzie throws the still burning cigarette onto the ground. "I take care of these fields, but I can't tell you why. I got no one now to leave 'em to."

Andrew looks over the fields, feels the heat already

rising from them, wonders if a gun still lies buried somewhere out there, just beneath the probing tines of the farm machinery. All these fathers and their sons, he thinks. DeSalvo, his son a drug addict and now divorced; O'Brien, his son dead at seventeen; MacKenzie, his son gone for good. He thinks of Billy with a pang.

"Well," says MacKenzie, "think I'd better get movin' before that sun gets much higher. My age, you can get heat stroke out here."

"I think any age you can get heat stroke in this," says Andrew, hopping off the tractor. "My regards to your wife."

"You stayin' or goin'?" MacKenzie asks.

"I'm going," says Andrew, shouting from the ground. "Soon."

"Best a luck to you, then," says the farmer, who puts the tractor in gear and lumbers slowly along the path.

Andrew waits for a truck to pass, then crosses the road. There is no sound of movement yet in the Closes' house. He looks at his own and thinks of his father. He wonders if his father was pleased with his son's progress through life, or if he considered him lost, like Sam MacKenzie.

But there is no one left now to ask.

SHE IS SITTING in the same chair, wearing again the blue dress with white buttons. He notes the part is askew today, but that her hair is freshly brushed. He is carrying the new pair of sneakers and the sunglasses.

He is relieved to see her sitting in the kitchen. He has imagined her in her room, unwilling to come down, to be with him again.

"Did she say anything?"

Eden shakes her head.

"I've brought you something," he says.

He puts the sunglasses on the table and bends down with the sneakers. He takes one foot in his hand. He has forgotten socks, he realizes, but no matter. "They're sneakers," he says, cradling her foot, sliding it into the unlaced shoe.

The fit, if not perfect, is adequate. He tightens the laces, then puts on the other shoe. He stands up and looks at her feet. The blue sneakers seem disembodied from her long white legs.

"You shouldn't have done this," she says.

But he is proud of his purchase. When they were kids, he is thinking, girls often wore sneakers without socks. It was the style then.

"And I've brought you these," he says. He picks up the sunglasses from the table and slides them onto her face. He moves the hair over her ears to secure the stems.

"What are these for?" she asks.

"They're dark glasses," he says. "To shield your eyes from the sun. I was worried the bright sun would hurt them."

"Nothing can hurt them," she says.

"How do they feel?" he asks.

"How do what feel?"

"The sneakers."

"All right."

"Let's go, then."

She stiffens. "Where?"

"I'm taking you to the pond."

"Why?" she asks.

"It's hot," he says. "And I feel like a swim. And I want to see it. I haven't seen it in years."

"The pond," she says.

"You remember it?"

"I remember it."

She turns her head. A fall of hair hides the side of her face, so that she looks, with her white skin and her dark glasses, with her long pale hair and her simple blue dress, like a film star making her first public appearance after a lengthy confinement in a rehabilitation center.

"It will be too dangerous," she says.

"Dangerous? Don't be silly," he says, knowing even as he says it that the remark is too glib, too easy.

He takes her hand; her fingers are cool. He feels a rough substance on her fingers and looks at them. "What's this?" he asks, massaging a gray patch.

She hesitates. "It's clay," she says. "I . . . I make things with it. They taught me when I was away."

"What things?" he asks.

"Oh," she says. "Just things. Shapes."

He tugs at her gently to make her stand.

"We'll go as we did yesterday," he says. "Side by side until we get to the path, then me in front and you follow."

She pulls her hand away from his but lets him take her elbow. She looks, he thinks, like a film star who may have been let out too soon.

The sun burns overhead through a zinc-white sky. The grass in the sullen light no longer appears green. Near the back stoop, the leaves of an old lilac bush hang mildewed and curled. On the radio this morning he heard that power blackouts, as a result of the heat wave, have already occurred in certain pockets of the county. The town pool reported record numbers yesterday. A tennis tournament at a local boys' camp has been postponed. At least one elderly woman has died of heat prostration.

He looks at Eden beside him, at the tiny seed pearls of sweat along her white brow. He stares at the small blue feet making footprints in the limp grass. Time has contrived to shorten the distance between them. He has grown very little since he was seventeen, whereas she is taller now by several inches. Still, though, the top of her head barely reaches to his shoulder.

With his free hand he pulls his own sunglasses from his shirt pocket and puts them on. He unbuttons the front of his shirt, yanks the tails out. He wishes he had on shorts. He has said, improvising, that he is taking her to the pond because he wants to swim, but in truth, until he said those words the thought had not occurred to him. He doesn't even have a bathing suit here. Yet the thought of plunging into the water, now that it is spoken, is seductive. He wonders if there will be small boys there seeking relief from the heat in the pond—or if boys nowadays prefer to stay inside their air-conditioned houses watching videos. He thinks of T.J.'s mirrored hallway and of his own twenty-seventh-floor office in New York.

When they reach the path, she makes a movement to shake his hand off her elbow. She touches the cornstalks on her left.

"I can go like this," she says. "It's easier for me."

He walks slowly in front of her. Beyond the point they reached yesterday, the path is sometimes barred by brambles, toppled cornstalks, densely grown underbrush. He uses his feet and hands to clear a way for her. He takes his shirt off and makes a fan of it, then a towel to wipe his brow. When he turns around to watch her, as he does often, he sees that Eden is stepping cautiously but evenly, with no apparent fear or hesitation. He tries to ascertain, from glimpses of her face, what her thoughts might be, but the set of her mouth below the dark glasses gives no clue. Rather she seems only to be concentrating on the map her fingers read and the progress of her feet.

Deep inside the cornfields—halfway, Andrew reckons, to the pond—he pauses for a moment to allow her to catch up, and it is then that he becomes aware of the sound, an intense resonant hymn of insects and small movements, punctuated at moments by the soughing of a dry sheaf or the quick whomp and flutter of a bird's wing, rising.

The path is shorter than he has remembered it and opens up to a grassy bank. Beyond the bank, the water shines like polished brass. Long vines have overtaken the trees, and the shade is denser at the water's edge than he recalls it having been years ago. A thick profusion of wild red lilies along the embankment, with the gold-colored water scintillating among and between the petals, stops him with simultaneous pleasure at their beauty and the guilty realization that she cannot see them. Should he tell her of them, he wonders, or is that worse?

On her own, she can go no farther than the cornfields, so he takes her hand and leads her to a damp grassy patch beneath the tallest tree, the tree most encumbered by vines and hence the one providing the coolest shade. She sits, leaning against the tree for support, her legs stretched out in front of her. She reaches for the hem of her dress and brings it to her face, wiping her forehead, her upper lip, the top of her chest. Her thighs, uncovered, are white, with a fine down of golden hairs. She smooths her dress along her legs, covering herself.

"You can tell me," she says.

"Tell you what?" he asks.

"How it looks. Is it how it was?"

He surveys the landscape nearest them. "It is," he says, "but more so. The trees are covered with vines. The water is much the same. Do you remember the color?"

She shakes her head.

"It's gold," he says, "from the minerals."

"Gold," she repeats.

"And here . . ." He stands up and walks to the mass of lilies. He snaps one off its stem and brings it back. He puts it in her hand.

"Do you remember these?" he asks. "They're lilies. Red. They've grown wilder, thicker along the banks. It's hard to say if anyone's been here recently. There's no obvious debris left behind, no trampling.''

The hymn he has heard before is quieter here. She fingers the long crimson petals in her lap.

''You're going swimming,'' she says.

''Oh, I don't know,'' he says, picking up a stone in his hand. He looks at the water. He would like a swim. The surface of the pond is glassy, undisturbed but for the arcs of water bugs.

''You could come too,'' he says. ''You could swim in your dress. It would dry in the sun on the walk back, and you could change before she got home.''

She shakes her head. ''I don't need to swim. I am just all right here.''

He tosses the stone from one palm to the other. She leans her head against the bark of the tree, and he can't tell if her eyes are open or closed behind the dark glasses. Her hands are in her lap, with the flower, wilting now in the heat. Even in the shade, the heat is enervating.

He throws the stone into the water. He stands up and unbuckles his belt. The clink of the metal sounds too loud in the silence. He slips off his clothes and his watch, lets them fall in a pile on the bank. He walks to the edge of the water.

The water at his ankles is cool but not cold. He wades out up to his waist, then lets his body drift slowly forward until he is floating. He raises his arm to begin a crawl, a lazy crawl to the other side. The distance seems longer to him than it did when he was a boy, but he attributes this to being out of shape.

He plunges his head under the water, feels the coolness drive the heat from his brain. He tries a breast stroke on the return lap, sees her through the rivulets of water that cascade off his head each time he comes up for air.

He turns and makes his way to the other side again, thinking that the rhythmic strokes feel good. But after

four laps, his arms begin to tire. He reaches the shore
closest to her, turns and thinks to make another lap,
but stops instead to stand when the water is chest high.
He looks across to the other bank, paddles idly in the
water, feels the pebbles when he puts his feet down,
then the claylike soil of the bottom. Lifting his feet off
the bottom, he lets his weight take him slowly up and
down beneath the water, blowing bubbles as he does
so. The water closes over his head and then breaks
again when he comes up for air.

He lies flat on his back, the water sloshing over his
belly. With the smallest of efforts, he can bring his toes
above the surface. He sculls quietly with his wrists.
Squinting, he can just make out a corona in the whitest,
most painful, part of the sky. It reminds him of something, but he can't quite seize the memory. He shuts his
eyes, lets his head float too, his brow and eyes sinking
below the surface, keeping just his nose and mouth free
to breathe. The sensation is delicious: the hot sun on
the exposed parts of his body, the coolness beneath.

Behind his eyes, images scintillate, shine, disappear. A leaf, translucent with the sun behind it, flut-
tering . . . Eden turning her head and smiling . . . The
sun glinting off T.J.'s sunglasses . . . A sunburst spar-
kling in the fender of his car . . . Billy with pennies
in his palm . . . A window somewhere throwing off
the shimmer of a rusty sunset . . .

A fish slithers under his left shoulder, startling him.
He tries to stand quickly, is thrown off balance, is
blinded by the water in his eyes. His toes scrape a rock
on the bottom. It's not a fish; it's her hand. She is
standing in the water up to her chest in front of him.
She is wearing her dress. Her arms are outstretched
for balance, but it seems to him she is reaching for
him.

He grasps her hand, pulls her off her feet so that she
is floating. The skirt of her dress billows up and around

her waist like a parachute. He leads her, as if executing a formal dance, until his feet leave the water and he must swim. He swims on his side, holding her elbow, letting her paddle with his support. He doesn't know what has brought her to the water—the heat, a desire not to be left alone—but he is glad to be beside her, to watch the concentration on her face as she makes her way in the unfamiliar water. He wonders if she has even once been swimming in nineteen years.

A third of the way across the pond, she breaks free of his hand, raises her shoulders and slices through the water with a knifelike crawl. She puts her face in the water, turns to the side for air, repeats the movements in perfect synchrony. Left behind, he swims ungracefully to catch up to her. Years ago, she was an excellent and tireless swimmer, making up in speed what she lacked in power.

"Make the turn now," he says, when they are near the other side.

She makes the turn but rolls onto her back, executing a smooth backstroke. He watches as each white arm rises from the brassy water with mathematical precision. Her hair swims around her, and her legs flutter, keeping her easily afloat.

"You can stand now," he says when they are near the shore.

Instead she makes a swimmer's turn and once again heads across the pond. He watches her for a moment, thinking to stay by her side in case she tires, panics; but so easy are her strokes that he is mesmerized, rooted to the spot. He lets her go.

She swims back and forth a dozen times. He is content just to watch her. When she is finished, she stands and pushes the hair away from her face. She is breathing hard. She rubs the water out of her eyes.

"You're still the best," he says.

She smiles, a real smile.

She has stopped twenty feet from him. He tries to

make his way to her side, but the water slows him down. She turns and walks unhurriedly toward the shore. He watches as she squeezes the water out of her hair, then moves around the grass near the water's edge until she finds a patch of sun with her feet. She lies down with her dress on.

He pulls himself out of the pond and stands at her feet, looking down at her.

"I don't think you want to do that," he says.

He means get the dress dirty. It is wet, and the dirt will stick to it. But there is something else he means. Her face is smooth, in repose. The little knots of tension he has seen there earlier are gone.

She doesn't answer him. He studies her. He is looking at a painting in a museum, a painting of a woman with alabaster skin in a blue dress on dried grasses—a masterpiece no one but himself will ever see. Her hair, in a twisted rope, lies to one side of her. He sees the softened knobs of her collarbone, the nipples of her breasts under the wet fabric. He sees the hollow space under the dress where the crease of her breast must be.

He crouches down beside her. Does she know he's there? he wonders. Can she "see" his awkward pose, awkward because of his nakedness?

He touches the rope of damp hair, her brow. She doesn't flinch or pull away, and he takes this as a sign that she is waiting. He touches the knob of her collarbone above the top button of her dress. He hears a sound like a small sigh escape her, and she seems to arch her back slightly.

He takes his hand away. A voice cautions him, tells him that if he does this, there is no turning back. It is not a casual act; she is virtually a child. He sees her as a child, feels again the secret dread in himself, about to touch something he should not. Images come to him from his childhood: Eden sashaying to the bus; teasing him at the pond; pressed against a brick wall.

He undoes the first button, kisses the skin underneath. It seems to him her legs slide together under her dress. She raises a hand, then drops it. The wet cloth is tight across her breasts. He undoes the second button, knows he will not stop now, and peels the cloth back. He kneels, bends his head to kiss her, and as he does so, he feels her hand at the small of his back.

She moves away from him and rolls over. She rises to her knees, stands, then slips off her dress and her underwear. She is smooth, carved but not muscled. Her breasts hang heavier than he has remembered from his dreams, and this is somehow reassuring. Her shoulders are thin, and there is a hollow place where her upper arm meets her body. Her pelvic bones are defined. Around him, the sun glints brilliantly off the water and through the foliage, causing in him a momentary dizziness. His mouth is inches from her flat belly, and he lets himself kiss her there. He lets his mouth slide along her as she drops to her knees in front of him.

He encircles her with his arms, pulling her face into his neck. He calls her name, an urgent summons, as if he were calling to her across the pond, or back across the years. Her name, spoken in that way, makes her shiver, and her poise deserts her then. He feels her break. It is a subtle movement in her shoulders, a letting go, so that he must bear her weight. She begins to cry. He presses her more tightly to him. He is glad that she is crying. There is too much that she is crying for, but he is glad, and he cannot stop himself from saying her name. He kisses her. He makes her open her mouth. He puts his knee between her thighs. She pulls her mouth away once, for air. He feels no hesitation now, no sense of caution. This is where his dreams have led him.

She knew it before I did, he thinks. *She knew it years ago, when I was still a boy.*

She seems unafraid now, though she has said the walk to the pond would be dangerous, and he misunderstood her. His balance lost, he takes her with him to the grass. Her thigh slides like silk over his, and her hair hides their faces like a cool tent. There is heat around them and the dampness of the grass, and a crow cawing irritably from the top of a tree. She clings to him, and he feels the sad frenzy of her nineteen lost years, but she is too shy to guide him or doesn't know how, and so he makes his own way, trying to be gentle, trying not to think of her as a child.

Later he will remember how a shiver rose from her belly and rippled out to her fists against his back. But he will remember, too, her unexpected delicacy. She doesn't make a sound, a silence he finds entrancing.

AFTERWARD she lies in the crook of his arm. He strokes the down on her upper arm. They both smell like the pond. She might be asleep; he cannot tell. He doesn't want to speak. In his mind he borrows a phrase from her, one that he has liked. *I am just all right,* he says to himself.

His body is tired, and he thinks it possible he might fall asleep with her—something he must guard against. He doesn't know the time but guesses there can't be more than an hour left, if that. He wonders if she can tell time here, where she hasn't been in years, where the sounds would be different from those at the houses.

He hears a rustling in the bushes. A small animal, he supposes, until he sees the boy. The boy is eleven, twelve. He comes near to the edge of the clearing, stops short when he sees Andrew and Eden. He has brown hair and glasses and freckles beneath a summer tan. He has a towel around his neck. His chest is bare. He stares at Andrew. Andrew returns his gaze but doesn't move. Then the boy turns and darts through the underbrush the way he has come.

Andrew smiles and wishes to himself that the boy will remember this scene all his life.

AFTER A TIME, he puts her head on the grass and unwinds himself from her. His watch is over by his clothes, and when he consults it, he is somewhat alarmed to see that they have only forty minutes left.

"Eden," he says, waking her. "We have to go now. Quickly."

She leans up on one arm. She seems dazed, disoriented. He helps her to her feet and retrieves the still wet dress from the grass. The dress is dirty and wrinkled. She raises the dress over her head and slips her arms through it, and it is then that he has his first doubts. The dress hangs on her, making her look suddenly very vulnerable. She slips on her underpants. Her hair is damp and tangled, with bits of grass and dirt in it. Her face is wrinkled with sleep. For a minute she seems like someone he had no right to touch, to expose.

"I don't know where the tree is, or where my shoes are," she says.

He finds the sneakers and the sunglasses in the place where they first sat down, but he hands them to her rather than putting them on her himself. The easy confidence he had before, or rather the trumped-up confidence—bordering at times, he has feared, on condescension—has left him. She is again a thing apart from him.

"When we get back," he says, trying again for a tone of authority he does not feel, "I'll take the dress and launder it and give it back to you tomorrow. Your hair should dry completely on the walk back. All you need to do is give it a good brushing and put something else on, but we have to be quick about it."

She nods once and lets him take her hand. He squeezes her hand tightly to recapture the intimacy just left. At the cornfields she goes before him, making her way with a more practiced ease and with more speed. He watches her outstretched arms, her fingers flicking gently against the cornstalks. On the other side of the fields, he takes her hand again and nearly runs with her to her back stoop. By his reckoning, they have only five minutes left. She can tell the time, too, here, on familiar ground, for he sees it in her face.

Once inside the kitchen, she begins to unbutton her dress. She slips the bodice to her waist and then steps out of both the dress and her underwear in one movement. She hands the bundle to Andrew like a child giving her clothes to a parent before she enters the bath. He takes them, moved by the ease with which she has done this, by the way she does not shield her nakedness with her arms. He is moved, too, though differently and more deeply, by her beauty, her beauty incongruous in this desolate kitchen, her feet in her blue sneakers so firmly planted on the worn linoleum floor. He aches to linger, to touch her again. He kisses her on the shoulder, slides a hand down her back. He can think of nothing right to say.

"Jim was my father," she says quietly.

He steps back, still touching her shoulder. "I know."

"No. You don't understand," she says. "I'm giving you something."

He is silent. "What are you saying?" he asks after a minute.

"I was his."

"He was your real father?"

"It's why she hates me."

Her meaning is clear, but his mind balks, unable to take it in.

"How is that possible?" he asks. "I remember the day. I was there when she brought you to the garden. . . ."

"The girl who left me was someone . . . he had been with."

"Girl?"

"She was sixteen."

"How do you know this? Did you know all those years?"

She tilts her head to one side, listens. "That's all," she says. She wrests herself from his touch, and he watches her disappear through the doorway to the darkened part of the house. Galvanized, he moves out the back door, down the steps and across the yard to his own back door. He is just inside with his bundle when he sees the Plymouth turn into the gravel drive.

HE DROPS the dress into the washing machine. The cellar is cooler than the rest of the house. He hopes she realizes in time that she still has the sneakers. He looks at the machine, tries to decide on the water temperature and the cycle. He cannot decide. He pushes buttons. The machine bucks once into life, then begins to throb rhythmically under his hand.

Upstairs, in the kitchen, the air is close, too thick to breathe. Two-twenty. The hottest part of the day. He sits at the kitchen table, brings a hand to his forehead, looks across to her house. He sees Jim sitting on the steps, waiting for Eden to come home. Jim's face, with its long flat planes, comes briefly into focus, then fades. Andrew would have said, indeed people did say, Eden resembled Edith, not Jim, but now he'd like to see the face to search for any likeness. All that comes is an image of height, ranginess, a loose charm when he wasn't drunk. All those years and no one knew. Or did they? Did his mother guess? Did Edith tell her? He sees his mother's back at the sink, slightly stooped, her hands in a stream of water from the faucet. An ache for his mother he is not familiar with knots his stomach. He walks to the fridge, thinking he should have some food, selects a beer instead, the closest thing at hand. Still standing by the fridge, he drinks it down like a Coke, immediately gets another.

Already his memories of Jim are shifting, changing shape to accommodate this new piece of information. He thinks of a scene he remembers from his childhood—Jim coming home from a business trip with presents for Eden, who is playing on a swing—but it means something different now. Indeed, everything about Jim is different now, moving slightly, giving way to something else.

The heat and his empty stomach and the beer, drunk too fast, leave him light-headed. He begins to move about the kitchen floor, pacing from the counter to the table, a slow pace in the heat. He takes his shirt off, drops it over a chair. He can still smell the pond on his skin. He imagines that he can still smell Eden on his skin too. He lets her come into his mind, his head dizzy with images of her. He tastes her skin, remembers how her shoulders felt when she broke. Her hair was dense, shading him. And then she was on her back, arching as if they might merge. She was easy, so easy, and so quiet. Nothing to show how she felt but the quivering.

He leans against the sink, puts his head in his hands. His head hurts badly at the back of his neck, up the sides toward the temple.

You remind her of the past, Edith said. You'll raise her hopes, her expectations.

He thinks of Billy, waiting for him, needing him. He thinks of Jayne in his office, of the job he must return to. He sees his mother, turning now to look at him, to ask him what he is still doing here. From the cellar, he can hear the washing machine switching into the rinse cycle.

He thinks, knows, he should not have made love to her. He feels dry and hollow. He has done the thing that Edith feared, was right to fear. He glances up. For the first time, the room looks to him exactly as it is: no longer a repository of memories—only a faded, shabby, lifeless kitchen.

He cannot tolerate the silence. He turns on the radio nearly as loud as it will go and takes the stairs two at a time. In his room, he changes into a dress shirt and khaki slacks. He empties the drawers, stuffs his underwear and socks into his leather satchel. Slipping on a throw rug in the hallway, he grabs a carton of mementoes on his mother's bed. His arms loaded, he makes his way downstairs and out the back door, letting it slam. He puts the suitcase and the carton in the trunk of the BMW. Back inside the kitchen, he allows the door to slam again. There is another carton in his mother's room, one in the living room. He takes them out to the car. Impatiently, he forces the cartons into the trunk. He is sweating heavily. The cloth along his spine is wet. Returning to the kitchen, he opens the fridge, thinking to throw away any food that might spoil. Instead, he takes another beer, quickly shuts the door. He lifts the phone out of its cradle, starts to dial T.J.'s number, replaces the receiver. He will call T.J. from the city tomorrow.

He finds his charcoal gray suit in his bedroom closet, picks up another carton in his mother's room. Pulling the kitchen door to, he lets the screen door bang shut one final time. He throws his suit and the carton, spilling the contents, into the back seat.

He puts the key into the ignition, but it jams. He tugs at it, tries again. There are shooting pains in his right temple. He thrusts the gearshift into reverse. He whirls around in his seat to back out the driveway, lets the clutch out too fast and stalls.

He slams the steering wheel with the heel of his hand.

He sees his mother coming toward him, and there is something important he wants to tell her, but the image fades before he can reach her. He sees Billy standing in the doorway of the house at Saddle River, watching Andrew pack on the day he left for good. He feels Eden break, mourning what he cannot comprehend. His head sinks below the surface, and he knows he is drowning. Billy is calling to him, but he cannot hear the words through the water. He cannot leave her, not now when she is causing him to drown. He lets the water close over his head. He feels the weight of his own body. He allows himself the sensation of sinking, of letting go.

He leans his head back against the headrest and opens his eyes. He realizes he has been crying.

He sees that he has left the lawn mower out beside the garage. A wasp flies through his open window and begins to crawl along the inside of the windshield. He takes a deep breath, shudders with a last spasm. In the near distance there are cornfields, and over them the heat shimmers.

You are thinking that my world is black. But it is not. When my eyes are open, there is thick fog. Dark fog that turns to white fog when I go to the window and the sun is out. I can make it brighten and then turn dark. The fog darkens, like before a rain.

You are something warm hovering over me.

You said my name, and until then, I had forgotten how it could sound. You were hungry too, for more than you could say. You are not like the others, not like my memories, but I have always known that you wouldn't be.

I am afraid now to dream of you.

I heard your door slam. And again. And I thought that you would leave me.

In the water, I was free.

I was his, which I knew and didn't. She burned me with it when she thought the time was right.

There is light coming into my world, but there is darkness too.

FIVE

SHE IS LYING ON HER SIDE, AWAY FROM HIM, WITH one knee bent, the other leg outstretched beneath her, while he traces small designs on her back with his fingertips. In the six days they have had at the pond, he has learned this about her—and, he supposes, she has learned this about herself: that she likes to have her back lightly stroked after they have been together.

Beneath them is a cotton blanket that he brings with him every day, and they have now found the coolest part of the clearing. Sometimes he marvels that they have not been intruded upon, or discovered, apart from the boy with glasses who saw them that first day and fled. He slides a hand down her side, along the curve of her hip. Her skin is smooth, like glass, despite the heat and the humidity. He would like to lie here all his life, he is thinking, just repeating that gesture.

She lifts a shoulder, then drops it. She means for him to keep touching her back. She tells him what she likes, not in words but in small movements and gestures, so that he has found himself alert to this communication, eager to move where he thinks she is directing him. This language, new to him, is exhilarating, heightening his pleasure. In all his years with Martha, she would never say what it was that pleased her, as if he must blindly guess at her desires, hoping to read her correctly, though he remembers that too often she seemed disappointed that he had not quite found his way.

In the hot days he has been with Eden, they have made no pretense of their desires. Just as she has no gift for small talk, she no longer knows how to be coy. On Sunday, the first day after they had been to the pond, she was waiting for him in the kitchen. He had brought the blanket, which he told her about. They walked in silence to the pond, and once inside the clearing, nearly dizzy with wanting her, he began immediately to help her off with the blouse and shorts and sneakers she had worn. The pitch of his need was keen, knife-edged—he felt only that he had been away from her for too many hours—and was matched by something both undernourished and generous in herself. And though there is within her a core of reserve he cannot yet penetrate—a repository of things she sees that are still unclear to him—their intimacy is intense, unlike anything he has ever known. Only much later that noon hour did he remember the blanket, abandoned at the edge of the clearing. He shook it out and unfolded it for them to rest on, establishing that day a pattern of resting afterward and then swimming.

When she swam that Sunday he made himself keep up with her. He didn't want her leaving him, if only for that. Twice while swimming, she exclaimed something he couldn't quite make out, and when she stopped, breathing so hard he could see her ribs rising and sinking, she was almost laughing. It has been, he thinks, a remarkable stroke of luck, finding the pond again, discovering together something that gives her so much pleasure.

Sometimes they have talked, though it surprises him when he is away from her how long their silences are, as if they had years together stretching into the future in which to unfold to each other all there is to know. Occasionally he feels an urgent need to ask her questions so that he will understand her secrets, so that they might reach another kind of intimacy, but he has learned, even in the brief time they've had together, that questions unsettle her, cause her to withdraw from him. What she gives, she gives in her own time, small parcels of knowledge.

"She told me in the spring, that last spring," she said, as they walked back to the houses on Sunday.

He was already learning to take a few seconds to determine what she was talking about.

"About Jim, you mean?" he asked.

"We were fighting, and she threw it at me. I picked up a glass and threw it at her. I didn't really try to hit her, and it broke in the sink."

He wasn't sure, but he thought he might remember that day, a day he was working under the car and he heard glass shattering.

"Why then?" he asked. "Why did she wait so long and tell you then?"

"They'd decided together never to tell me, because of what he'd done. But she couldn't stand it anymore. She wanted me to know how he was," she said. "To make me see him differently."

HE HAS given her small parcels too, though of a different nature. One day he fashioned a picnic of sorts out of tuna-fish sandwiches and grapes and cold water in a thermos and cookies from a bakery for dessert. On Tuesday, he bought her a gold necklace, which she wore while she swam. On another day, having searched the county until he found it, he brought her a book in braille from a library in a town nearly twenty miles away. It was *My Ántonia*. She had told him, when he asked, that she had been taught braille when she was first in the hospital but hadn't had a book in braille for years, not since Edith stopped bringing them home shortly after Eden came back to the house to live. He watched her finger the raised dots, trying again to recall the letters. Each day he has brought the book and watched her read. He wanted her to take the book home with her, to hide it in a drawer, but she said no, she didn't want to risk Edith's finding out they'd been together.

"She must suspect something," he said.

"She never says. I'm very careful."

"Why don't we just tell her and get it over with?"

"Tell her what?"

"Tell her we're going to be together when we want to."

"She won't leave, then. She won't go to work."

"But why?"

"She's afraid of you."

"Afraid of me? That's ridiculous."

"It isn't that easy," she said.

HIS LIFE now has achieved a simplicity he would have said was impossible. He lives for the hours between ten and two. He wakes early, with the dawn, and labors on the house. In the coolest hours of the day, he has repaired the torn screen, finished the gutter, repainted the back stoop and sanded the woodwork on the mantel in the living room. He is sometimes vaguely aware that he is doing this work so that he can put the house up for sale, but in the six days since he tried to leave and failed, he has resisted thinking of the future. He cannot now imagine getting into the BMW and driving away for good, nor can he quite sort out the consequences if he doesn't. As a result, he has resolutely decided not to think about it, to savor each day as it comes to him, to experience his days as organic, without a master plan. He has noticed, however, that the things inside the cartons have begun to come out, to spread themselves gradually again over the house. And on Monday, as he was meant to do, he went to T.J.'s office, but not, as T.J. had intended, to drop off the key. Instead he told T.J., who swiveled in a gray chair, eyeing Andrew warily, that he wanted another few days to accomplish all the repair work on the house he had set out to do. He felt he owed it to his parents, he explained rather lamely, to leave the house in good condition. T.J. had let his chair snap straight up with a thwack and had stood, adjusting his belt. "OK by me, pal," he had said, not looking at Andrew, "if you're sure you know what you're doing."

His afternoons are as rhythmic as the mornings. After he and Eden have been together each day, he drives to the mall in search of gifts for her she cannot keep. He has become, as a result of this habit, a devotee of the mall. He has bought her a peach-colored cotton sundress and a copy of *Ethan Frome,* which he plans to read to her. He has bought her a box of chocolates, which they devoured one day after swimming. He has bought her sunscreen lotion for her face and a wide-brimmed straw hat. Today he has bought her something special, the most ingenious of his purchases.

"I'm going swimming," she says, stretching and sitting up.

"I'll come with you," he says.

"No. I can do it myself now."

He is about to protest, but stops. There is no reason she can't swim on her own. Her sense of direction is uncanny. He has noticed that she has entered and come out of the water at exactly the same spot each day. He wonders how she does it: does she feel the path with her feet, or does she hear her way?

Propped up on one elbow, he watches her walk to the pond, wade out up to her waist, then dive forward to begin her crawl to the other side. He likes watching her swim. Her strokes are neat, mathematical, and he takes pride in seeing her strength return with each passing day. She can easily finish twenty laps now, and if they had more time, she might do thirty.

He lies back with his hands under his head. He thinks he hears, very faintly, a distant rumble of thunder. The strangling heat wave, now in its eighth day, has broken all records. It is as if the entire town and its environs were waiting breathlessly for the siege to

break. He hopes it is thunder that he has heard, and
that it will come soon, this afternoon, bringing with it
a soaking, rinsing rain. He imagines the rain, bounc-
ing up from the cracked ground, dripping from the wet
leaves, falling onto his face and shoulders as he shuts
his eyes and turns his face gratefully up to a cloud-
burst. . . .

He wakes with a start, annoyed to see he has been
dozing. He has no idea how long he has been unconscious: seconds? minutes? He stands awkwardly and
too fast, feeling hollow as he does so. He scans the
pond. There is no sign of Eden. He glances around
the clearing, but she is not there either. He calls her
name, the first time hesitantly, the second time
abruptly, as he runs to the water's edge.

"Eden!" he shouts, as if he were cross with her.

The surface of the pond is eerily smooth.

"Holy Christ!" he yells now, flailing into the pond.
His heart is loose inside his chest. His lungs are huge
balloons, pushing against his ribs. The water is mo-
lasses. It is like the nightmares he used to have as a
boy when he couldn't run fast enough in his dreams.
"Jesus God," he cries as he pitches forward to swim,
not knowing in which direction to head.

To his right, he sees a ripple, than a hand. She rock-
ets straight up in the water not twenty feet to the side
of him, panting hard. She smiles. She listens for him.
She waves in his general direction.

"What the hell are you doing?" he snaps angrily,
trying to catch his breath.

"I'm just swimming," she says, surprised by his
tone. "What is it?"

"I thought you'd . . ."

He turns and heads back toward shore. He holds his
chest where his heart is palpitating and walks around
the perimeter of the clearing, with the other hand on
his hip. She does not follow him, remains in the water
where he has left her. When he circles close to shore,

he sees her making waves with her fingers, idly stroking the surface. He lunges into the pond, pulling his feet high and clear until the water reaches above his knees. He dives forward in her direction. He bobs in front of her, lifts her in his arms, cradling her, then rolls her in the air and lets her belly-flop into the water. She comes up sputtering, gasping. She makes a broad sweep with her forearm, spewing the water in his direction. He dives, catches an ankle, drags her under. He holds her there, kisses her, but she pushes at his shoulders, propelling herself to the surface. When he comes up for air, she is laughing. He grabs her around the waist, pulls her onto her back, slides her over himself. She turns abruptly, plunges his head under water, and leapfrogs over his body. When he stumbles to his feet, he sees that she is already halfway to shore. She runs dripping up onto the grass, quickly feels with her feet where the blanket is and sits down, hugging herself. Home free.

"You're an asshole sometimes, you know that, Andy?"

The word is a song note he thought he might never hear again. It lifts him up, makes him as buoyant as a child's inflatable toy in a pool. He bobs happily, watching her, then slithers out of the water to the blanket. He sits beside her.

"I fell asleep," he says, "and when I woke up I was disoriented. I thought you'd . . ."

"Drowned?"

"Yes."

She touches his shoulder, runs her hand down his arm. "I'm sorry," she says.

"I just feel . . . ," he says.

"I'm responsible for myself."

"It's more than that."

"It's hard to believe now," she says, "but I once wished that *you* would drown."

He looks at the surface of the pond, returned to its glassy, golden state. "I love you," he says.

She squeezes his forearm. "You think you know me, but you don't."

"I know enough."

"I could say I love you too, but I don't know what it is."

"I do," he says.

"I wish I could see your face when you make love to me," she says after a long silence.

He turns to look at her. He hoots. He drapes his arm around her shoulder.

"I'm glad you can't," he says. "I probably look ridiculous."

After a time, he consults his watch. "I've brought something for you," he says. "I'd better give it to you now."

She no longer protests when he gives her presents, and he likes that. He reaches for the plastic bag he brought with him to the pond.

"It's a battery-operated cassette tape recorder," he explains, taking her hand and letting her touch the small rectangular object. "It's easy to operate, and I've brought you some books on tape to listen to." He fetches the boxed cassettes from the plastic bag. "Short stories by Chekhov," he reads, "and *Smiley's People* by John le Carré."

She fingers the buttons on the tape recorder.

"And here's the best feature." He pulls from the bag a set of headphones. Smoothing her hair behind her ears, he adjusts the headphones and plugs in the jack. "Listen to this," he says.

He snaps the cassette of Chekhov into the tape recorder. "Nod when the sound is the right level," he says. He turns the volume up slowly, and she nods. He watches her listening. He pushes the stop button and moves the headphones off her ears.

"When you have these on, no one can hear the tape.

You can play it in your room, and she won't hear you. It's small, so it can easily be hidden.''

''I don't know,'' she says cautiously.

''Trust me. Here, give me your hand, and I'll teach you how to use this.'' He takes her fingers and shows her how to read the buttons. Play. Stop. Eject. Record. Play. She holds the black box, listens to the words on the cassette. If he can find the right cassettes, he can give her an entire world that has been lost to her all these years.

She pushes the stop button, takes off the headphones.

''When are you leaving?'' she asks.

Leaving. It is a question he has scrupulously avoided asking himself for six days. ''I don't know about that,'' he says.

''You'll have to go. You have a life you have to go back to. You have a job and a son.''

He flops back onto the blanket and rubs his eyes with the heels of his hands. ''I don't want to talk about that now,'' he says.

''Now *you* have things you don't want to talk about.''

''It's different.''

She puts the tape recorder aside and crosses her legs, supporting her weight on one hand.

''In the beginning,'' she says, ''I was asleep. Then I cried for a very long time. And then I felt guilty and knew I was being punished.''

''Punished for what?''

''For how I'd been.''

He is silent.

''You remember,'' she says.

He ponders this confession. It is another parcel, a small piece of the puzzle. She has given it, he thinks, because she wants him to tell her something, to give her in return a clue about the shape of her future. It has, however, the opposite effect. It irritates him, makes him suddenly want to know more, as if she had merely teased him.

"It's not enough," he says rashly, not looking at her. "Tell me more."

"There isn't . . ."

"Tell me all of it."

"There isn't any more."

"I don't believe you. Was it Sean?"

"I don't remember."

"You know you said it, though. Someone has told you you said it."

"I know I said it one time, but I don't remember it. I have no memory of that time. Please don't do this." Her voice rises at the last sentence.

Even with his eyes shut, the sun is so bright behind his lids he has to squint. He wishes he had his sunglasses on. He sits up quickly, knowing he has gone too far. He touches her thigh with the backs of his fingers. He notices that her hand is shaking.

"I'm sorry," he says.

She sits perfectly still—though inside, he knows, there must be a turbulence he can only guess at. It is, he thinks, a finely honed skill, her poise, a means of coping with too much darkness, too much silence, too many bad memories.

"Is that thunder?" she asks.

He listens and hears nothing. "I don't know. I heard something like thunder earlier. I hope it is, though. Then maybe this awful heat will break."

"I don't want it to break," she says.

"Why?"

"Because then it will be something else, and we'll be different."

He slides his arm along her back and draws her down so that she is lying now on top of him.

"There isn't time," she says. "I can feel it."

He stretches an arm and looks at his watch behind her head. "It's exactly one-oh-seven," he says. He

kisses her, pressing her head down toward his face
with his forearms. She moves slightly, making small
adjustments to accommodate her breasts, her hip-
bones.

"I think the place likes us," she says. "I think it
wants us to stay here."

And as he looks past her head at the trees above
them, he believes that what she has said is true—that
there is about the pond and its clearing an unmistak-
able benevolence. Once it offered them its seasons of
childhood games. Now, years later, overgrown and
neglected, it shelters them as lovers.

WHEN HE enters his kitchen, arms full of grocery bags
from the A & P, and a plastic bag from the mall dan-
gling from his fingers, the phone is ringing. He lets
his bundles fall to the kitchen table, lifts the receiver.

"Andrew?"

"Jayne."

"You sound short of breath."

"Oh, a bit. How are you?"

"I'm fine, Andrew. I think the real question is: How
are you?"

"Better. Better," he says vaguely.

"I've been asked to call. . . ."

"I know. I should have called in."

"You *are* coming back?" she says.

"Yes. Soon. Is it very bad there?"

"Everything that can go wrong . . ."

"And Geoffrey?"

"The usual. Well past hysteria."

Through the kitchen window, Andrew can see a long
blanket of tarnished silver clouds advancing on the
western horizon.

"Jayne, before you say any more, I've decided to
take some vacation time. There's a lot owed me, but
I'm thinking in terms of another week, ten days."

There is a pause.

"Jayne?"

He thinks that perhaps they've been disconnected, but just before he is about to hang up, he hears a male voice on the line.

"Andrew."

The one spoken word brings Geoffrey, all six feet four inches of him, clearly into focus. He will be standing at Jayne's desk, his free hand fussing with the knot of his tie. Andrew can see the black aviator frames with the smoky tint, the neatly trimmed black mustache with flecks of gray, the black wing tips, glossily polished.

"Geoffrey."

"Sorry about your mother."

"Thank you."

"But that's not why I called."

"No."

"It isn't a convenient time right now for a vacation. The agency is collapsing under the weight of this project even as we speak. We may have to scuttle them altogether and start anew with someone else. We need you, Andrew, to tighten the reins, to get this thing under control. The product's been ready for six weeks."

"I know."

"So you'll come in, then. Tomorrow?"

"No."

"Then when?"

"I'm not."

"Come again?"

"I can't. Not right now. I'm sorry, Geoffrey."

There is a long silence.

"I think you should give this some more thought, Andrew. Consider what I've said."

"I'll do that."

"I want you to call in tomorrow. Talk to me after you've thought about it. You can take a month's vacation when this is over."

''It's not the vacation per se, Geoffrey. It's that I can't leave here right now.''

''I don't want to have to say your job is on the line.''

''No.''

''We don't want that to be a consideration.''

''No.''

''So don't back me into a corner on this one, OK, buddy?''

''No.''

''Is that all you have to say?''

''I think so. This isn't personal, Geoffrey. I'm not trying to cause a problem.''

''Then don't.''

''I'll call you.''

''Do that.''

Andrew holds the phone to his ear long after he has heard the click on the other end. He replaces the receiver and walks to the left side of the window so that he may have a better view of the blanket of clouds on the horizon. He hears, distinctly now, a long roll of thunder in the distance. It is as though a town were waiting for an advancing army to liberate it.

The office must be in worse shape than he thought, for Geoffrey to have threatened him—though Andrew knows the threat is almost certainly an empty one. He would have to be AWOL a lot longer than this for Geoffrey to let him go. This knowledge, however, is oddly disappointing. Getting fired now would come as a relief, absolve him of responsibility for the future.

The phone rings again.

''Andrew?''

The chemical reaction in his larynx deflates his voice by half an octave.

''Martha.''

''Where are you?''

''I'm here, obviously.''

''I mean, why aren't you in the city? You were only going to take a week.''

"I've decided to stay on a bit, take some vacation time."

"Vacation time? But what about Billy? He's been expecting you."

Andrew winces. This fact, which has lain at the back of his thoughts for six days, kept in check by Andrew's attention to the details of his house and of providing for Eden, spirals out of its niche and floods the whole of Andrew's consciousness.

"It's only another week," he says, in a voice that has risen a notch. He clears his throat. "I need to sort some things out."

"Andrew."

"What?"

"You sound odd. Is everything all right?"

"No. Not really."

"What is it?"

"I can't talk about it now. I'm sorry. Tell me how Billy is."

"He's great. All tanned and healthy. But I think you're going to have to talk to him."

"I know. Put him on."

He waits, his chest tight, for his son's voice.

"Daddy?"

"Hi, Billy. What are you doing?"

"Me and Mommy are making a battleship with my Legos. I can't go outside 'cause it's raining. Are you coming to get me now?"

"No, Billy. Not today. I'm still at Grandma's house."

Andrew hears a long sigh, like that from an old man. The sigh enters his own body, goes right to his bones with a shudder.

"Billy?"

"Tomorrow can you come?"

"I can't tomorrow. But soon. I'll come as soon as I can. I love you and miss you."

"I love you too, Daddy."

"I went swimming today in a pond. And guess what color the water is."

"Green?"

"It's golden."

"Are there fish in it?"

"Lots of fish."

"Can we go there sometime?"

"Sure. We'll see."

"Grandpop took me fishing in the ocean."

"Did you catch anything?"

"Nope. Well, kind of. I caught a lot of seaweed."

"You be good, OK, Billy?"

"OK."

"And I'll come soon."

"OK."

"Can I talk to Mommy now?"

"OK. Bye, Daddy."

"Bye, Billy. I love you."

Andrew falls into the chair by the phone, rests his head on his hand.

"So you don't know when you'll be here," Martha says. Drag and exhale. Away from him, she has lit a cigarette.

"I'll let you know."

"You know, Jayne called here this morning. She wanted to know if I knew what was going on."

"There's nothing going on. I'm just exhausted, that's all. I need some time."

"So you say. I'll try to handle Billy. But don't wait too long. You've never not come when you've said you would. I'm not sure he understands this."

"Give me another week. That's all. I'm sure I can sort this out by then."

"You don't sound good."

"I'm actually very good. That's the funny part."

"I don't know if I like this," she says. "You're not making a lot of sense."

"Don't worry. Everything will be all right. Give Billy a kiss for me."

"Andrew?"

"Yes?"

"You take care of yourself."

He stands up, heads immediately to the fridge. Taking out a beer and opening it, he holds it in one hand as he removes the groceries from the paper bags and puts them in the fridge and the cupboards. A half gallon of ice cream he has forgotten about has leaked into the paper bag. Halfway through this chore, he opens the screen door, stands on the back stoop. From there he can see nearly the entire horizon line where the army is advancing. It is a slow-moving storm, beginning only now to flutter the leaves in the trees overhead. Soon the leaves will turn their backs and shine silvery as the clouds slide across the sun. He can see a distant flash of lightning, can hear another slow rumble of thunder.

The phone rings again. He doesn't move. It rings seven times, and then it stops. When he's sure the caller has given up, he reenters the kitchen and throws the empty beer can into the wastebasket. He is nearly through the kitchen on the way to his bedroom when the phone begins to ring again.

"Andy-boy."

"T.J."

"Everything OK, pal? I thought you'da blown town by now."

"Not quite."

"Well, anyway, I got some good news for you."

"What's that?"

"I just had a call from your neighbor, Edith Close. She's sellin' too. Moving right away, she says. This is fantastic. With both houses on the market, we can get a much better deal now."

* * *

THROUGH THE NIGHT, storms rattle the town, wave upon wave battering the gates, pausing for a time, then beginning again. The skirmishes—lewd light shows beyond his screen, punctuated by splintering cracks of thunder overhead—sever Andrew's dreams, causing him to start and wake a dozen times before dawn. In the morning, nothing has changed but the rising of a gray curtain of light that reveals the trees' wild careening and a lawn strewn with debris—branches, twigs, leaves and dead hydrangea blossoms. He wakes a final time, his mouth dry, his body soaked from a tenacious humidity that will not break. The sheets on his bed are grainy from too many days of dampness. He curls himself off the bed and slips on the jeans and shirt and sneakers that lie in a pile on the floor. Stumbling into the dim bathroom, he flips on the switch there and is puzzled for a moment when the overhead light doesn't go on. To check that it is not simply a blown bulb, he reaches behind him for the light switch in the hallway and finds there, too, only a deadened circuit. He walks heavily down the stairway, through the living room and out to the kitchen, pausing only long enough to drink a glass of water.

Outside the air feels charged: he thinks he can smell a faint trace of ozone. It is not raining, but he knows the calm is deceptive as he surveys the sweep of the sky over the town and sees no break in the clouds in any direction. He heads down the gravel drive, past a faded green shutter that has fallen from an upstairs window at the Closes' house during the night. At the road, he stops. He has no destination, merely a desire to leave the two houses for a time so that he can think. To his right is the town, with its pockets of subdivisions encroaching farther and farther along the straight road out toward his house. To the left is a nearly empty expanse of road through farmlands and cornfields, leading to the next town. He turns left.

He walks on the asphalt, his hands in his pockets,

stepping into the ditch from time to time when he hears the whining of a truck or a car. He marvels at the amount of debris on the road and wonders where it is that the wires are down, causing the blackout. He wonders, too, if the luncheonette has opened for breakfast, if T.J. and his wife are even aware, in their insulated capsule, that storms have shaken the county. He tries to imagine how they will survive without their air-conditioning if they, too, have lost their power. He wonders if the women and their babies are getting ready to go to the mall now, or if they will stay home today.

He walks perhaps three or four miles before he is aware of just how far he has traveled. He has managed not to think too strenuously, which, he realizes, is what he wanted all along. He has reached a spot in the road on either side of which are only cornfields. An angry burst of thunder takes him by surprise, for he has not noticed any lightning preceding it, and it seems to him that the thunder is close, just off his left shoulder. The sky, too, is darkening, as if it would return so quickly back to night. He thinks now that he should turn around, that in his drowsy state he has come too far. It is foolish, he knows, to be walking on an open road, so far from shelter, with the promise of another storm.

He starts to make a turn, when he sees, in the middle of the road up ahead, not fifty feet from him, a small shape that seems as though it shouldn't be there, that doesn't look like a tree branch or a blown cornstalk. He squints at the shape, trying to make out what it is, torn between investigating it and retreating toward his house. He moves a few steps forward, in order to see more clearly, thinking he can discern the outline of an animal. It moves slightly, raising its head. A pencil-thin dagger of lightning in the cornfields to his left lights up the scene: the wet road, the waves of undulating fields, the huddled shape. He feels raindrops on his hair and shoulders—an announcement of yet another storm, followed immediately by a drumming shower. He jogs to the shape, crouches down beside it. A beagle's head turns toward him, its eyes calm and sorrowful. The dog looks at Andrew, as if for an explanation of this calamity, and lays its head down, still watching the man. A bolt of lightning appears to strike the road not a hundred feet from Andrew, startling him. The crack of thunder is so sudden and so sharp the dog lifts its head again. Andrew sees that the creature's hind legs have been crushed, and there is a smear of blood, about three feet long, on the asphalt—washing away now in the rain—where the animal has tried to drag itself. Andrew peers up and down the road. In the distance, coming from the town, he sees the headlights of a vehicle. Another bolt of lightning and then another, a pair of jagged wires piercing the space around himself and the dog, make him shudder involuntarily. He has always, even as a boy, harbored a fear of lightning. He bends down and tries to slide his arms under the dog. It gives a faint moan. The headlights of the car are more distinct now, moving fast along the road. Andrew lifts the animal into his arms, feeling the dead weight of the hindquarters. The dog raises its head, tries to reach its nose to Andrew's face. He carries it to a grassy patch beside the road and lays it down as gently as he can. The car whizzes past, showering Andrew and the dog with a fine spray. The center of the storm is upon them now, spewing out its stabs of lightning with abandon. Andrew crouches toward the ground, so as not to be a target, then lies on the grass on his stomach beside the dog. The thunder is so loud—or his sudden fear of the accompanying lightning so paralyzing—that he cannot move, save to cover his head with his arms and hands. He chooses not to watch, but he knows, his breath held, then released in spasms, that all around them there is lightning, dancing gaudily in the cornfields. His spine tingles with the image of his exposed back as an electrical field, inviting the ferocious charge. He stretches his arms out in front of him, feeling the earth. The thunder rises like the crescendo of an orchestra gone mad. He presses his brow hard into the grassy soil and waits.

When he hears the thunder subside, he raises himself off the ground to a sitting position. He tries to clear the rain from his face with his sleeve. The dog's eyes are closed. He puts his hand on the animal's head, lets his hand caress the inert body. The dog has stopped panting, is not breathing at all.

"It's all right," he says, stroking the wet fur. The rain soaks them both, indifferent to the living and the dead. He thinks about the dog's silence on the brink of death. Did its hind legs not hurt? he wonders.

And then, so completely drenched that he has begun to shiver, he thinks about injury and damage done. The thoughts come warmly and familiarly into his brain; it was what he was trying to dream about all night, an exploration rudely thwarted again and again by the nocturnal chaos of the storm.

Can damage be erased, redressed? he asks silently.

"And who of us is not damaged?" he asks aloud.

He think of T.J., lost to his belief in the morality of material things.

He thinks of Martha, twisted from an early age by an anger that refused to explain itself or leave her.

He thinks of Geoffrey, with his wing-tip shoes and his expensive dark suits, committed ten hours a day to the drama at the top of a glass and steel building.

And he thinks of himself, engaged so long in the same enterprise, forfeiting the thing he cared most about—the daily fatherhood of his son.

Is Eden any more damaged than himself? he wonders. Than any of them? And was it folly to imagine that he could, by loving her, ease the hurts of her past? Or she his?

A rusty green pickup truck sails past Andrew, stops short, nearly hydroplaning on the wet pavement, and

backs up to where Andrew is sitting. A middle-aged
man, wearing a once white T-shirt and a brown felt
hat with a brim, leans across the front seat and rolls
down the window. Andrew can see the gray stubble
on his cheeks, an eyetooth missing.

"That yer dog?" he asks.

Andrew shakes his head.

"What you want to do with it?"

"Bury it," says Andrew.

"Well, then, throw it in the back. You live around
here?"

Andrew nods, tells him where he lives.

"Better get in," says the man.

HE BURIES the dog under the hydrangea tree. It is a
frustrating process in the rain, since the hole he makes
with a spade keeps filling up with water and falling in
at the sides. It has to be a largish hole and fairly deep
to accommodate the dog and to keep stray animals
from digging at it. When the lightning comes again,
he has to retreat to the kitchen for a cup of coffee. He
looks out the window at the dog and the half-dug hole.
The lightning stops, and he goes out to resume the
digging. At times he wishes he had not decided to do
this, because he knows he has to think now, to plan,
to make lists about the immediate future. He is afraid
to have an idea and then not remember it later. But
when the hole is fully dug, the dog placed inside it,
the soil raked over, he is glad that he has done this.

SHE ISN'T sitting in the chair when he enters the
kitchen. She is at the sink and turns immediately when
he opens the door. Her face seems agitated, hard to
read. She is wearing a long blue seersucker bathrobe,
and she is rubbing her arms with her hands as if she
were cold. He has been worried all morning that Edith
would not go to work, and when he heard the Ply-

mouth start up, he raised his head toward the ceiling in grateful thanks.

"What's going on?" he asks at once. He does not go to her. He senses she wouldn't want that yet.

"She found the tape recorder."

"How?"

"I thought she was taking a nap. She said she was going to. I put the headphones on and was listening to the stories when she came into the room. I should have heard her long before she ever got to my room, but with the headphones on, I couldn't."

"I'm sorry."

"She took it."

"What did she say?"

"She didn't say anything. She just left."

"Do you know she's selling the house?"

She nods. "I heard her on the phone. But how do *you* know?"

"It was T.J.'s agency that she called."

"Ah."

"Come over to the chair and sit down," he says. "We have to talk."

"What is there to talk about now?"

"Let's go upstairs," he says, "to your room. I want to lie down with you, talk to you that way."

"No," she says quickly. "Not my room. I'll come sit down."

She makes her way to the chair and perches on it reluctantly, as if about to hear a lecture she intends to resist. She folds her hands in her lap. Her face, he now sees, has become, on the surface, impassive, struggling to keep in check a face underneath.

He reaches across for her hand. She gives it unwillingly.

"Tonight," he says, "I'm going to pack up the house for good. When I come tomorrow, I'm going to help you pack. Then we're going to get in my car and drive to my apartment in New York. We'll leave a note for

Edith. When we get to the city, I'm going to take a short leave of absence from my job. We'll get you settled in a good program for the blind, but we'll be together, live together.''

He is improvising now. Until this minute he has been unable to think beyond the drive south, the exhilaration of that open highway.

She begins to shake her head.

''What?'' he says.

She says nothing, but he can feel her retreating even further, inch by inch.

''What is it?'' he asks more forcefully.

''I can't do that,'' she says. ''I can't leave.''

''But why?''

''I wouldn't know how.''

''I'll be with you every step of the way. It doesn't have to be the city; we can go anywhere.''

''You have a son,'' she says. ''And I have Edith.''

''You have Edith?'' he asks incredulously.

''I have to have Edith and she has to have me. There are things about this you don't understand, things about me you wouldn't like if you knew.''

''There's nothing about you I couldn't deal with. I love you. I've told you that. It's simple.''

''No; that's just it,'' she says. ''It isn't simple at all.''

She withdraws her hand, rises and edges toward the sink.

''I won't leave here without you,'' he says. ''There's nothing more important in my life that I have to do.''

She hunches her shoulders forward, rests her weight on her hands at the lip of the sink. He can see the shape of her back, her waist beneath the robe. Her hair is tangled, not brushed. There are dishes in the sink she has not washed yet. She runs her palms along the porcelain rim. She takes hold of the faucet, massages it with the heel of her hand.

The silence worries him. He feels that he is losing

ground. "I won't leave without you," he says again, "and I won't let—"

She cuts him off. She whirls around quickly from the sink. "I've changed my mind," she says. "I want to go upstairs now."

He guesses she is doing this to stop him, to divert him from his campaign. But he imagines that lying next to him, she cannot fail to hear him.

He follows her through the dining room, the living room, up the stairs and, after they have reached the landing, through a darkened doorway.

A flash of lightning through the sole window lights up the room, illuminating hundreds of faded pink roses on the walls. The paper is peeling badly, revealing another, grayer paper beneath it. Someone years ago, perhaps when Eden was a baby, thought to cover the more somber paper with one befitting a little girl, but having no expertise in wallpapering, as was the case with Jim and Edith, merely covered the one paper with the other. Oddly, he or she also papered the slanted ceiling over the bed, but there whole patches have come away, laying bare a crumbling plaster. The bed is tucked under the slanted ceiling, one side against the wall, with only a foot of space above the edge of the bed where the wall and ceiling meet. The bed has no headboard, only an iron footboard, painted white, but chipped in so many places it looks more mottled than painted. A worn pink chenille bedspread is drawn up neatly to the single pillow. The floor, wide plank boards, is painted a chocolate brown. On the other side of the room is a small desk of maple with a stained green blotter on its surface. There is a radio on the blotter and a hairbrush. Beside the hairbrush is a sealed plastic bag with what seems to be a large lump of moist clay inside. On the chair in front of the desk is the blue sundress.

Another flash of lightning, followed almost immediately by a shuddering crack of thunder. He looks out the window at the rain and at the trees whipping back and forth. The shade at the top of the window is torn along the bottom, and he sees that the panes have not been washed in a long time.

Nearly noon, and it is as dark as a heavy dusk.

It is the first time he has been in her room as an adult, though when he was a boy he was sometimes here while Eden collected a baseball glove or her mittens. Then the room was not barren, at least not as he remembers it. The desk was cluttered in those days with a record player and her records and her sports paraphernalia. Sleeves and legs of clothes spilled from the dresser. In the corner, he remembers, she kept her hockey stick and skates. He thinks, too, he must have been here on a stormy day, like this one, but he can't, for a moment, recall what it was they did here. He has a vague memory of endless games of Monopoly, stretching long past the point when he'd have been glad to concede the game to her if he could have brought himself to do it—or did they go to *his* house on rainy days?

He surveys the room again, returning to the moment. The weight of it hits him now. He imagines how she must sit here with the darkness falling. He wonders if he would be able to stand that, or would he have to find a light? There is a light, a wall lamp near the door. It must be for Edith, for when she comes during the evening.

He watches Eden sit on the edge of the bed, as if momentarily preoccupied with choices, then lie back close to the wall. She raises one knee slightly, and the robe falls open when she does so. She stretches out an arm to indicate that he should come.

There is something uncomfortable about her posture. He tries to read her face. Already she is eons away from him.

He sits in the chair by the desk. He would like to know what she has in its drawers, whether the "things" that she makes are there. The radio is an old one, of round brown plastic. He wishes they could go back to the kitchen, start again.

"I'm lonely over here," she says.

The voice is one he hasn't heard in years. He remembers the afternoon as clearly as if he were at the pond this moment. *You can touch my blouse,* she said, and the voice was the same. But then he was a boy, and he resisted her.

He bends down to loosen the laces of his sneakers. They are still soaked from his walk. He thinks of the dog under the tree. He would like to tell her about the dog. He takes off his shirt, unbuckles his belt. He lays his clothes on the chair, over the blue sundress.

He walks to the bed, lies down beside her. He thinks only that he will hold her, bring her back. But under his weight, when he moves toward her, the bed creaks abruptly and loudly in the silence—the old iron springs protesting a man's additional weight. Yesterday, he thinks, they might have laughed together, but now the sound makes her freeze, as if she had badly miscalculated, as if she had not anticipated this echo. Quickly, he presses his hand against the small of her back, drawing her closer, but she is stiff against his embrace.

"Eden," he says, but she doesn't answer him.

He can feel her fear, or something like fear, along the tendons and muscles of her back. The fear is contagious and travels up his arm to his own chest. Alarmed, thinking he can stop the current by a bold gesture, or by seizing her to him more tightly, he roughly shifts her hips under his. The bed creaks again. He kisses her, but her mouth is empty.

"What is it?" he asks, the fear gathering in his chest like a cloud.

He raises her arms and pins her hands up behind the pillow.

"What is it?" he asks, shaking her wrists.

She lifts a knee as if to twist him off her, but he presses her leg with his own and holds her to the bed under him. He looks at her closed eyes, the almond eye. She turns her face away.

"Who was here before me?" he whispers hard into her ear.

She gives a cry and strains toward the wall. He lets her go but wraps an arm around her abdomen and pulls her buttocks against him. He puts a hand at the back of her neck, bending her forward. He raises the skirt of her robe until it is bunched at her waist. A sensation, as swift as a kick, moves through his chest when he sees her exposed, too white, too vulnerable. But he is lost now to reason, letting his fear guide him. Holding her hipbone with his free hand, he slips inside her from behind. She cries out again as if he had hurt her, but he doesn't believe he has hurt her. It is something else she is resisting. He can see the buttons of her spinal column rising from her buttocks until they disappear beneath her robe. He moves his hand down to the place where her thigh joins her hip and holds her there.

"Tell me who," he insists, his voice no longer a whisper.

She reaches for the edge of the bed nearest the wall to anchor herself against his pounding. He can see her shoulder quiver with the strain. Beyond her shoulder is the faded paper with the roses and its brittle cracks. But he is suddenly confused, not in her bed but in the pond, grabbing for her hand because she has gone under.

"I was his," she cries out to the wall. The voice is taut, stretched, too high-pitched.

"Who?" he says hoarsely to her back. He holds her tightly now, diving beneath the water to reach her, nearly there.

"*Jim's.*"

It is a wail that comes to him from across the pond.

He breaks the surface. The cry reaches him, buffets his ears like a high wind. He takes the name, looks at it, remembers it.

He stops, halted in frenzied midsentence. His eyes refocus on the blue and white stripes of the seersucker cloth. His body slips away from her of its own accord.

He makes a sound like a man coming up for air. He rolls onto his back.

Outside, the lightning comes again, but it is nothing and barely registers. The thunder is more muted than it was when they entered the room. The storm, he thinks, must be moving on. The panes rattle in the loose window frame as if from a farewell gust. He glances over at her desk, at the clothes on the chair, at the clay on the blotter. His eyes stray back to the slanted ceiling directly over him. He squints at the paper. There are tiny holes surrounding the crumbling plaster, he now sees. *Of course,* he thinks, *from the shooting.* And there will be other tiny holes in the room too.

He forces himself to a sitting position. He stands and walks across the room to the window. The window sticks, then gives. On the lawn between the two houses, he can see eddies of leaves and twigs, twisted into dust devils by the wind. On the horizon is a seam of bright light beneath the cloud bank.

Her robe is still raised to her waist. He walks back to the bed and bends across it. He lifts her hand free of the edge, where she is clutching it. He smooths the robe over her legs. He walks to the chair and sits down.

He watches as she turns onto her back. She wipes away a patch of sweat near her temple with the palm of her hand. Already, through the open window, there is the faintest suggestion of a chill in the air.

On either side of the well of the desk are the drawers, the bottom drawers the deepest. He opens the one to his right. Inside is a forest of gray clay shapes. He lifts out one of the small sculptured pieces and puts it on the blotter. It is a figure of a nude woman, sitting on a straight-back chair, not unlike the one he is on. Her head is bent forward, and her long back is curved. One leg is stretched out, the other bent. The sculpture is about fifteen inches high, but he can make out the fine depressions to the side of one eye. The hair, thick and tangled, cascades down the back of the chair. It is an extraordinary likeness, but it is not just the likeness. It is the remarkable softness of the body against the square shape of the chair.

He looks over at Eden on the bed. She has to have heard him open the drawer. He draws out another. It is again a self-portrait, a woman in a sundress with buttons down the front, bending to the floor to pick up a shirt. He runs his fingers along the folds of the skirt, admires the way it opens as the woman has bent forward.

''These are wonderful,'' he says.

She says nothing, turns her face slightly away from him.

''This is what you meant,'' he says.

He takes another from the drawer. It is a woman in a nightgown, lying on her side.

''She brings me clay,'' she says. ''But they dry up after a while, and they break.''

''But they could be kiln-dried, couldn't they? Or reproduced in metal? They're beautiful.'' He feels a sensation, something like relief, that she has had this—and then another sensation, one of admiration, that she has been able to create such beauty in this barren room.

She hugs her arms as if she were again cold. She rises to a sitting position. Another gust whistles against the window.

''I'm sorry,'' he says. ''I should never have forced you like that.''

''It's all right,'' she says.

He runs his fingertips along the nightgown of clay.

"I went for a walk this morning," he says, "and I found a dog lying in the middle of the road. It had been hit by a car and couldn't move. But it was still alive. I carried it to the side of the road. I lay down beside it while a storm passed over, and when I sat up it was dead."

She draws the robe more tightly around her legs.

"A man came by with a pickup truck and let me bring the dog home. I buried it this morning under the hydrangea tree."

She hunches her shoulders forward and rubs her arms.

"But the thing about the dog is it never cried," he says. "Do you remember any of it—the skating, the railroad tracks, the baseball?"

She tilts her chin up, as if thinking.

"I was remembering this morning," he says, "after I found the dog, that day you were hit with the puck on the cheekbone. Do you remember it? Sean had whacked it, and it caught you right under the eye. Your face turned white, but you didn't cry. I'll never forget it. You never made a sound."

She stands up and walks to the window, her back to him. Her arms are tightly wound over her chest.

"He was always in my bed," she says, "from the very beginning. He would lie down with me to tuck me in when I was little, and sometimes we would sleep side by side."

"You don't have to tell me," he says.

She rubs one of the panes with a finger. "She didn't like it, his being with me, but there wasn't anything she could do. She didn't want to touch me herself."

He watches her from the chair. She is making perfect circles on the glass.

"When I was older, she told him I was too old for him to be doing that. She could say it then, so he stopped. But she started working nights, and he came when she was away. It started then, when we both knew we were hiding from her.''

As we have, he thinks suddenly but doesn't say.

She turns toward him, leans against the sill. ''I never said no, not the first time, not ever. It was what I had to offer him. To offer anyone.''

He massages the sculpture in his hands. There is nothing he can say. He could say, *It wasn't your fault,* but the phrase seems meaningless, the word *fault* without reference. It is an intimacy he doesn't entirely comprehend. He knows there must be consequences, ramifications to this unnatural life she has had, and perhaps he could say it was this that made her the way she was then, but these would be shallow suppositions, made without understanding.

His eye falls to the chocolate floorboards by her feet. Somewhere on these floorboards, Jim died and Edith found him, and then his father found all of them. The ground lurches when he tries to bring Jim into focus. Soon his memories of Jim will have to be recast, redrawn again. And of Edith too, he thinks dizzily.

''Did she know?'' he asks.

She doesn't answer him directly. She leans her head back against the window. ''I've had all these years to ask *why,* and I still don't know the answer. I knew the answer better then; I could feel it. Now I can't. She wasn't cold to him. It wasn't that. He liked young girls. He needed to drink before he came to me, but he was always gentle, he never hurt me. It wasn't like you think. I don't know the word you would give it. I don't even remember his face now.''

He puts the sculpture on the blotter, walks to where she is. He lays his hands on her shoulders, pulls her head to his chest. He is afraid to form the question, knowing that her answer will be permanent, unshakable. But he has to know.

''You'll come with me now,'' he says. He tries to

say it casually, though she must hear his heart racing beneath his voice.

She doesn't make him wait. She nods, a small gesture.

The balloon inside his chest expands, bursts. He lifts her, taking them both by surprise, and carries her to the bed. She is weightless, no longer resisting him. He drapes her gently on the pink bedspread. He sits on the edge of the bed, looking down at her, holding her by the wrist. Then he is bending over her, kissing her while he unties the sash at her waist. His hand finds her skin, and she moves to make room for him to lie beside her. He tries to free her arms from the robe, and she helps him. His stomach and chest are suffused with warmth—she must feel the heat radiating from his pores. He slides over her, hunkering down. She is feeling his face, reading him. He tastes the salt at the edge of the almond eye. She murmurs something he cannot quite make out. He thinks she is saying his name into his ear. She opens her thighs and guides him, and he feels, as she takes him in, a gathering there of more love than he thought was inside him. She moves against him slowly: there is no time against which to measure this. She has her arms hooked around his shoulders from underneath. He feels her curl a foot around his calf. Soon they will drive south on the thruway, toward the city. He will buy her clothes, and she will wear them, and she will cast her portraits in precious metals. He will make it up to her; he will give her what was taken from her. The bed creaks merrily and loudly under their double weight. He pictures a pair of ribald characters in a play he read somewhere years ago, and he wants to tell her of this lusty image. He bends his head down to kiss her breasts. He wants to tell her of the drive south, of all there is ahead of them. He is full of images, like bright bits in a kaleidoscope. They are with Billy, and Andrew is making pancakes for the three of them. They are under his mother's quilt on his bed in the city, drinking wine. They are in a concert hall, listening to a piano. He slides his mouth along her neck, reaches his hands down underneath her to hold her there.

But she is pushing at his shoulders. He doesn't understand. He is confused, thrust too quickly away from her, away from the images. He feels her fingernails cut into his skin.

He rises up to see her face, and there is terror there. He hears, too late then, what she has heard, on the floorboards. He whirls around to face the doorway.

Edith is standing just inside the door with something large and strange in her arms—a sight as incomprehensible and as meaningless in the universe they have just created as a code he will never decipher. He struggles for sense, for clarity. He hears Eden cry out behind him. Instinctively, he raises an arm, a hand, to separate himself from the apparition in the doorway, even as it brings the large and strange thing closer to its face. He wants to shout *Wait,* and perhaps he does. The adrenaline hits his thighs then, his calves. He leaps up.

It is the leap of an athlete, a left fielder grazing the sky for a fly ball, a goalie catapulted off the ice to make a save. He will catch the ball, the puck. He knows it. He cannot fail.

But it is not Andrew the gun is intended for.

SIX

THE NIP IN THE AIR TASTES OF COLD WATER. EVEN ON this second Saturday in September, he can see his breath, the steam rising from the mug of coffee. The maples are already turning, in the sunlight, a translucent pink, and he knows that down by the pond the leaves of the birches will be the color of brass.

He finds T.J. in the dining room of the Closes' house, standing with his hands in his pockets, surveying the stripped walls. The shades and curtains in the room have been removed, so that the sun makes the newly washed windows gleam. A few last remnants of the old paper, a mildewed and darkened pattern of cabbage roses, fill a plastic trash bag by the doorway.

"I brought you these," says Andrew, handing T.J. a pair of stained jeans and an old blue plaid flannel shirt. "And I brought you a cup of coffee."

"Thanks." T.J. cradles the coffee. "I called Didi, told her I'd be hanging out with you for a while. The kitchen looks great, by the way. Like an ad for *Country Living* or something."

Andrew laughs. But he is pleased with the kitchen. He has sanded away the green paint on the walls and cabinets, replaced it with a semigloss white. He has torn up the cracked linoleum and sanded and refinished the wide old plank flooring underneath. He threw away the shades and gave the table and chairs to the Salvation Army. The kitchen is now pristine and simple, waiting for new owners to walk in and claim it.

He likes standing in the center of the kitchen, drinking his morning coffee there. His only regret is that Eden cannot see what he has done. She has rubbed her bare feet along the satin finish of the floorboards, felt the glossy paint on the cupboards, smelled the fresh tang of new paint in the room. But he could tell, by looking at her face, that to her the room was still green and dark, still contained too many memories. After that day he did not ask her again to "see" his work, and she has not returned to her house, not even when he emptied and packed her own room. She stays now with him at the other house, across the yard.

T.J. finishes the cup of coffee and sets the mug on the sill. Andrew watches as T.J. strips off his brown leather jacket, his expensive safari pants and a vivid lime green and blue cotton sweater. He puts on the flannel shirt Andrew has brought, zips up the jeans.

"You look better," says Andrew. T.J. acknowledges the dubious compliment with a wry grimace.

Actually, Andrew is thinking, T.J. doesn't look well at all. His face has lost its color, and new vertical lines have appeared in the center of his forehead. Although his stylish clothes are the same, the panache seems to be gone.

"How is she?" asks T.J.

"Good. She's sleeping."

"I thought she looked very good when I came around . . . you know, right after. I woulda been back sooner, but you both looked like you needed to be left alone for a while."

"Thank you. We did. But it's better now."

T.J. surveys the dining room. "Where do I start?" he asks.

"I've got the walls down to the plaster, sanded the woodwork," says Andrew. "I'm going to paint the walls a linen white, do the trim in the same color, but a semigloss. I've only got one roller, though. Which would you rather tackle—the walls or the woodwork?"

"I can do the walls," says T.J.

"OK. Give me a hand with the dropcloth, then."

The two men unfold the dropcloth and draw it up to the baseboard. T.J. crouches down, opens a can of paint and begins to stir it with a wooden stick. Andrew, with his own can of paint, does the same.

"It was a great save, whatever you did," says T.J. "I've heard the story now twenty times, and each version is a little different. You're a goddamn hero in the town, you know that?" The statement is an invitation. T.J. looks at Andrew.

Andrew shrugs, a gesture that belies the memory of that moment—the many epiphanies in that single frozen leap.

"I hit the barrel with my hand," he says. "The shot deflected to the ceiling. Then I took the gun. In fact, when I did that, she just sat down."

He remembers how she walked to the chair, and how she folded her hands in her lap, resolutely refusing to look at Eden, who had, in the tussle, risen to her feet and was tying the sash of her robe. Andrew, naked, had held the gun, with the barrel pointing toward the floor, and had told Eden, in a voice that wasn't entirely composed, to go to the phone, dial the operator and ask for DeSalvo's number, then to call DeSalvo and ask him to come out at once. If he wasn't at home, to call the luncheonette. Curiously, his nakedness in front of Edith Close had caused him no embarrassment—in retrospect, he imagined it was because they had all passed, in an instant, onto another plane of guilt and shame—but he walked nevertheless to the chair on which Edith was sitting and lifted his clothes from behind her. He sat on the bed, the gun beside him, and dressed, his hands shaking so badly he couldn't tie his sneakers. He had said to Edith— feeling like a poseur with the gun in his hands, slightly raised in her direction—to go down to the kitchen. Following her, not knowing exactly what would transpire when DeSalvo arrived, he began composing fragments of stories to see if they might hold, might be plausible, until he reached the kitchen and glanced at Eden, in her robe, at the table, and saw in her body and on her face that she knew that she was free now. She would say whatever she would say, whatever she had longed to say.

"You called the police?" asks T.J.

"I called DeSalvo. I thought I needed advice at that point more than I needed anything else. Later he called the police, and they came and got her."

"And she told the whole story?"

"No. It was Eden who did that. After they had taken Edith away, DeSalvo and I sat down with her, and she told us everything. She was very calm, very clear about it. It was a relief to her. . . ."

T.J. scrapes the drips off the paint stirrer, lays it on a piece of newspaper. He pours a measure of thick creamy liquid into the paint tray. "So it was Mrs. Close all along," he says.

Andrew nods, stands and holds his brush as steadily as he can against the strip of molding nearest the wall.

"She found them in bed together?" asks T.J. The question is rhetorical, or a request for confirmation. T.J. has heard this part of the story oft repeated now from people in the town. For the town, the revelations have been titillating and deeply satisfying, closing an unresolved chapter in its history.

"He was leaving Eden to go back to his own room because he knew Edith would be home soon, but she'd come earlier and they hadn't heard her."

"We all thought Mr. Close was at the movies and came home with Mrs. Close that night," says T.J.

"So she said."

"I guess no one was going to question the story of a grieving widow and a badly injured child."

"Well, they didn't."

Like a flashbulb popping in front of his eyes, the

image of Edith Close being pushed to the ground by the ambulance attendants comes briefly into focus. He hesitates, then says to T.J., "They didn't think to question the grieving widow, because she really *was* grieving. You understand that it wasn't Jim she meant to shoot?"

Andrew is surprised by his own desire to tell T.J. these facts—after all, he and T.J. have so little in common now—but there is, in the telling, a kind of relief for himself too. Perhaps it is the shared activity of the work that brings on the atmosphere of confidence, or possibly seeing T.J. in old clothes.

T.J. puts the roller down, turns to Andrew. "And he got in the way?"

Andrew nods. "Something like that." Andrew wonders now if Jim, too, had leapt to make a save.

T.J. shakes his head, gives a low whistle. "She tried to kill her own daughter?"

Andrew nods. "His daughter."

T.J. stares at Andrew, trying to take this in. He turns, resoaks the roller in the tray, lifts it to begin another long strip. "You ever guess that about him?" he asks. "About him and Eden?"

It is a question Andrew has thought about in the three weeks since Eden told him about herself and her father. He knows the answer is no, he did not imagine this of Jim. And yet the clues may have been there, he now thinks. He remembers the way his mother would watch Jim caress his daughter on the steps. "Sickening," she would say, and he thought she meant Jim's indulgence. But perhaps she felt something else too, something she couldn't articulate or even bring to clarity in her thoughts.

"Watch for drips," says Andrew. He opens one of the windows to let out the paint fumes. Immediately, clean air fills his lungs. When he has finished the painting, he will rent the sander again and refinish the narrow oak floorboards. The Salvation Army has taken away the rug and the furniture—indeed, they have taken most of the furniture in the house. Almost nothing, apart from a mahogany sideboard in the dining room, was good enough for auction.

"T.J.," says Andrew. "There's something I feel bad about."

"What's that?"

"Well, for a while, maybe a half hour or a day—I can't remember—I thought it might have been you. Those guns . . ."

"Forget about it. You were under a lot of strain. You weren't thinking clearly."

"You didn't tell Sean, then?"

"No, and I don't know who did, though the news spread fast that morning. His father maybe. My guess is that Sean went crazy when he heard it, didn't know what he was doing."

Andrew watches the shiny paint cover the dull sanded surface. Painting, like mowing, he is thinking, is rewarding work. He cannot tell T.J. how obsessed he has become with this house—seized by the notion of transforming it, sanding it clean, airing it out so thoroughly that the past, like the paint fumes, will drift out the windows and be dissipated in the clean September air. The work has been pleasurable, apart from the one day he was forced to enter Edith's room and remove the belongings there. The room, with its drawn shades, its bleak furnishings and its lone picture of Jim on a dresser, depressed him so much that he sat for long minutes on the worn bedspread, unable to proceed further. The worst moment was opening her top dresser drawer, as he had done in his own mother's bedroom. He was tempted merely to lift the entire contents into paper bags to take to her lawyer, to be given to Edith at the hospital with the suitcases of clothes, but a kind of prurient curiosity compelled him to linger over the items, fingering them, imagining them as clues to an enigmatic woman: a postcard from

Jim from Buffalo, dated 1959; a pale blue nylon night-gown that appeared not to have been washed in years; a valentine from Jim that referred to an evening of intimacy; a certificate stating that Edith Close was a licensed practical nurse. Astonishingly, or perhaps not surprising at all, there was not a single trace in this dresser drawer, as there was in his own mother's drawer, that the woman had ever raised a child, that a daughter had ever shared her home. Not a single memento, school paper or photograph. He put the contents in a shopping bag and left the drawer open, unable and unwilling to touch it again.

"What'll happen to her, do you think?" asks T.J.

"You mean Edith?"

"Yeah."

"I think they'll put her away."

"The loony bin?"

"Probably. Even if it comes to trial, which I'm not sure it will do. Eden doesn't want that. No one really wants that."

"She's there now?"

"She's under observation. Sixty days."

He tries to picture Edith under observation, remembers her in the kitchen waiting for DeSalvo to come. She stood the entire time, refusing to sit at the table. Andrew still held the gun, though he knew it wasn't necessary. There was no place now that she would go.

He had not been in a room with the two grown women before, and he thought how palpable the tension was between them, like an electric current running from the table to the place where Edith stood, a current so alive he himself did not want to intersect it. And yet the minutes in which they waited for DeSalvo were silent ones. Neither woman spoke to the other or turned her head in the other's direction. Andrew felt his presence to be intrusive, foolish. He sensed that even without him, the two of them would have waited passively for whatever was to happen next.

Indeed, the shooting now seemed like a nonevent, something he might have dreamed—so much so that he was mildly embarrassed to see DeSalvo, over-weight and breathless, sprint from his tiny car to the back door, a revolver in hand. That gesture, and his own posture with the gun, seemed hyperbolic—too much for the small, plain kitchen. DeSalvo felt it too, first looking wildly from face to face, then slowly lowering his own gun. He had handcuffs, but Andrew said he was sure they would not be necessary. He did think, though, that it would be better if Edith was taken away from the house, and it was then that DeSalvo called the police station. Again they waited in the kitchen. DeSalvo had the sense not to ask yet what had happened. Andrew thought that he should ask DeSalvo if he wanted a cup of coffee. He longed to show him the blown ceiling in the bedroom, to lend their vigil in the kitchen credibility, but he knew that would have to wait until the uniformed officers had come.

After a time, they heard the sirens. Andrew raised a shade and saw two cars pull into the driveway. Men leapt from opened doors as they had been trained to do, and at once there were too many people in the kitchen. DeSalvo took charge then, giving orders, and the tone of his voice and the flashing lights outside reminded Andrew of the other time when police cars had come to the two houses. A man took Edith by the elbow, gently, as if she herself were the victim, as if it were she who was in shock. She never said a word, never looked back, had no gesture of farewell for the woman at the table, the woman who was meant to be her daughter, the woman she had tried twice to rid herself of.

"But she still wants to sell the house?" asks T.J.

The question brings Andrew back to the present. "So she told her lawyer," he says. "Regardless of what happens, I don't think she'd be able to come back here. Not now."

"No."

T.J. lifts the roller, makes another straight sweep the length of the wall. "So where'd she get the gun?" he says.

Andrew catches a drip, stands back to study the color. "It was here," he says. "It was always here."

"Where?"

"You think the linen white is OK?"

T.J. looks over at the woodwork. "It looks fine to me."

Andrew dips the brush again into the paint. "In a trapdoor under the floorboards of Edith's bedroom closet," he says. "Jim had bought the gun years ago, in the same aimless way be bought everything. He had a farmhouse in a remote part of town, so he thought he should have a gun—just like the way he used to buy seeds and then never plant them. He taught Edith how to use it in case a burglar came while he was on the road, and he had my father build a box—a kind of safe—under the floorboards for him. The funny thing is I *remember* when my father did that. I hadn't realized, I don't think, that the box was for a gun, but when Eden told us about it I remembered the weekend my father built it. It was a joke in our house, how Jim had seen the plans in *Popular Mechanics* but, like always, got my father to do all the work."

"So Edith stashed the gun there after she shot Jim?"

Andrew stops painting, glances at T.J. He is aware of a feeling of vague discomfort. It wasn't part of the story Eden told, or could have told. She'd have been unconscious then. The discomfort rises to a heat at the back of his neck.

"I don't know," he says to T.J. "She must have."

T.J. sets the roller in the trough, stands back to admire his work.

"Whaddya think?" he asks Andrew.

Andrew examines the wall. "Like a pro," he says.

"Feels good," says T.J. "I haven't done this kind

of work in years. Tell you what. I'll do another wall for you, then I gotta go. Tom junior's got a soccer game.'' T.J. picks up the roller, starts on the second wall.

''I envy you, you know that?'' he says.

''Envy me? Why?'' asks Andrew.

''Starting fresh. Your life is like this room.''

Andrew is about to speak, but T.J. cuts him off.

''Tell you the truth, I could use a fresh start right now.''

''Why?'' asks Andrew. He faces T.J., who is keeping his back to him.

''The till is empty, Andy-boy. Worse than empty, you follow me. I made some bad investments. . . .'' There is a pause. ''I may lose the house.''

Andrew watches the deliberate way T.J. raises the roller, pretends to be smoothing over a rough spot. The flannel shirt is torn along the shoulder seam. He senses that it has cost T.J. to tell him this.

''Me and Didi, we're supported by what we have,'' says T.J. ''That goes, and I don't know. I don't know how we'd be together without all the stuff, but I don't have good feelings about that. Sometimes I think the till is empty there too.''

T.J. stands back to survey his work again, still avoiding Andrew's gaze.

''No one starts completely fresh,'' says Andrew carefully. T.J. says nothing. ''I'm on a leave of absence now,'' Andrew adds, ''but soon I'll have to go back to my job. Maybe not full time. In fact, probably not—as a consultant possibly. I have to have an income, and that's the most efficient way I know how to get one right now. I've got a son to provide for—whom I *want* to provide for. . . .'' He thinks of Billy with a tightness in the center of his chest. This is now the longest he has ever been away from his son, but Andrew and Eden will drive to New York soon, and he will have Billy there. He knows that it will be hard for

Billy to understand Eden's presence, but he cannot spare his son this. There are things now he cannot control, such as Martha's revelation, just a week ago, that she is getting married again—to a psychiatrist. She had planned to wait to tell him, she said, until she saw Andrew in person, but she had grown annoyed with his delays. Andrew found, over the phone, that he could not respond to this piece of news—immediately he was assaulted with visions of another man throwing grounders to Billy, another man tucking his son in at night. Andrew hopes the psychiatrist, whoever he is, will not be one of those shrinks who insist that everyone in the family unburden himself of his feelings. "I've got to see Eden settled," Andrew says, shaking off the insupportable image of another father for Billy, "with tutors or a good program for the blind. I want to get her set up with . . . Hang on a minute."

Andrew sets his brush down, retreats into the living room, reappears with an object in his hand.

"What do you think of this?" Andrew asks.

T.J. moves closer for a better look. He touches the surface, runs his fingers along the curve of the back, the straight chair back.

"That's beautiful. Where did you get it?"

"Eden made it. It's what she does."

"Jesus."

"But this is clay. She says it will break after a time. She's made dozens of them over the years. And they're all gone. When I think . . ."

"Can't you spray it with something to make it last?" asks T.J.

"I don't know much about the process, but I think it either has to be fired in a kiln, which she never had access to, or she could do them in wax, get them cast in a metal like bronze. My idea is to sell my condo, get us set up in a bigger place downtown, give her some room to do these."

"Yeah," says T.J. He raises his eyes from the sculpture to Andrew's face. The glance is brief but naked. Andrew sees, on his old friend's face, a look of envy mixed with regret. T.J. pulls away first, pivots toward the wall.

Andrew wraps the sculpture in newspaper, returns it to the carton in the living room. He and T.J. work in silence. T.J. paints three of the walls, leaving only the wall surrounding the window that opens onto the gravel drive. Then he changes back into his own clothes. He gives Andrew the jeans and shirt, as if handing over another persona, one he is reluctant to part with.

"Listen," he says to Andrew. "Later on, say four o'clock or so, you want to go for a run with me?"

Andrew accepts the clothes. He watches T.J. slip his arms into his leather jacket. T.J. lifts a pair of sunglasses from his pocket, puts them on. He seems to retrieve something with this gesture.

"Sure," says Andrew. "Why not? I'd like that."

T.J. rests a hand on Andrew's shoulder. He opens his mouth as if to speak, then seems to decide against it. Andrew follows him through the kitchen. He holds open the screen door as he watches T.J. saunter toward his Prelude. His walk is sharper now. T.J. leans against the car, twirls his keys. He looks over at Andrew's house. "You've really done a lot for Eden. I mean, you've really saved her."

"No," Andrew says quickly. "I think it's the other way around."

T.J. looks up at the sky as if searching for a cloud. "Why didn't Eden leave?" he asks. "Why didn't she just get out?"

Andrew hesitates, but only for a second. "Where could she go?" he says. "What could she do?"

T.J. thinks, then slowly nods. "I'll be back around four," he says, folding himself neatly behind the wheel. Andrew watches the red car back out the drive and swing in the direction of town.

He lets the screen door slap behind him, stands on the stoop, his hands in the pockets of his jeans. The stoop is sturdy now; he finally repaired it last week. He leans against the railing and looks north over the cornfields—a crisp ocher against a bright blue sky. The answer is not sufficient, he knows. The true answer is one Andrew feels but cannot say. To know it as he does, T.J. would have to have seen Eden that first day Andrew came upon her in the kitchen. He could say it was guilt, complicity, fear of Edith's harming her again—but Andrew knows it is more than that. It was, he thinks, an absolute forfeit of will—a sacrifice made deliberately to survive her deprivation.

HE WALKS across the grass, deep green now and soon in need of cutting. The BMW in the driveway is growing dusty, as his father's Fords always were. Looking at it, he can't help but think of the first time he took Eden out in it, just two weeks ago. It was a clear day, crisp like this one, with the first real hint of fall. Perhaps it was the cooler temperatures, or a feeling it was time, but he knew when he woke that morning that he would take her out, that she was ready for an excursion. In the week since the aborted shooting, he had been to the mall and had bought her some clothes, so that she was wearing that day a new pair of jeans and a vivid blue-green sweater that he had picked because it matched the color of her eyes.

"We'll just drive," she said, seeking reassurance, when they got into the car.

"We'll see," he said, not committing himself, backing out the drive and turning onto the straight road through the farms and cornfields. He had discovered, in the short time he had been with her, that she responded to new experiences better if he simply announced that they were going to happen. Asking her

if she wanted to do something was likely to make her
anxious—though there had not been anything yet that
he'd suggested that she hadn't, in the end, enjoyed.

There wasn't a lot of traffic on the road. He took the
car up to sixty, edged it toward sixty-five. The clean
air made the farms and the fields look washed, and he
wished, as he knew he would wish a hundred thousand
times in the years to come, that she could see what he
could see. He was still tentative about verbal descrip-
tions. He wasn't certain that they helped her—nor even
if, after nineteen years, she could "see" his portraits.
The visual world, he was coming now more fully to
understand, would not be what they shared.

He pressed a button to lower the window on his
side, so that she could feel the speed, the air, the day.
The wind buffeted her hair; she raised a hand to keep
it off her brow. Slowly, he lowered the window on her
side, telling her that if it was too much for her, she
should say so. Her hair, luminous when the sun hit it,
swirled up and around her head like wild bits of silk.
She tried to shelter her face with her hands, then gave
up and sank back into the headrest. He took the car
up to seventy. For the first time ever in his adult life,
he wished he had a convertible.

He drove for an hour, changing direction, changing
the type of road when he could or when he had an
inspiration. He took a small back road he knew was
full of twists and turns, took it just a shade too fast so
that she would feel it. She laughed when the centri-
fugal force pressed her up against the door; once she
grabbed for something to hang on to, got the gearshift—he took her hand. He felt reckless, faintly like
a teenager with his father's car, a thought he enjoyed—
the vestigial memory of the boy pretending to be a
man, with his girl beside him in the car—until the
thought made him sad, and he put it away quickly: She
had missed all of that, all that went with those years,
and he would never, no matter how many times he

took her out, no matter how fast he drove, be able to give it back to her.

After a time he took the straight road back, but when he reached the houses he said nothing and bypassed them. He looked to see if she knew, but she was still lying against the headrest, her eyes closed, and appeared to be lost to the sensation of the moving car. It wasn't until they got closer to town and passed a school playground, where there was a soccer game in progress on the field, that she leaned forward, listening.

"Where are we?" she asked.

"You'll see," he said.

She stayed bent forward, alert, listening now to the once familiar sounds of men with hedge clippers, children squealing to each other from bicycles, the slightly thicker traffic of a small village. He parked in front of the luncheonette.

"Where are we?" she said again.

"I thought we'd get some lunch."

"No," she said unequivocally, shaking her head.

"I don't have anything at the house to eat," he said.

"That's just an excuse."

"Look, it has to happen someday."

"Maybe, but not here, not now."

He sat back in the car, looked across to the gas station, thought a minute.

"I'm going in to have lunch," he said. "You can come with me or you can sit in the car."

He ran his finger along the humps in the steering wheel, waiting for an answer.

"All right," she said after a time.

He didn't know if the "All right" meant all right, she'd stay in the car, or all right, she'd go with him, so he decided to interpret the answer to his benefit. He walked around to her side of the car, opened the door. She hesitated, then got out. He took her hand.

"Trust me," he said.

"You've been saying that for days."

"Well?"

The shooting had happened only a week before; she was a celebrity, the source of rich gossip. Few had seen her in nineteen years, but with the exception of the Vietnamese man behind the counter, who would not have known who she was by sight, may not even have understood all of the stories that had passed from stool to stool that week, everyone in the place looked up, stared at Eden.

Without question, Andrew thought, there were times when he was glad she couldn't see.

But she knew. They took a table by the window, slightly away from the counter.

"Are they looking at me?" she asked, her head lowered.

"Lift your head up," he said. "Look at my voice."

She did so.

"DeSalvo's here," he said. The former police chief had waved when they entered. He would give them a minute, Andrew knew, then come over, a gesture of solidarity as much as of friendship.

"And some men I don't know, and . . . ah . . ."

"Who?"

"Henry O'Brien," he said quickly.

"Oh," she said.

O'Brien was glaring at Andrew and Eden, as though frozen, as though stricken by the sight of an unwelcome vision from the past. The other men, politely, had gone back to their sandwiches—though Andrew noticed that they contrived, by reaching for the salt or the napkin dispenser, to look surreptitiously in Eden's direction. Only O'Brien continued to stare openly.

"Will he cause a scene?" asked Eden.

"No," said Andrew. "I don't think so." But the truth was, he didn't know. O'Brien's eyes were rheumy; he'd already been drinking. There was a slow wave of anger moving across his brow.

The Vietnamese man came to the table. Andrew read Eden the menu from the blackboard. "I recommend the Turkey Health Club, but not the Pepsi," Andrew said to her.

"Fine," she said.

Andrew ordered.

"Raise your head. Look at my voice," Andrew said again to Eden.

She did so, but she kept her face tilted slightly toward the window, away from the men.

"You're beautiful," Andrew said. "You have nothing to be ashamed of."

She shrugged.

"You're the most beautiful woman in here," he said.

She grimaced, then smiled. "It sounds to me like I'm the only woman in here," she said.

"Well, there's that," he said, enjoying her smile.

Out of the corner of his eye, he saw O'Brien put his leg to the floor, about to stand. Andrew stiffened but kept his gaze on Eden. He hadn't known O'Brien would be here; he should have looked before he brought Eden in.

O'Brien swiveled, bent to stand, swayed a bit. Even if Andrew wanted to get Eden out, there wasn't time. For one incredible moment, he actually thought he might have to fight O'Brien. He tried to envision the scene, could not imagine himself landing a punch on the man's face.

But DeSalvo had seen O'Brien move too, perhaps even before Andrew had. "Henry," DeSalvo said, instantly behind O'Brien, slapping the red-haired man on the back, lowering him onto the stool. "How ya doin'? How ya doin'?"

O'Brien, momentarily restrained by DeSalvo's beefy hand, mumbled something Andrew couldn't hear.

"Al, cup a coffee for my friend Henry here," DeSalvo said in a loud voice, so that all could hear.

"Talk to you in a bit, Henry, but I gotta go say hello to my friend Andy before he blows town."

DeSalvo walked to Andrew's table and, in a gesture that took Andrew by surprise, bent to kiss Eden's cheek, the way a man like DeSalvo might casually greet the wife of an old friend.

"Thank you," Andrew said, meaning O'Brien but also the kiss.

"Mean son of a bitch," said DeSalvo under his breath, "but I'll give you some advice." DeSalvo stood to his full height, hitched his navy blue jogging pants. "You enjoy your sandwiches," he said. "Take your time. That's OK. But Henry's a powder keg even under the best of circumstances, you follow me."

Andrew nodded. He watched DeSalvo return to the place where O'Brien was sitting, take the outside stool, so that he was blocking O'Brien's view of Eden. Andrew could just see the back of O'Brien's head, the longish hair curling over the collar of his jacket, the bright pink skin leading to his ear. No one could help O'Brien now. That was damage that could not be erased, undone.

When DeSalvo had gone, Eden took a bite from her sandwich and said, "I told you it was a bad idea."

He looked across at her. Her hair had taken a beating from the wind. Another woman would have combed her hair in the car before going into the luncheonette. Andrew realized that he would have to be alert to these small gestures for her. The blue-green sweater, a loose cotton, hung neatly from her shoulders, exposing a small white crescent of skin at the neckline. She had the sleeves pushed to the elbows. He reached for her wrist, rubbed the back of her hand. His heart lifted at the sight of her across from him, raising the sandwich to her lips, her hair framed by a Coca-Cola poster behind her—lifted at the thought of the two of them doing something as ordinary as eating in a luncheonette.

Andrew took a bite of his own sandwich.
"It wasn't entirely a bad idea," he said.

WHEN HE enters his own house, he listens for sounds of movement, hears none. There are dishes in the sink he must wash later. He walks through the house and up the stairs, making his way quietly along the floorboards of the hallway, thinking he will not wake her yet. But when he enters his mother's room and sees her lying beneath the quilt, her hair in a braid that trails along the pillow, he cannot resist the impulse to sit on the bed beside her. She stirs slightly, and he says, *It's Andrew*. She smiles in her sleep, before she comes fully to consciousness.

He looks at his watch. He *should* wake her now, he thinks. He has discovered, sleeping with her, that she has lost the common distinction between night and day. She sleeps only three or four hours at a stretch, twice a day, often getting up to prepare herself a meal at three in the morning. He would like to retrain her to a rhythm they could share.

"Where have you been?" she asks drowsily, reaching immediately to touch some part of him. It is her way of looking at him, making contact. She rubs a hand along the cloth of his sleeve by her side.

"I've been with T.J. He came by for a visit, stayed to help with the dining room. You should wake up now. It's nearly noon."

She smiles again. He thinks she is sometimes amused by his efforts to guide her into a normal routine. He wonders if this effort on his part isn't his way of reclaiming for himself some sense of order in his small universe. These have been extraordinary days, extraordinary events, beyond his ken—brought now barely under control.

She yawns, bringing a hand to her mouth.

"I'm hungry," she says.

"Good," he says.

He walks to the window, lifts it open. "It's a fantastic day," he says. "Can you feel it?"

He bends, peers down into the yard. Perhaps it is looking through the encrusted screen that does it—that makes the sound come unbidden into his thoughts. The dream *did* get it right, he realizes suddenly. It was through his own sodden sleep that he first heard a woman's voice cry out, and he thought it might have been his mother. Then there was the second cry, a hoarse shout, that of a grown man, and immediately the frightened squeal of another female, a child still, as he himself was then. And finally, after the shots, the reedy, high-pitched wail, the tendril of smoke rising to the sky, gathering momentum—the anguished voice of Edith Close. He hears again the terrible keening.

"Eden," he says too loudly, shaking off the other sound. "There's something I have to ask you."

"What?" She props herself up and raises the quilt to cover her bare arms. The chill from the day outside has reached her. He returns to the bed, sits on the edge beside her.

"After Edith shot Jim, what did she do with the gun? I mean, how did she get rid of it so fast? My father was there within minutes."

She hugs the quilt around her. She says nothing.

"Eden?"

"I wish you wouldn't ask this," she says.

"Why?"

She doesn't answer him. He waits.

"Tell me," he says. "I have to know."

"It was your father," she says quickly. "It was your father."

"My father?" He lifts his head up sharply to look at her. "My father?" he asks again, unconsciously mimicking her.

She bites her lip, then releases it, giving up a last parcel.

"He saw what she had done, thought he knew why she had done it. Maybe he knew or had sensed it, about Jim. He took the gun and put it back in the box he had built. After the police had finished with him the next day, he came and got it and kept it in his garage. I think he thought she shouldn't go to jail for shooting him. It would have repulsed him, about Jim and me. He didn't guess, then or ever, that it wasn't Jim she meant to kill."

"Did Edith tell you this?" he asks.

She turns her face to him. "We'd long passed the point of having secrets," she says.

Andrew tilts his head back to study the ceiling. He sees his father's face, returning across the gravel drive, the barrel of the rifle limp along his leg. Will there be no memories, no portraits, left intact? His imagination skids out from under him, careens around the room.

"And my mother?" he asks finally. "Did she know?"

Eden nods.

Andrew says nothing, waits.

"After your father died, she came to the back door with the gun. She said, 'I don't have to have this anymore,' and she left."

There is a clock on his mother's dresser. He can hear it ticking. He sees his mother bent over the other side of the bed, making the bed, smoothing the quilt, looking up at him. Already there is something in her posture, in her face, that has changed forever. He remembers the way she would turn away from him, deflect him, whenever he asked about Eden. In time Eden will tell him other stories, small stories of this conversation or that, of that event or this, so that away from them, the houses, too, will change, and the landscape of his childhood will grow branches, sprout wings.

"Is there anything else?" he asks.

"No."

"Would you ever have told me if I hadn't asked?"

"I don't know. I was hoping you wouldn't ask, but I don't know about ever."

From where he is sitting he can see most of the room—the room in which his parents slept, made love, created him: the two screen windows, the pale green wallpaper, the light overhead on the ceiling. Did his parents lie here arguing in suppressed whispers, he wonders, trying to comprehend and possess the object his father had taken to the garage? An object that would alter the homely pattern of their days, that would not let itself be forgotten for even one day, no matter how deeply hidden? And would his father have confided his vision of the scene he had witnessed, his understanding of that horror?

Eden's hairbrush is on his mother's dresser now; his own toilet kit and a list he has written are on his father's. Some of his clothes are still in his suitcase on the floor, hers in a carton on the chair. They will leave soon, drive south to the city.

He slips his hand under the quilt, finds the hem of Eden's nightgown and raises it to her waist. He lays his hand on the flat of her belly, feeling the warmth there. He likes to imagine it is already rounded, swollen, but he knows it may be weeks yet before the shape will change. He is impatient for this to happen, impatient for the visible signs.

"This is everything," he says, touching her.

Her face is ripe with sleep or her condition. She lays her own fingers over his where they are resting.

He leans forward to kiss her at the side of her face. As he does so, he moves into a patch of sunlight coming through the window, forming a bright square on the pillow and the headboard. The sun hits the side of his face, warms his face with its heat. He shuts his eyes. He feels her skin with his mouth, under his hand.

If only his luck will hold, he is thinking.

* * *

Your hands erase the memory of others.

A part of you is inside me, and I will always have that.

You have made me give up all the secrets, and I am lighter now.

You talk of days stretching after days, and you believe in them. I do not believe in them, but I believe in this day.

Your mother's quilt has a sweet smell. She had secrets too, and she is lighter, glad that I have told them.

Your face shimmers in the water, and I sometimes think that I can see it.

I will feel and smell my baby, but I will never see its face.

We will leave this place and not come back, and in our dreams it will turn to dust.